A Magical Moment . . .

"Are you saying that Daisy is going to be all right, my lord?"

He grinned. "It would appear so."

Justin was never quite sure how it happened, but the next thing he knew Miss Thornhill was in his arms, laughing and crying and hugging him with all her might. Without a second thought, he hugged her back.

Then from the sheer joy of the moment, and because it seemed the natural thing to do, he kissed her trembling pink lips. To his surprise she returned his kiss with an exuberance which more than made up for her obvious lack of expertise. He felt a brief moment of triumph. She was an innocent. Whatever else that Adonis, Drew Wentworth, might be to her, he was not her lover. Then forgetting all else, he abandoned himself to a passionate exploration of her warm, responsive mouth. Pleasure rippled through him. He felt as if all the sunshine hiding behind the dark clouds over London had suddenly flooded the small room with a light so bright it filled every inch of his being. Long minutes later, he reluctantly lifted his lips from hers. She stared up at him, her eyes wide with astonishment. "My lord," she gasped, "whatever are we doing?"

Justin viewed her flushed face through a haze of desire. "I believe it is called kissing."

The Unlikely Angel

Nadine Miller

Ø
A SIGNET BOOK

SIGNET
Published by the Penguin Group
Penguin Putnam Inc., 375 Hudson Street,
New York, New York 10014, U.S.A.
Penguin Books Ltd, 27 Wrights Lane,
London W8 5TZ, England
Penguin Books Australia Ltd, Ringwood,
Victoria, Australia
Penguin Books Canada Ltd, 10 Alcorn Avenue,
Toronto, Ontario, Canada M4V 3B2
Penguin Books (N.Z.) Ltd, 182–190 Wairau Road,
Auckland 10, New Zealand

Penguin Books Ltd, Registered Offices:
Harmondsworth, Middlesex, England

First published by Signet, an imprint of Dutton Signet,
a member of Penguin Putnam Inc.

First Printing, April, 1998
10 9 8 7 6 5 4 3 2 1

To my brilliant cardiac surgeon, Dr. James Smith
Thank you for giving me back my life

and

To my good friend, Linda Smith
Thank you for being there when I needed you

AUTHOR'S NOTE

The scene in the slaughterhouse was based on an actual event, as recorded by Mr. Arthur Lee, an early Victorian social worker. He and his sister met with a similar response when they attempted to better the lot of the "savage amazon butchers who labored in the greatest slaughterhouse in all of England."

Chapter One

"I am sorry to disturb you, my lord, but I fear I must inform you that a rather formidable person of the female persuasion has ensconced herself in the vestibule and refuses to leave until she speaks to you."

Justin Anthony Warre, Viscount Sanderfield, looked up from the hand of cards he had just been dealt by his friend, Reggie Lynch, the Earl of Rutledge, and scowled at his elderly butler. Wimple had an annoying habit of appearing out of nowhere to make dramatic pronouncements that must instantly be dealt with whether or not one felt so inclined. They almost always turned out to be the proverbial tempest in a teacup, but some inexplicable instinct warned Justin this particular tempest would not blow itself out so easily.

"A woman? To see me?" he asked warily. "How odd. What lady other than my mother would dare visit my bachelor establishment?"

"She most certainly is not Lady Warre, my lord."

"No, of course not. Mother is in Bath taking the waters."

"Nor is there any likelihood she is acquainted with her ladyship," Wimple declared with chilling certainty. Stiff as a ramrod despite his venerable age, he showed no sign of departing the salon without explicit orders as to the disposition of the "formidable female" who had invaded the viscount's London town house.

Justin took a closer look. Did he just imagine it or was the fastidious Wimple's wig askew? His color a trifle high?

The old man blinked away a drop of perspiration trickling into his right eye, and Justin stifled the urge to chuckle. Always the perfect retainer, the inestimable butler would never consider performing an act as personal as mopping his brow in the presence of his employer—no matter how much he might disapprove of that employer.

"What makes you so certain the caller is not a friend of my mother's?" Justin queried. "I've made the acquaintance of no other lady since my return to London."

Wimple's nostrils flared. "The deduction is simple, my lord. She would never be received in her ladyship's drawing room because she could not by any stretch of imagination be termed a lady. She is accompanied by neither chaperon nor maid—and she is not wearing gloves."

"Good God! The creature must be as common as dirt!" Reggie sounded properly horrified, but Justin caught the twinkle in his friend's eye as he raised a glass of brandy to his lips.

Wimple, however, took the earl at his word. "My feelings exactly, my lord. Furthermore, she has an umbrella—a very large, black, gentleman's umbrella—the sort no proper lady would consider carrying."

Justin glanced at the streaming window on his right and the murky, rain-washed square beyond it. "One could hardly fault her for such prudence on a day like this," he said with a shiver. His blood had thinned during his long stay in the Greek isles, and he found November in London unbearably wet and cold. Nothing short of the death of his older brother could have lured him back to the dreary place. As soon as his lawyers completed the legal details of his succession to the title, he planned to return to sunny Athens and the work he'd begun on the translation of a recently discovered letter purported to have been written by Aristotle to his pupil Alexander the Great.

Wimple's raspy voice trailed off into silence, reminding Justin he hadn't listened to a word the old man had said. He placed his cards facedown on the small gaming table he shared with Reggie and regarded his elderly butler gravely. "Now, what was that you were saying about the lady's umbrella?"

"I said the fault lies not so much in the umbrella as a proper accessory, as in its use as a weapon." Surreptitiously, Wimple pressed his properly gloved hand to his midriff.

Reggie choked on his brandy. "Never say the virago poked you with her umbrella!"

Wimple gave an indignant sniff. "She did indeed, my lord—

and at this very minute she is holding John Footman at bay with the lethal thing."

A grin spread across Reggie's long, angular face as he turned to Justin. "So, my shy friend, it appears this determined female, whoever she may be, has breached the ramparts of your closely guarded bachelor fortress. As I see it, you will either have to hear her out or find an umbrella of your own and engage her in a duel." He smiled. "I shall be happy to act as your second should you choose the latter course."

Those who knew him well claimed the Earl of Rutledge was a man who would laugh at his own funeral. Most men who had fought in the bitter Peninsula battles came home silent and somber. Reggie had stepped off the ship in Dover at the end of August as jovial as ever.

Justin could see that, true to form, his friend was thoroughly enjoying both this present bumblebroth and Wimple's exasperation. Justin, himself, saw no humor whatsoever in the situation. He found dealing with any woman unnerving—and the one currently demanding his attention sounded more impossible than most. He scowled. "Damn it, Reggie, must you make a joke of everything?"

Reggie sobered instantly. "Sorry, old sod. I know females are a touchy subject where you're concerned."

Justin gave him a quelling look and returned to the problem at hand. "Did this woman who is terrorizing the staff happen to mention her name or divulge what it was she wanted to see me about?" he asked his sour-faced retainer.

"She did not see fit to impart the nature of her business, my lord—and while she did give her name, she offered no card so I cannot be certain I can repeat it correctly."

Justin ground his teeth in exasperation. "Do your best, Wimple."

"As I recall, Miss Thornhill was the name she mentioned."

Reggie's eyes widened. "Not Miss *Theodosia* Thornhill?"

"I believe that was the creature's full name, my lord."

The earl gave a hoot of laughter. "Heaven help you, Justin, it's Terrible Tess Thornhill who's camped in your entryway!"

"You know her?"

"Never met her myself, but I know plenty of men who have."

Justin stared in amazement at his grinning friend. "Are you saying that the woman currently threatening my footman with her umbrella is a common harlot!"

"Lord no! Anything but. She's the spinster daughter of Ishmael Thornhill, a rabid evangelical—though I've heard tell the old zealot hasn't spoken to her since she took up residence in the stews."

"Ishmael Thornhill? I recognize the name. Why would the daughter of one of London's wealthiest merchants choose to live in the slums?"

"She's a militant do-gooder, that's why. Opened some kind of foundling home in the St. Giles Rookeries and started pestering every wealthy man from Mayfair to Threadneedle Street for donations to support her little bastards. It's only by pure luck I've managed to avoid her myself, for I'm told she's a sorceress when it comes to parting a man and his blunt." Reggie chuckled. "The she-cat talked poor Willy Haversham into donating six months' gambling money to her cause last time she got her claws into him."

Reggie rolled his eyes in mock horror. "Now she's come to wheedle a healthy donation out of the new Viscount Sanderfield—and I'll wager a monkey she'll get it too. A shy, reclusive fellow like you is no match for Terrible Tess Thornhill."

Justin breathed a sigh of relief. If money for the less fortunate was all the dried-up old spinster wanted of him, he would gladly donate his share and send her on her way. He turned to his butler, who still hovered in the doorway. "Show Miss Thornhill in, Wimple."

"Yes, my lord." Wimple promptly disappeared, to return minutes later and announce in a voice heavy with disapproval, "Miss Theodosia Thornhill."

Gripping his stout Malacca cane, Justin propelled himself out of his chair to stand upright. Reggie rose beside him as Wimple stepped aside to reveal the umbrella-wielding she-devil who was terrorizing the household servants.

Justin took one look at the woman Reggie had called "Terrible Tess Thornhill" and felt his knees go weak. He had probably seen a more beautiful woman at some time in his life—though he could not at the moment say when. He was absolutely certain he had never before seen one as gloriously alive or as spark-spitting angry as the rain-drenched vision who stalked through his doorway.

Indeed, to describe Miss Thornhill's reaction to the welcome accorded her by Wimple and his staff as mere anger would be tantamount to calling a full-fledged hurricane a brisk breeze. Unmitigated rage flashed in her huge emerald eyes and drew her lush pink lips into a tight line; two bright spots of color flamed in her creamy cheeks, and even the honey-gold curls peeking from beneath her wilted green bonnet bounced with indignation.

She took a deep breath and shifted the offending umbrella from her right to her left hand—seemingly unaware of the provocative picture she made, with her water-soaked pelisse molding her high, proud breasts and outlining her nicely rounded hips. Reggie's soft gasp told Justin the effect had not been lost on his rakish friend; he had a feeling his own mouth was gaping, but he couldn't for the life of him close it.

Silence hung like a thick, chilling fog over the small salon into which Tess Thornhill was finally directed after her tussle with Viscount Sanderfield's surly servants. Her gaze swept the sumptuous embossed silk wall covering, the heavy wine velvet drapes, the unseasonal fresh-cut flowers on a delicate half-moon table, and she found herself comparing the tastefully furnished salon with her own garish quarters in the stews.

She glanced down at her bare, work-roughened hands—so out of place in such elegant surroundings. Damn and blast! Why hadn't she thought to hunt up her one pair of decent gloves? She had lived so long with the desperately poor, she'd all but forgotten how to look or act the proper lady.

Not one, but two, men had risen when she'd stepped through the doorway, but she settled her attention on the shorter of the two. His uncanny resemblance to one of the children in her care instantly branded him the rakehell viscount she sought.

Still, he was not at all as she had pictured him. Slender and slightly above average height, he was a surprisingly pleasant-looking fellow with warm, amber eyes, and a mouth that—when he finally closed it—tilted in a shy, crooked smile that instantly triggered a strange fluttering sensation in the region of her heart.

His unruly brown hair was sun-streaked, his skin unfashionably tanned—probably from summering at one of his country estates. The very thought squelched any residual flutterings and replaced them with a familiar surge of anger at the gross injustice of the British social system. Such indolent libertines as the viscount invariably enjoyed long, lazy summers in the cool, green countryside while the helpless products of their conscienceless rutting sweltered and often starved in the hellish filth of the London stews.

She stared at him, waiting for some kind of greeting. None was forthcoming. No "Good afternoon, Miss Thornhill," nor even a polite "May I present my friend, Lord . . ." The man was not only a rake—he was an unmitigated boor as well.

"You are Viscount Squanderfield, I presume," she said coldly when the waiting became unbearable—then heard her own startled gasp at her slip of tongue. A hot blush flooded her cheeks. Dear God, she'd inadvertently addressed the scoundrel by the name she'd privately dubbed him.

The viscount blinked as if he'd sustained a blow, and to her utter amazement his lean cheeks colored with a flush to match her own. "I take it you are a devotee of William Hogarth's brilliant engravings, Miss Thornhill?"

"I am . . . acquainted with them, my lord," she stammered. "As a matter of fact, my great-aunt, Jane Thornhill, was his wife."

"Ah! I too enjoy his manner of exposing the foibles of what we choose to call polite society." The viscount's expression was grave, his voice as soft as warm clotted cream, but his eyes glinted with unmistakable humor. "Tell me, was it *A Rake's Progress* or *Marriage à la Mode* in which the reprehensible viscount figured?"

For the life of her, Tess couldn't remember. Her mind was a blank, her tongue in a knot. As a last desperate measure, she had bearded the dragon-viscount in his den in the hope of appealing to any minuscule spark of decency lingering in his jaded soul. Now, less than five minutes in his presence, she'd handed him an unpardonable insult.

Well, there was nothing for it but to ignore her faux pas and get on with the business at hand. She raised her chin a notch to where she could stare down her nose at him. "I have come here, my lord"—she said in her haughtiest tone of voice—"to demand an explanation as to why the rent on the Laura Wentworth Home for Abandoned Children was recently doubled."

The viscount's eyes widened with obvious astonishment. "The Laura Wentworth Home? Why I . . . that is, I really cannot say offhand." He glanced toward his companion—a tall, gangly fellow with a face like that of a melancholy horse. "What say you, Reggie? You are more knowledgeable about London and its happenings than I."

The man called Reggie shook his head. "Haven't the foggiest, old sod."

Tess gritted her teeth in frustration at the incredible gall of these two titled fops. Did they think she was taken in by their ridiculous clown act? "Do not pretend that you are unaware you are the owner of the tenement building housing the orphanage, my lord," she snapped. "For I have seen your name on the lease. I suppose next you'll tell me the name Bessie Wattling means nothing to you."

"Wattling?" The viscount looked even more puzzled. "I don't believe I've had the privilege—"

"How dare you treat the situation so lightly!" Tess took a firmer grip on her umbrella and advanced a step farther into the salon. "Or are you so devoid of conscience, you cannot even remember the names of the women you have ruined? Women driven to sell what men like you have already taken from them!"

The man called Reggie made a strange choking sound, which Tess ignored. His elegant blue superfine jacket, gray watered-silk waistcoat, and impressive collection of fobs and seals branded him a dandy. Such mindless fribbles were always surprised that anyone would have the courage to take their kind to task for sins against their so-called inferiors.

She fixed the red-faced viscount with an accusing stare. "I cannot pay the exorbitant rent you ask, my lord. If you persist in this thievery I shall have to close my home. Is your extravagant lifestyle so important to you that you do not feel a single qualm about dispossessing innocent children to support it? Even when one of those children is your own bastard?"

"My own . . ." The viscount took a step back, stumbled and righted himself with the help of his cane. His eyes fairly popped from his head. "I am afraid there has been a slight mistake, Miss Thornhill."

"A *slight* mistake?" His horse-faced companion guffawed. "Monumental is more like it, all things considered. Tell me, ma'am, how old is this child the viscount is supposed to have fathered?"

"Daisy is three years old and the resemblance is unmistakable," Tess declared defiantly. Though, in truth, if it were not for that resemblance, she would find it hard to believe this soft-spoken man with the kind eyes was the care-for-nothing rake who had forced his attentions on an unwilling maidservant.

The taller man gave a triumphant snort. "Aha, he has you there! Justin returned but two months ago from a seven-year sojourn in Greece."

"So you see, Miss Thornhill," the viscount added, "as my friend, the Earl of Rutledge is trying to tell you, I could not possibly be—"

"Little Daisy's father," Tess finished for him, feeling herself wilt with embarrassment beneath his calm amber gaze. "Well, that's that then, and I suppose you think I should offer an apology for accusing you unjustly on that one count," she sputtered. "But you'll hear the gates of hell slam shut before you hear that, my lord, for that's not the only charge I hold against you—and if you'd ever laid eyes on Daisy, you'd know very well that if you weren't the one to seduce poor Bessie Wattling, then it had to have been a close relative posing as you." She gulped a quick breath. "For Bessie was most adamant that the unconscionable rake who'd trapped her in an upstairs linen closet and then tossed her into the street when he found he'd gotten her with child was none other than Viscount Squander . . . Sanderfield."

Tess had a tendency to chatter when she was unsure of herself, and she could never remember feeling more unsure than she did at the moment. In truth, she felt as if she'd stepped into a bog of quicksand and was sinking deeper with every word she uttered.

The viscount, blast him, exchanged a telling look with his friend, then favored her with another of his shy smiles that made her knees tremble like leaves in a windstorm. "The fact that I was not acquainted with the unfortunate Miss Wattling does not mean I am unmoved by her unhappy fate or by the plight of her child.

Indeed of all abandoned children," he added gravely. "If you would take a seat, Miss Thornhill, we can discuss the problem you appear to be having with your children's home. I've just recently acquired the title and attendant properties, you see, and odd as it may seem, I really did not know I was a slum landlord."

All of which only made Tess feel worse. She hesitated, torn between the desire to turn tail and run and the unlikely hope that if the viscount was not quite the blackguard she'd supposed him to be, he might possibly lower her rent if she stayed long enough to apprise him of the cost of feeding and clothing a houseful of hungry, growing children.

"Please be seated, Miss Thornhill," he repeated. "I'm sure the earl would like to sit down; I know I would—and we can't, you know, as long as you remain standing."

Tess felt the flush in her cheeks deepen at his reminder of her lack of social acumen. Quickly, she dropped onto the nearest chair and, lowering her eyes to escape the viscount's warm gaze, found herself staring at his boots. The supple leather and subtle stitching proclaimed them the work of a master bootmaker of Hoby's caliber. But no amount of superb workmanship could disguise the fact that the viscount's left foot was grossly deformed.

Justin cringed at the shock he saw registered on Miss Thornhill's face and reminded himself he should be used to the reaction people had when first they viewed his odd-shaped boot. Somehow he never was. Some gaped; others made a point of looking everywhere but in his direction. Justin endured them all in silence—a silence that all his life had set him apart from those who dared not mention the fact that the youngest grandson of the powerful Duke of Arncott was a cripple.

Inexplicably, he felt compelled to force Miss Thornhill to acknowledge what he had always been more than content to let others pretend to ignore. He tapped the toe of his boot with the tip of his cane. "In case you're wondering, I have a clubfoot—or 'devil's foot,' as my Scottish nanny called it."

Beside him, Reggie made another strangled sound and Justin realized that for once his friend wasn't laughing. Heretofore he had been the only person with whom Justin had ever discussed his deformity.

Miss Thornhill merely raised her remarkable eyes and stead-

•

fastly met his gaze without a hint of pity. "I guessed as much," she said with the same unvarnished candor with which she had admitted to unjustly accusing him of seducing the hapless Bessie Wattling. "Can you walk on it?"

"Yes." Justin swallowed hard, taken aback by her unexpected question but at the same time constrained to be completely honest with her. "However, my gait is somewhat awkward."

Once again she fixed her gaze on his misshapen boot. "Does it hurt?"

"Only if I stand on it too long."

She favored him with a brilliant smile that literally took his breath away. "Well then, it's not so very dreadful after all, is it?"

"No, I guess it isn't at that," he agreed. Though he had to wonder how anyone as whole and perfect as the lovely creature sitting opposite him could possibly know what it was like to be handicapped by a crippling birth defect. He studied her closely, trying to gauge if she, like his grandfather the duke, found him less a man because of his deformed foot.

The unbidden thought shocked him to the core. He had long ago quit worrying what any woman thought of him. In point of fact, the only woman with whom he'd had any close contact in the past seven years was the lusty widow he employed as his housekeeper in Athens—and Sophia gave him no reason to feel uneasy about his affliction in her presence. She merely took care of his physical needs with the same careless ease with which she cleaned his house and cooked his meals. It was the perfect arrangement for a near recluse who felt more at home in the fourth century B.C. than in the nineteenth century A.D.—or so he had always told himself.

"Now about this children's home of yours, Miss Thornhill," he said, changing the subject to one that left him feeling less vulnerable. "I have two questions. The first one is: Who is this Laura Wentworth for whom the home is named?"

"Laura was my best friend—my sister in spirit, if not blood." Miss Thornhill's lovely face contorted with pain. "She died giving birth to the illegitimate child of the titled rake who seduced her."

Which, Justin decided, explained Miss Thornhill's animosity

toward him and probably all other men with titles prefixing their names. He wished he'd never broached the subject.

"And your second question, my lord?"

"Ah yes, my second question. It is of a less personal nature, I assure you," he said gently. "I was unaware that the rents had been increased on any of the Sanderfield properties. Did my man-of-affairs give his reason for doing so?"

"Willard Drebs has only one motivation for anything he does, and that is greed." She took a white-knuckled grip on her umbrella handle, giving Justin the distinct impression she was imagining it to be Drebs's scrawny neck. "I have made numerous improvements to the building, at my own expense, in the five years I've inhabited it. Obviously a mistake on my part, for now he informs me that as it stands today, it could be more profitably used as a bawdy house."

Justin registered Reggie's gasp of astonishment. Miss Thornhill was not only disarmingly honest; she was also embarrassingly frank about a subject that was considered beyond the pale by most proper ladies. Accustomed as he was to Sophia's earthy manner of speaking, Justin found himself more intrigued than shocked by his visitor's frankness.

He watched Miss Thornhill's expressive eyes flash with anger over the injustice done her and found himself remembering a priceless emerald he'd once seen in whose cool green depths a white-hot spark of fire had smoldered. "Fire and ice," he murmured, more fascinated than ever by his volatile guest.

"I shall be happy to consider your request to lower your rent, Miss Thornhill." To his dismay, Justin heard his voice crack like that of a lad still wet behind the ears. The woman had the most amazing effect on him. Just looking at her made his pulse quicken; imagining what it would be like to take her in his arms made his blood race through his arteries.

He shifted uneasily in his chair but managed a shaky smile. "In all fairness, however," he continued, "I must warn you that since Willard Drebs was entrusted to handle my brother's affairs for many years, I feel obliged to personally inspect the building before I make any decision regarding the rent."

"You want to inspect my children's home?" Miss Thornhill squeaked, staring at him through eyes wide with astonishment.

Beside him, Reggie groaned audibly. Justin ignored both reactions to his statement. He knew full well he was acting the fool; for once in his life, he didn't care. He had to see this glorious woman again—even if it meant resorting to such a paltry excuse to do so.

"I shall be happy to welcome you to the Laura Wentworth Children's Home," Miss Thornhill said, looking every bit as happy as a condemned prisoner eyeing the hangman's rope. "But I have to wonder if you realize it is located in one of the most notorious sections of the stews? I cannot believe you would want to venture into such an area, my lord." She dropped her gaze, and Justin gained the distinct impression she was once again staring at his misshapen boot.

He stiffened. "Do not be misled by my infirmity, Miss Thornhill. I am perfectly capable of protecting myself."

Tess felt heat flood her cheeks. "I did not mean to imply you were a . . . a . . . " She gulped, leaving the sentence incomplete, but the words "helpless cripple" hung in the air between them as surely as if she had actually said them. "I merely meant that someone accustomed to the elegance of Mayfair might find the London stews a bit shocking."

"I thank you for your consideration, Miss Thornhill, but I assure you I have seen slums in Paris, Rome, and Athens that would surpass anything the London stews has to offer." The viscount regarded her gravely. "Since I plan to return to Greece very shortly, I should like to conduct my inspection as soon as possible. Would the day after next be convenient with you?"

Tess could think of a hundred reasons why a visit from the viscount would not be the least bit convenient the day after next nor indeed ever, but she mutely nodded her agreement.

"Friday morning it is then." Once again, the viscount treated her to a glimpse of his beautiful, shy smile. Then leaning heavily on his cane, he limped to where the ornate bellpull hung beside the fireplace and rang for his insufferably stiff-necked butler to show her the door.

With sinking heart, Tess descended the shallow steps fronting the town house and climbed into the hackney coach she'd hired to carry her from the Rookeries to Mayfair and back. Settling herself on the faded squabs, she glanced up at the window of the town house to find the viscount watching her, his lean, sun-bronzed face devoid of all expression. She was tempted to wave him good-bye, but all things considered, the gesture seemed somewhat inappropriate.

Slowly, she released the breath she hadn't realized she was holding. Lord love her, she'd done it again—let her incautious tongue run away with her. She'd insulted the man not once but three times, and questioning the wisdom of his visit to the stews had obviously wounded his pride. Always a bad mistake with a man.

The coachman cracked his whip, issued an order to his spavined nag, and the coach lurched forward. Tess covered her nose with a square of perfumed linen to mitigate the sour smell of human sweat, and God only knew what else, that permeated the interior of the cab. Somehow the stench seemed even more rank than she remembered, after inhaling the scent of the fresh flowers gracing the viscount's salon.

A cold, numbing sensation traveled her spine. What would a man accustomed to such subdued elegance think of her precious children's home? She and her volunteer helpers had scrubbed and painted and sawed and hammered to transform the filthy, varmint-ridden tenement into a habitable dwelling. With the aid of charitable donations—some of which she had to admit were a trifle colorful—she had furnished it in what had seemed a truly splendid manner just a few hours ago. Now, remembering Willard Drebs's opinion of her accomplishments, she had to wonder if the viscount, too, would judge it more suitable for a brothel than an orphanage.

She shivered, chilled as much by her gloomy ruminations as by her rain-soaked garments. There was nothing for it but to control her acid tongue and persuade the man to give her what she wanted. What was the saying? *One attracts more flies with honey than vinegar.* Surely the adage applied to titled flies as well as those of the common swarm.

From a purely practical standpoint, she had one thing in her favor. Most men were fools where a beautiful woman was concerned—and she was not unaware she'd been blessed with a bounty of what her lifelong friend, Drew Wentworth, termed "remarkable physical attributes." If nothing else, the burning looks the viscount had cast her way would have convinced her of that.

She had never quibbled at resorting to batting her eyelashes at paunchy bankers and lecherous noblemen to obtain the donations she'd needed in the past. Why should she balk at using such feminine tactics on the viscount when he held the power of life or death over her beloved children's home?

Another saying came to mind: *All's fair in love and war.* Who could deny the war she was waging against the poverty, disease, and ignorance of the London stews was every bit as horrendous as any battle Wellington had fought on the Peninsula.

She sat up straighter and glanced out the window at the busy street down which the coach was traveling. She always felt better about a problem once she'd formulated a plan to solve it—and this time the plan was ridiculously simple. Charm a man who was already attracted to her into giving her what she wanted.

It was not what she would have chosen to do. Under different circumstances, she might have found Sanderfield rather likable, despite his title. But desperate situations called for desperate measures, and every feminine instinct she owned told her that turning the shy viscount up sweet would be as easy as taking a sugarplum from a baby.

Chapter Two

Long after the hackney coach carrying Tess Thornhill had disappeared from the square, Justin stood at the window recalling the look on her face when she'd reluctantly agreed to show him her children's home. For one brief moment, something akin to fear had darkened her eyes and her grave expression had added a new, breathtaking dimension to her beauty.

But there was so much more to Miss Thornhill than mere beauty. One would expect a woman endowed with a perfect face and a figure that made even a cynic like Reggie gasp in admiration to be vain as a peacock. By rights, she should be devoting every waking minute to thinking about the gowns and jewels and other gewgaws with which females adorned themselves. Instead, the remarkable Miss Thornhill spent her time and energy lavishing her love on children no one else wanted—the kind of love he had been denied by the frivolous woman who had borne him.

"Devil take it, Justin, are you going to stand there all afternoon mooning after the woman like some green lad who just discovered girls are different from boys?" Reggie's voice cut into his thoughts like the thrust of a rapier. His carefree friend sounded unusually aggravated, and Justin instantly wheeled around to face him.

"I am not mooning," he declared, though he knew full well he was doing that very thing.

"Bah! You look as though you've been poleaxed; you have since the moment she appeared in your doorway. What in God's name are you thinking of? The hellcat from the stews is not for you—or for any other man who values his peace of mind."

Justin felt his hackles rise at Reggie's uncomplimentary description of the lovely Miss Thornhill. "She is the most glorious creature I have ever laid eyes on," he declared. "And the most fiercely maternal. A magnificent golden lioness protecting her helpless cubs."

"An apropos analogy." Reggie stalked to the sideboard to refill his brandy glass. "She does remind one of a feline—claws and all. Namely the great, tawny cat that prowls its cage in the Tower of London zoo."

Justin opened his mouth to protest, but Reggie ignored him and continued his diatribe. "Any man with an ounce of sense where females are concerned could see Terrible Tess Thornhill is the worst kind of termagant—as would you if you'd spent less time studying ancient Greeks and more time studying modern females like the rest of us."

"Nonsense." Justin limped back to his chair, sat down, and picked up his hand of cards. "You're judging her by the gaggle of empty-headed incomparables from which your family expects you to choose your countess—or the greedy dolly birds you set up in that tidy little house on the outskirts of London. You would feel threatened by any woman with passionate beliefs and the courage to pursue them."

"And you don't?" Reggie's eyes widened in disbelief. "Then, my friend, I begin to think you even more a fool than your grandfather claims. For there's no more troublesome creature on earth than a strong-minded female."

The reference to the autocratic old man who held him in such disgust touched a sore spot in Justin. "I doubt that how I view the opposite sex has any bearing on the duke's disappointment in me as his heir—any more than my whole-of-limb brother's contempt for all women was what won him unqualified approval," he said bitterly.

Reggie had the grace to flush. "Devil take it, Justin, I was out of line with that remark and I apologize for it. But I'll not apologize for warning you off Tess Thornhill. Good God, man, for the sake of your sanity, stay away from the woman."

Justin tossed his cards on the table, completely out of the mood for the game of whist he and Reggie had been playing when Miss Thornhill arrived. "And tell me, if you will, what I should do for the sake of the child, Daisy, who is in her care? Have you any doubt that the unscrupulous rake who fathered her was my brother?"

"None whatsoever," Reggie admitted. "Oliver was trapping unsuspecting maidservants in clothespresses when you and I were still in the first form at Eton. But I sincerely hope you are not planning to support all the little bastards the randy fellow left behind when that yacht of his capsized."

Justin smiled in spite of himself. "Hardly. I doubt I inherited pockets deep enough to tackle such a monumental project as that."

"Then do not try to persuade me it was simply concern for the child's welfare that led you to make that asinine appointment to 'inspect your property' in the London stews."

Now it was Justin's turn to flush. "Whatever my reasons, they are not your concern. May I remind you, as I did Miss Thornhill, that I am quite capable of taking care of myself in the roughest of areas."

"As well I know. I'll never forget how you saved my bacon with that handy cane of yours in a back alley of Athens last time I visited you. But we're not discussing street fighting here. When it comes to a woman like Tess Thornhill, you, my friend, are still a babe in leading strings."

"Now wait just a minute—"

Reggie waved his objection aside. "I have never presumed to give you advice before; I only do so now because you're like the brother I never had."

Justin gritted his teeth. "I know that, but—"

"Hear me out, my friend. Admire Miss Thornhill if you must; lower her rent if you will. You can certainly afford to, and I'll not argue that the poor little devils in that home of hers are probably better off because she champions them. But for the love of God, keep your distance from the witch. A naive fellow like you would be a good deal safer stepping into that lion cage at the Tower than tangling with the likes of Terrible Tess Thornhill."

A wise man once observed, "The two persons from whom no gentleman can hope to keep a secret are his butler and his valet."

Justin was no exception to this rule. The two elderly retainers he'd inherited from his brother and father before him had taken his measure at first glance and decided they had their work cut out for them if they were to turn the reclusive new viscount into a creditable member of the peerage.

Each in his own way had attempted to educate the new master to the responsibilities of his lofty position. But with a full two months elapsed since he'd returned to England to claim his title, they had to admit he'd yet to show the slightest interest in any of the activities a young unmarried man of his wealth and station was expected to take up. Though cards and invitations by the dozens arrived daily, they sat unopened on the bookroom desk while the new viscount buried his nose in one or another of the dusty volumes he'd brought with him from Greece.

Not once had Wimple been ordered to ready the town house for entertaining guests on a moment's notice, as had been the habit of the previous two viscounts. Except for the lawyers who arrived daily with their ledgers and portfolios, the only visitor the new viscount received was his longtime friend, the Earl of Rutledge—and then only for a quiet game of whist.

Not once had Pruefrock, the valet, been called upon to dress the new viscount in proper evening clothes—nor, for that matter, even been allowed to tie his cravat in the stylish Waterfall or Mathematical the previous viscount had favored. Pruefrock had lived in dread of being sacked the first month he'd served his new master, for the viscount appeared to have little use for the services of a superior valet when all he required of a manservant was to keep his shirts ironed and his boots polished. But Lord Justin was a good-natured fellow and, living up to his name, a just one as well. To date, he'd showed no sign of replacing any of the staff he'd inherited.

Still, in more ways than one, he was a bitter disappointment to the two old men who had served one or another of the Viscounts Sanderfield for the past fifty years. And now, to top it all, there was this dither over the Thornhill woman.

"By George, he's going to do it—call on that impossible creature at her home in the stews." Wimple stepped away from the door against which he'd had his ear pressed for the past half hour. "The earl, God bless him, has the Thornhill woman pegged to the tuppence, but I could have told him the viscount wouldn't listen to a word against her. It was plain as the nose on his face, the young fool was besotted with her at first glance."

Wimple straightened his wig, which had slipped over one ear during his monitoring of the earl and viscount's conversation, and headed for the butler's pantry and the supply of crested notepaper on which he penned his daily missive to the head of the Warre family. "Well, the duke will want to hear of this. It is exactly the sort of thing he warned me to watch out for."

Pruefrock pried his eye from the keyhole, dabbed the perspiration from his brow with a lace-edged handkerchief which had once been the property of the former viscount, and followed in Wimple's footsteps. It galled him no end that a butler had been entrusted to keep the Duke of Arncott informed of the comings and goings of his grandson, when everyone knew it was a man's valet who was privy to his most intimate secrets. Besides, he rather liked the shy, young viscount, despite his unfortunate taste in clothing. The lad never failed to compliment him on the gleaming perfection he achieved on his sadly mismatched boots.

"He's an odd duck, the new master, and that's a fact," he remarked, settling onto one of the two chairs that had sat in the exact same spot in the butler's pantry for as long as he could remember. "No telling what sort of woman would strike his fancy. But better the harpy from the stews than none at all—if you takes my meaning. I don't mind telling you I was getting a bit anxious on that score, with him back in London a full two months and not so much as looking at a female."

"Humpf! No need to worry about such as that. He is a Warre, after all, in spite of . . . everything." Wimple poured two glasses of fine French brandy from the bottle he had recently liberated from the viscount's well-stocked cellar and handed one to Pruefrock. "One would have hoped, however, he would show a little more taste in his selection of a female companion once he acquired the title. Lord Oliver may have been a bit of a rip with the upstairs maids and the Drury Lane doxies, but he never made the mistake of being seen with one of them in public—a fine line that has apparently escaped Lord Justin."

"And just where was Lord Justin supposed to learn about this 'fine line'?" Pruefrock demanded. "As I recall, the family kept him hidden away in the country until he was old enough to be sent off to school, with naught but a prune-faced Scotswoman for company. Only one as ever cared a fig about him was Lady Anne, God rest her soul."

Wimple gave Pruefrock a withering look. "I can see you've no understanding of the nobility, despite your years of service," he said stiffly. "The Warres are a proud family—and the old duke the proudest of them all. He can scarcely be faulted for not wanting to admit publicly that one of his grandsons was born less than perfect."

He paused to refill his glass. "The duke has suffered mightily this past year. I don't know which was the greatest loss to him— the granddaughter he doted on or the grandson who was his heir. Lady Anne's death broke the old man's heart, but Lord Oliver's death left him no choice but to acknowledge Lord Justin as his rightful heir—which had to put a dent in his pride."

"Serves the old buzzard right," Pruefrock mumbled to himself. *As if a gimpy foot was reason enough to treat the lad like he was some kind of freak.* He drowned his disgust with the duke in a healthy swallow of brandy, though he'd take a glass of hearty English ale over the miserable Frenchie brew any day.

He was sorely tempted to throw caution to the winds and express his opinion of the treatment his young master had received at the hands of his autocratic grandfather, but he immediately thought better of it. There was no telling what information would find its way into those infernal notes Wimple was always penning—and His Grace, the Duke of Arncott, was the last person any man in his right mind would want to cross.

With Reggie's dire warning ringing in his ears, and a pepper-box pistol tucked in the waistband of his trousers, Justin set out for the East End of London two days later. The pistol was to pacify Pruefrock. For once, his punctilious valet had overstepped the limits of the master-servant relationship to demand his young employer arm himself before he set out on his junket into the notorious stews.

"The place is a sewer, my lord," the old man declared as he and Mrs. Pennywacker, the rotund housekeeper, saw Justin off. "I know it well, for wasn't I one to take my pleasure in the gin shops of Fleet Street when I was your age." He shuddered. "You'll be taking your life in your hands once you cross into the East End, for the dregs of humanity roam the streets of the stews—flash-house whelps, pimps and prostitutes, soldiers home from the Peninsula, and sailors released from His Majesty's navy—many of them crippled—if you'll pardon the expression—and all of them destitute."

"Chimney sweeps and their climbing boys, moneylenders, fish-wives, and more bog trotters than you'll find in the whole of Dublin," Mrs. Pennywacker added.

She viewed Justin through rheumy eyes, her round, apple cheeks pink with agitation. "Vicious as starving rats they be, wot with times so hard. I've heard tell they'd as soon murder a man for a shiny button as a gold watch fob."

Pruefrock nodded his agreement. "What's more, there's to be a hanging outside Newgate prison this very afternoon—and I don't have to tell you what kind of crowd that will draw. Think on it, my lord. Every cutpurse and cutthroat in London will be on the streets."

Though he was sorely tempted, Justin refrained from asking how two members of his household staff came to be so intimately acquainted with his plans for the day. It was obvious there had been an ear to the keyhole during his interview with the fascinating Miss Thornhill. Actually, he felt more touched by his elderly retainers' concern than annoyed at their snooping. He was not accustomed to having people worry about him, and he found the experience both gratifying and embarrassing.

Consequently, he not only agreed to fortify himself with the pistol Pruefrock provided, but also agreed to carry a similarly armed groom—Mrs. Pennywacker's young nephew from Yorkshire—with him in his curricle as well. He drew the line, however, at strapping her kitchen knife to his boot. Arming oneself to the teeth to call upon a young lady seemed a trifle excessive.

However, an hour later he found himself wondering if he should have taken the advice of the two old quizzes more to heart. His first look at London's notorious East End was a shock. It was not that he was a stranger to the seamier side of life. He had been honest when he'd told Miss Thornhill he had seen the vilest of slums in Paris, Rome, and Athens. He had seen even worse filth and poverty when he'd walked the narrow, crooked streets of

Bombay and the back alleys of Constantinople in search of a document bearing the signature of the Emperor Constantine.

But somehow he had never equated the squalor and misery he'd witnessed in those foreign cities with the capital of his own country. For good reason. He had been fresh out of Oxford when he left England, and he knew nothing of London except the little he'd gleaned during the fortnight he had spent at the Pulteney Hotel in Piccadilly prior to sailing for Greece.

In his mind, London had always been gracious hotels, fine food, and such pleasant places as Hyde Park, Hatchards bookshop, and Hookum's Library. Unlike his devil-may-care older brother, he had never sowed his wild oats in the brothels and gambling hells of this other, darker London.

Slowly, he guided his pair of handsome Cleveland Bays down the narrow, congested cobblestone street to which Miss Thornhill had directed him. On all sides, peddlers and pedestrians stopped to watch his progress and before he'd maneuvered a city block, he'd collected a dozen or more ragged urchins as an entourage.

He found himself wishing he had a conveyance less conspicuous than the gaudy red-and-gold curricle he'd inherited from his brother. But it was either that or the even more ostentatious closed carriage with the family crest which had once belonged to his father. He would not be in England long enough to warrant purchasing a rig more to his own liking.

"Look for a blue door," he ordered his groom, raising his voice to be heard over the din of cart wheels and the cries of vendors hawking their wares. "I was told it's all that distinguishes the building we seek from the others in this godforsaken hellhole."

He glanced about him at the dilapidated tenements lining the odoriferous, garbage-littered street. Like a bizarre chorus of drunken ballerinas, they leaned higgledy-piggledy against one another for support, giving the impression that should one of the ramshackle structures topple over, the rest would soon follow suit.

"There it be, my lord," the groom declared, pointing to a door the color of a newly hatched robin's egg. With a smile for the incongruity of the brave splotch of color in the sea of gray, age-grimed stone, Justin brought his curricle to a stop before a building bearing the sign THE LAURA WENTWORTH HOME FOR ABANDONED CHILDREN.

Immediately, he was surrounded by a crush of unwashed humanity, the stench of which not even the brisk November breeze could fully dissipate. "Phew! The ripest hog pen in Yorkshire smells better'n this lot," the young groom declared, wrinkling his nose disdainfully.

"Well now, look who's come to see 'ow t'other 'alf lives," a ruddy-cheeked old harridan pushing a soup and stew cart catcalled as Justin struggled to calm his nervous nags. "If it's Carlton 'ouse yer lookin' fer, guvnor, ye made a wrong turn at the last corner."

A tinsmith, his wares piled high in a wooden barrow, rattled past. "But likely ye'll find 'is fat 'ighness at Florabelle's grinding 'ouse next street over," he added with a toothless grin for the laughter his allusion to the unpopular Prince Regent occasioned.

More earthy remarks concerning the prince, his collection of ne'er-do-well brothers, and the nobility in general followed from a wizened little secondhand clothing merchant, whose makeshift stall butted up against that of a purveyor of well-worn boots. In spite of himself, Justin felt a grin spread across his face. The clothing merchant's comments were shockingly disrespectful, but he seemed good-natured enough—as did his raucous audience. All but one young, red-haired boy, who stood back from the crowd, staring at Justin with hot, angry blue eyes.

Something about the surly youngster held Justin's gaze—a look of sharp intelligence in his pinched face, a proud rigidity in his rail-thin body that set him apart from the miserable creatures surrounding him. Justin found himself inexplicably drawn to this child of the slums who, for some unknown reason, showed every sign of hating him on sight.

Shaking off the uneasy presentiment crawling his spine, he tore his gaze from the boy, instructed his burly groom to guard the carriage, and made his usual clumsy descent from the driver's seat. Instantly, a hush fell on the crowd at the sight of his misshapen boot. "Lord luv us, the toff is devil-marked," an old crone in a mobcap croaked in a hoarse whisper Justin felt certain could be heard a good mile down the Thames.

"Devil-marked" . . . "devil-marked" . . . "devil-marked,"

echoed through the crowd of curious spectators like a breeze rustling through dry autumn leaves. A familiar tide of angry frustration swelled within Justin; these denizens of the stews were even more cruel in their ridicule of one of nature's freaks than their counterparts in the *ton*. With grim determination, he limped forward, clearing a path with his cane as he went. The crowd fell back before him—all but the red-haired boy, who stubbornly stood his ground at the foot of the stairs leading to the blue door.

Justin brushed past him and felt a sharp tug on the pocketbook he'd thought to pin securely inside the pocket of his greatcoat—a precaution he'd often employed to discourage the wily thieves of Athens. Instinctively, he swept his stout cane between the young pickpocket's legs, sending the boy sprawling facedown on the grimy cobblestones. Balancing on his good foot, he planted the misshapen boot of the other one in the small of his quarry's back.

"What in heaven's name are you doing to my young assistant, my lord?" The female voice was sharp with indignation, and looking up, Justin beheld Tess Thornhill swooping down the stairs like an avenging angel.

Instantly, his breath caught in his throat; she was even lovelier than he remembered. Today she was dressed in a plain wool gown with the long sleeves and prim neckline he associated with proper Methodist ladies, but the color—he blinked—was the vivid, shocking scarlet worn only by the most daring members of the demimonde. Apparently Miss Thornhill's taste in clothing was as unorthodox as her choice of doors—and as he'd suspected at their first meeting, she, herself, was the same illogical combination of hoyden and Puritan as that of her unusual gown.

She paused on the step above him, her hands on her hips. "Well, my lord, I am waiting for an answer to my question."

Justin gathered his wits. "Good morning, Miss Thornhill. I should think it would be obvious I am defending my person and my pocketbook against this light-fingered little weasel." He glanced down at the scrawny figure beneath his foot. "And I must say, if this is an example of the kind of staff you employ, I can understand why your coffers are empty."

Miss Thornhill gasped. "Damn and blast," she muttered under her breath, darting the boy a look that fairly singed his mop of carrot-colored hair. She transferred her fiery gaze to Justin. "I apologize for Danny's inexcusable behavior. Nevertheless, I must insist you let him up off that filthy pavement this very instant."

Justin removed his foot from the boy's back, but not before he had leaned forward to take a firm hold on the collar of his thin jacket. With a swift, fluid movement, he yanked the culprit to his feet just as the cadaverous proprietor of the used boot stall stepped forward to address the audience forming behind Justin. "Wot call, I asks ye, 'as a bloomin' lord to be 'ere in the stews in the first place? And wot right 'as such as 'e to be accusin' a poor orphink like Danny of tryin' to nick 'is poke? Next we knows, 'e'll be turnin' the lad over to the watch."

Angry murmurs of agreement circulated through the crowd. The young miscreant was obviously one of their own.

"I think it best you release the boy, my lord," Miss Thornhill said grimly. "Tempers are short hereabouts and the mood of the crowd can turn ugly very quickly." She glanced toward the stolid groom, who had drawn his pistol and stood ready to come to his master's defense. "Someone could be badly hurt—or worse. I cannot believe your pocketbook is that important to you."

Justin tightened his hold on his squirming captive. "I attach little importance to my pocketbook," he declared. "But this piece of misguided humanity"—he scowled into the boy's defiant blue eyes—"might just be a commodity worth salvaging. Tell me, Miss Thornhill, what chance will your young assistant have of becoming a man of integrity if he is not made to accept responsibility for his actions as a lad?"

Tess felt a flush of embarrassment heat her cheeks. "A point well taken, my lord," she admitted grudgingly. "But I doubt you are the proper person for the task."

The viscount blanched, but didn't relinquish his hold on the boy. "Perhaps not, Miss Thornhill, but since it is obvious no one else has made an effort to counsel the lad to date, I believe I shall give it a try."

Tess's cheeks grew even hotter. She had long ago recognized the keen mind hidden beneath the boy's rough exterior. Time and again she had taken him aside and begged him to give up the dangerous profession he had learned in one of London's most infamous flash houses. But to no avail. As soon as her back was

turned, he augmented the pittance she managed to pay him by relieving some unsuspecting gentleman of his purse.

Now this privileged aristocrat with his elegant greatcoat and his
fine carriage and matched pair dared openly castigate the young
pickpocket in the presence of men and women to whom thievery
was an accepted way of life. Didn't the fool know what hatred his
kind engendered in people whose stomachs rumbled with hunger
and whose bodies had never known the luxury of a warm winter
coat? The Viscount Sanderfield would be lucky if his sanctimonious prattle didn't earn him a clout on the head or a knife between his ribs.

She gnashed her teeth in frustration. Damn and blast. The idiot
left her no choice but to back him up. She could see her rent dou-
bling again if her landlord came to harm on her doorstep.

"The truth, Danny!" she demanded of her hapless assistant.
"Did you try to rob the viscount of his purse?"

Danny's eyes narrowed, silently accusing her of going over to
the enemy. "Wot if I did?" He raised his chin defiantly. "Wot's 'e
doin' 'ere anyhow? We don't want the likes of 'im sniffin' round
little Daisy."

So that was what this unfortunate business was about! Tess felt
a stab of guilt. She should have thought to warn Danny of the viscount's impending visit. The boy was too observant by half—a
natural artist, always scribbling likenesses of everyone around
him on whatever scraps of paper he managed to get his hands on.
He would be certain to see Sanderfield's uncanny resemblance to
the little girl he adored and draw the wrong conclusion as to the
reason for his visit to the childrens' home.

Tess stepped closer to the viscount and his captive. "Listen to
me, Danny," she said in a quiet voice meant only for his ears.
"The Viscount Sanderfield is not Daisy's father, though I grant
you he looks a great deal like her."

The young street urchin gave a disbelieving grunt. He had been
fiercely protective of the little girl since the day her mother had
left her at the home "for a day or two" and promptly disappeared,
never to return.

"No, I'm telling you the truth. I made the same mistake until I
learned he had been away from England for the past seven years."
Tess laid a hand on the boy's arm. "I promise you, he is not here

to take Daisy away from us, but merely to negotiate the rent on the building he owns."

Danny relaxed noticeably, but he stared at his captor with wary eyes. "Wot'll 'e do to me if I admits to 'avin' me 'and in 'is pocket?"

Tess turned an imploring gaze on the viscount, who was obviously listening to their exchange. "My lord?" she asked, registering the pensive look in his amber eyes.

"I shall overlook the boy's malefaction this once if he'll give me his solemn promise he'll never again put his fingers in any pocket but his own," he said gravely.

Behind him, the crowd shifted restlessly. Murmurs of "Don't listen to the toff, laddie-o" and "Who's 'e to be sayin' wot's wot 'ere in the stews" mingled with the sound of shuffling feet and the clip-clop of horses' hooves as a heavily loaded wagon lumbered by.

Danny's ginger brows drew together in a frown. "Don't know what a 'malefaction' is, but I knows a flimflam answer when I hears one. Never's a long time!"

"That it is," the viscount agreed. "But I'll not settle for less."

"You drives a 'ard bargain, guvnor."

"And you play a dangerous game, my lad. Last I heard, cutting a man's purse was still a hanging offense. You're lucky I've no stomach for sending a mere bantling to Newgate." The viscount loosed his hold on the boy's collar and held out his hand. "Are we agreed then?"

Tess held her breath, half expecting Danny to bolt and run. Like all residents of the stews, he harbored a deep distrust of the nobility. Furthermore, he was stubbornly independent; he would not take kindly to being backed into a corner.

"Don't see as 'ow ye leaves me no druthers. Ye twiddles a mean stick . . . fer a cripple," the boy said sourly, but to her surprise, Tess saw a look of grudging respect cross his thin, young face.

"A fellow born with a handicap like mine would be trampled underfoot unless he learned to defend himself," Justin said matter-of-factly.

"Ye've the right of that, guvnor!" Danny glanced around the circle of onlookers for corroboration, and Tess felt a subtle less-

ening in the tension gripping the crowd. Here and there she saw
nods of approval for a man who asked no quarter because of his
affliction.

With an expressive shrug of his narrow shoulders, Danny
clasped the viscount's outstretched hand. "You're a right 'un,
guv-nor, and I'll keep me side of the bargain, though I never
thought to shake 'ands with a bloomin' toff."

The viscount chuckled. "Nor I with the likes of you, my lad.
But I offer my hand in good faith, something I'd not do to a fellow whose word I couldn't trust."

"Likewise," Danny said, appearing to grow an inch or two before Tess's very eyes.

Solemnly, they shook hands while the surrounding spectators
collectively held their breath. The viscount was the first to break
the silence. "We'll talk about this later, lad. You'll need an in-
come to take the place of your former . . . profession, and if all
goes well here today, I may be in need of a building manager."

"I'm your man, guvnor. I knows every nail in the bloomin'
building. Put most of them there meself." He stole a sheepish
glance at Tess. "With a bit of 'elp, of course."

"Of course." The viscount's amber eyes twinkled. "I'll let you
know when and where I can arrange a meeting to discuss the
proposition I have in mind."

"Well you come out on top o' that one, Danny," the soup and
stew hag declared, and a murmur of assent went around the
crowd. The drama over, the spectators began to disperse, taking
Danny with them to bask in the glory of the brief excitement he
had brought to an otherwise bleak November day.

Relief flooded through Tess—and conversely, a deep resentment that a complete stranger, and a member of the hated aristocracy to boot, had extracted a promise from the boy that she had
been unable to obtain with two years of serious effort.

She clenched her fists in frustration. Males, whatever their age,
were bewildering creatures—and the viscount was the most bewildering of all. There was something dangerously seductive in
his shy smile and dulcet voice. She had felt the spellbinding pull
of that seduction within moments of meeting him; now her cynical young assistant had fallen victim to the man's elusive charm.

She would be heartily relieved to put this day behind her and see the last of the troublesome fellow.

Forgotten was her solemn vow to be so docile and sweet-natured she would charm her landlord into giving her the reasonable rent she so badly needed. With an angry swish of her skirt and a glare to match it, she turned her back on him and rapidly mounted the stairs.

"Are you coming, my lord?" she asked impatiently when she realized he was not directly behind her. "I should like to get this business of the tour over with as soon as possible. I have other pressing matters to attend to today, as I'm certain have you."

The sharpness in her voice instantly wiped the smile from Justin's face. "At your service, ma'am," he said, and cringed at the look of shock—or was it pity—on her face when she realized her precipitous flight up the steep stairs had left him far behind.

She pressed her fingers to her lips as if suddenly remembering she should have been more considerate of a man with his affliction, and once again the unspoken words "helpless cripple" hung between them.

Humiliation. Anger. Despair. Justin felt gripped by all three with an intensity he hadn't felt in years. Inclining his head in a stiff gesture that was not quite a bow, he took a firmer grip on his cane and made his laborious way up the stairs toward the glorious woman he feared would always be just beyond his reach.

Chapter Three

Tess registered the desolate look on the viscount's face and instantly guessed he'd misconstrued her reaction to his slow progress up the stairs. The fellow was far too sensitive about his affliction. She had made her inconsiderate dash toward the door for the simple reason that she had been so caught up in the confusing emotions he engendered in her, she'd forgotten all about his blasted foot. Now he had something else to hold against her.

Well, there was nothing for it but to push on with this miserable inspection and pretend nothing was amiss. "I may as well warn you, my lord," she said as she opened the daring blue door which had become her trademark with the local residents, "the Laura Wentworth Home does not conform to the prevailing concept of an orphanage." She raised her chin a notch. "Nor will it ever, as long as I am in charge of it."

Since Justin could think of nothing to say in reply to Miss Thornhill's audacious remark, he simply followed her lead and crossed the threshold, only to stop short and stare about him in amazement. From her colorful door and flamboyant scarlet dress, he had deduced she was an "original." He could see now he had seriously underestimated her. She was, in fact, a dyed-in-the-wool eccentric who happily ignored the opinion of polite society.

For, instead of the somber gray ambience usually associated with charity institutions, a rainbow of colors met his astonished eyes. The walls were the vivid yellow of a spring buttercup, the ceiling the same blue as the door, and the multipatterned carpet beneath his feet rivaled any he'd seen in Persia for sheer brilliance of hue. Two gilt-back benches, upholstered in the same scarlet damask as Miss Thornhill's gown, flanked the doorway and beyond them stood a life-size marble statue of Cupid, complete with bow and arrows. If he didn't know better, he'd swear he'd just stepped into a Paris bordello.

He looked up from his perusal of the amazing carpet to find himself staring into a huge gilt-edged mirror which reflected the scarlet-robed Miss Thornhill, his own soberly-clad person, and a startling leaf-green staircase that wound like a mammoth coiled serpent into the upper regions of the building. He knew he was gaping, but the hinges of his jaw seemed incapable of closing.

Miss Thornhill tossed her head defiantly. "If you're wondering how we came by such lovely colors of paint, the entire lot was donated to us by Miss Florabelle Favor, a . . . a local entrepreneur. It was what was left over when she redecorated her . . . business establishment." Miss Thornhill's cheeks flamed, leaving Justin little doubt as to what kind of business establishment the generous Miss Favor operated. "There are those who might consider the color scheme a trifle vulgar, but the children and I find it to be vastly cheerful. And who could be more in need of cheer than abandoned children?"

"Who indeed?" Justin echoed faintly.

His lovely guide nodded toward the serpentine stairwell. "I doubt you'd care to climb two flights of stairs to inspect the sleeping quarters." Her flush deepened, as if she'd suddenly become aware she had again alluded to his infirmity. "Suffice it to say each child has been allowed to choose the color for his or her own cubicle from the paints we had in store. The results are really quite amazing; children can be very imaginative when given the freedom to be so."

Her smile held a momentary tinge of sadness. "I was never allowed such freedom of choice as a child. I used to long for a bit of color in my drab life. I vow I will never be without it again."

Justin found himself envisioning a bright, inquisitive little girl stifled by the restrictions imposed on her by her coldly pious father—and applauding the woman who so valiantly defied them. "With me it is flowers," he said without thinking. "I have always been drawn to their beauty and fragrance. But boys are not supposed to care about such things, you know." *Especially boys who are the grandsons of the Duke of Arncott.*

"Luckily, I was left on my own at one of my family's small country estates for most of my childhood years. The gardens were tended by a young Italian gardener named Luigi, whose favorite saying was, 'A man's spirit is never so low it cannot be raised by the sight of one of God's perfect flowers.' "

He laughed self-consciously, thinking how like one of those perfect flowers was the vivid woman standing before him. "Naturally I dared not share this bit of Latin wisdom with my fellow students at Eton and Oxford, lest I be thought unmanly. One of the few benefits of succeeding to the title has been the privilege of demanding a continual supply of fresh flowers about me at all times."

Tess remembered the unseasonal bouquet gracing the salon of his town house and felt a tug at her heart strings when she pictured what life in the English school system must have been like for him. She'd heard tales of the cruel ragging of the younger students by upperclassmen; a boy with a crippled foot would have been a prime target for the pranksters.

She pulled herself up short. Blast him! He was doing it again— revealing glimpses of himself which forced her to acknowledge he was nothing like the typical callow aristocrat she had expected him to be. A woman in her position could ill afford to indulge in such maudlin sentiments about a peer of the realm. She pushed past him, determined to show him the balance of the home as quickly as possible and send him on his way.

"This is the common room in which the children take their meals and study their lessons," she said briskly, throwing open the pair of tall double doors which she had personally painted a deep magenta. It had seemed such a delightful color at the time; now, viewing it through the viscount's eyes, she wondered if she might not have been wiser to choose something a little less flamboyant.

Justin noted the frown creasing her brow and wondered what he had said that upset her this time. He appeared to have a talent for rubbing her the wrong way. He gritted his teeth. Women were such bewildering creatures, even the best of them. How could any man hope to stay in their good graces for long?

Limping forward, he found himself in a large, high-ceilinged room, dominated by a long plank table that was set with a dozen or more earthenware soup bowls and tin spoons. Beside each setting was a chunk of crusty bread. No wonder Miss Thornhill was miffed with him; he had apparently timed his inspection to coincide with the children's noon meal.

He smiled to himself. How convenient. He would simply have to cut this first visit short and make an appointment to see the rest of the facility—and the intriguing Miss Thornhill—on yet another day. Proper etiquette dictated nothing less.

Feeling inordinately pleased with himself, he made a show of carefully examining the room in which he found himself. Like the entrance hall, it was painted a cheerful shade of yellow—all except one wall, which was papered in a vast mural of a lush meadow framed by a copse of white birch trees. Dozens of woolly lambs gamboled about on the grassy sward, and in their center stood what looked to be a gigantic goat on whose head rested a crown of daisies.

He took another look. Good God! The creature was not the common species of hoofed animal he'd first suspected it to be; it was instead some artist's rendition of that half-man, half-goat phenomenon, the Greek god Pan. And a lascivious rendition at that.

Miss Thornhill tucked a stray curl into her somewhat unruly chignon. "The wallpaper was also donated by Miss Favor," she said matter-of-factly. "Luckily for us, she is not well-versed in mythology. I have to believe she had the god Bacchus in mind when she ordered it from a shop in Paris, but she asked for Pan—and this was the result."

She avoided looking him in the face, but Justin felt certain he caught a glint of humor in her eyes. "I imagine Miss Favor may have been right in thinking that some of her patrons might take offense at the horns protruding from the fellow's head, not to mention the body of a goat attached to his torso."

"I daresay they might." With a great deal of effort, Justin managed to keep a straight face.

"But the children love it," she continued, a note of sadness creeping into her voice. "None of them have ever seen a meadow, you see." She sighed. "Still, I've no doubt the mural was one of the things which inspired that jackal, Willard Drebs, to declare my lovely children's home should be turned into a bawdy house."

"I suspect it might have had something to do with the expres-

sion on the god's face," Justin managed, though he was choking
with laughter.

Miss Thornhill's eyes widened. Stepping closer to the mural,
she made a minute examination of Pan's leering visage. "I do believe you may have hit upon the truth, my lord," she said, her
shoulders shaking with mirth. "Oh, dear, I've never before taken a
really good look at the wicked fellow." She pulled a square of
linen from her sleeve and blotted her streaming eyes. "But you
must admit it is a lovely meadow."

"Never seen one lovelier," Justin agreed, wiping tears of mirth
from his own eyes. Devil take it, he had never heard a woman
laugh as heartily as Miss Thornhill. Nor could he remember having ever enjoyed anything as much as this highly improper conversation with the uninhibited original. Frantically, he racked his
brain for reasons to call upon her once his tour of the home was
completed.

Emboldened by their brief repartee, he decided it was high time
he suggested they agree to address each other less formally. But
before he could form the words, a door slammed somewhere in
the nether regions of the building. A babble of voices echoed
through the corridor outside the common room, followed by the
patter of little feet and a childish trill of laughter.

"Speaking of the children, I do believe they've returned from
their daily walk," Miss Thornhill declared, blotting her eyes one
last time before tucking the square of linen beneath the prim
white cuff of her scarlet sleeve. "I usually take them myself, but
since you were coming, I prevailed upon my good friend, Drew
Wentworth, to supervise them today."

"Wentworth? The same name as the woman for whom your
children's home is named."

"Drew is Laura's brother. The three of us were inseparable as
children. Even now, I rely upon him greatly. Without his help, I
would never have been able to establish the children's home,
much less keep it open these past five years."

Justin felt as if someone had suddenly doused him with a buck-
etful of cold water, washing away every last vestige of the mirth
he had felt just moments before. Leaning heavily on his cane, he
drew a calming breath and wrestled with the disturbing idea that

there was a man in the intriguing Miss Thornhill's life—one on whom she "relied greatly."

The piping young voices drew nearer. "Ah, here come my charges at last, my lord." Miss Thornhill gave him one of her brilliant smiles, sending every drop of blood in his veins soaring to the temperature of molten lava. "Now you'll be able to see for yourself the kind of flowers I grow in *my* garden."

"That I shall," he agreed. But his gaze was riveted, not on the bright-cheeked, vividly garbed children who clustered in the doorway, but on the angry blue eyes of the tall, black-haired man who stood in their midst.

Justin blinked, taken aback as much by Drew Wentworth's spectacular appearance as by the malevolence he displayed. This "good friend" on whom Miss Wentworth depended so heavily was a veritable Adonis, whose perfect classic features and magnificent physique made Justin more aware than ever of his own physical deficiencies.

But why the instant hostility on the part of the handsome fellow? Justin was accustomed to curiosity, sometimes even revulsion, on the part of strangers who spied his misshapen boot for the first time. The look in Wentworth's eyes was neither of those, but rather pure, unadulterated hatred—a bizarre reaction to someone he'd never before laid eyes on. The only plausible explanation was that Wentworth held all men of title to blame for his sister's disgrace and death.

The flush staining Miss Thornhill's cheeks proclaimed she too was aware of her "good friend's" insulting behavior. "May I present Mr. Drew Wentworth, my lord," she said in a voice sharpened by strain.

Wentworth gave a stiff little nod in Justin's general direction, which more closely resembled an outright snub than a cordial greeting.

"I believe I mentioned that *my landlord*, Viscount Sanderfield, would be making an inspection of the children's home with a view to negotiating a more equitable rent than that imposed by his man-of-affairs," she continued pointedly, leveling a look on Wentworth that Justin found himself fervently hoping she never had occasion to turn on him.

Wentworth appeared unfazed by her set-down. "I shall leave

you to it then, sweetheart," he declared somewhat breezily. "For I have business elsewhere."

Sweetheart! Miss Thornhill's blush deepened and Justin found himself wondering just how intimate a relationship she shared with the handsome cit. He took a tighter grip on his cane as a sudden urge to rearrange a few of the fellow's handsome features came over him—a reaction Wentworth instantly registered, if the triumphant look that crossed his face was any indication.

"Incidentally, *sweetheart*," Wentworth remarked just before he exited the room, "Daisy had a rather nasty fall. I managed to bandage the cut on her leg with my handkerchief—despite her objections, of course—but you might want to douse it with one of those evil-smelling medicines of yours."

Justin's gaze shifted to the tearstained face of the small child, thumb in mouth, who hovered on the edge of the group of chattering children. She, in turn, regarded him with unfathomable gray eyes that seemed to stare into his very soul.

He felt his heart lurch in his chest. From her silky dark hair and heart-shaped face to the perfect little dimple in her chin, she was the living image of his beloved sister, Anne, when a child of four. With one notable difference. Lady Anne Warre had been the merriest of little girls—a creature of light and laughter, while this child of the London slums appeared far too grave and withdrawn for her tender years.

A wave of pain tore through him. Once again he felt gripped by the terrible grief that had held him in its black vise when he'd learned of Anne's death, and he fought back the unmanly tears that threatened to spring to his eyes. "Annie," he gasped, unaware he'd spoken aloud his childhood name for the little sister he'd adored, until the sound of it echoed in the suddenly silent room.

Miss Thornhill regarded him anxiously. "My lord, are you ill? You've gone white as paper."

"I am fine," he managed, though he nearly choked on the words. "It is just that the child bears an amazing resemblance to my sister, Anne, who died this past summer when my brother's yacht capsized en route to France."

Miss Thornhill's lovely emerald eyes misted. "And you lost both siblings in one cruel stroke of fate. Oh, my lord, I am so deeply sorry. Such grief is beyond bearing."

He stared at her, startled by the sincere sympathy he saw mirrored on her expressive face. What a pitiful sort of fellow he must appear to elicit such unexpected compassion in a total stranger. Squaring his shoulders, he resolved to keep his feelings more carefully hidden in the future.

That resolution was put to an instant test as, without warning, he felt a sharp tug on his trouser leg and looking down, found the child, Daisy, at his knee. For a long, bewildering moment, she assessed him with her disturbing gaze. Then, to his surprise, she raised her arms in the age-old plea of children in need of adult comfort.

Without a second thought, he braced his cane against a nearby table and picked her up. A cumulative gasp of amazement rose from the bevy of children surrounding him, and looking up, he found Miss Thornhill staring at him with what could only be described as utter incredulity.

"I cannot believe this," she declared. "Daisy never lets any stranger come near her—and she is particularly terrified of men. Could it be she senses—"

"That we share a special bond?" Justin interrupted her before she could put into words the ugly truth of the child's parentage. He had always despised his brother's penchant for deflowering servant girls and village maidens, and leaving the results of those liaisons scattered across the length and breadth of England.

He caught himself up short. But who was he to judge Oliver or indeed any man? He was no saint himself where women were concerned. He'd freely taken his pleasure in the arms of the lusty Sophia for the past seven years and before that in those of any number of practical-minded ladies of the demimonde who were all too willing to overlook his physical disability once he crossed their palms with silver.

The child squirmed in his arms, breaking his train of thought. He scowled and instantly felt her nestle trustingly against his shoulder and reach out a hand to tenderly stroke his face. The memory of Anne's small hands ministering to him in just such a manner sent a new wave of grief coursing through him.

"Daisy is an unusually perceptive child, my lord. She senses your pain and wants to comfort you." Miss Thornhill spoke in the soothing tone of one addressing the seriously ill, and once again Justin cringed with embarrassment.

"But I really should examine her knee," she added, quickly reverting to her usual practical manner, and relieving him of his burden, proceeded to do so. "It is a deep cut," she declared a moment later. "She must have fallen onto some sharp object. I'll have to clean it and put some of what Drew calls my 'evil-smelling' concoction on it. But I'll wait until after luncheon to do so. Daisy is a brave little girl, but my doctoring will seem less painful with some good, hot soup in her stomach."

With a quick hug, Miss Thornhill set the child on her feet and with brisk efficiency, busied herself herding her charges to their places at the table. Minutes later, a thin young woman with lank brown hair and a severely pockmarked face carried a black iron kettle through the open doorway and began ladling its contents into the soup plates.

The happy sound of children's voices filled the room; to Justin's untrained ears, they all seemed to be chattering at once. All except Daisy, who sat sucking her thumb—alone and silent between two empty chairs near the head of the table.

"She is a quiet little thing, your Daisy," he remarked when Miss Thornhill once again joined him.

"Her affliction sets her apart from the other children. The only one she is close to is Danny."

"What affliction?" Justin's gaze instinctively flew to the little girl's slippered feet; they had looked perfectly normal to him.

Miss Thornhill stepped closer and spoke in a voice meant for his ears alone. "Daisy can't . . . or won't talk. She hasn't said a single word the entire year she's been with us—at least not when she's awake. Sometimes she cries out when she's having one of her nightmares, but even then the sound is unintelligible—an eerie kind of wail, more like an animal in pain than a human child." She sighed. "But we have hopes; the physician who donates his services to the children's home can find nothing wrong with her vocal cords."

Anger darkened her magnificent eyes. "I have to believe Daisy's problem stems from the cruel abuse she suffered at the hands of the man her mother was living with—and the horror of watching the poor woman beaten to within an inch of her life time and time again by the drunken beast."

Justin flinched at the thought of the misery his brother's senseless rutting had caused the hapless maidservant and her tiny daughter. He knew he would never rest easily until he had done his best to rectify the situation. He cleared his throat. "Where is Miss Wattling now?"

"Bessie is dead. Her battered body was found in an alley behind a Fleet Street tavern less than a fortnight after she left Daisy with me." Tess Thornhill's voice sounded oddly flat and devoid of emotion, and Justin gained the impression that such a finding was not all that uncommon in the stews.

"I'm certain my father and his pious friends would deem her death another example of 'the wages of sin,'" she continued in the same dispassionate manner. "But it seems to me that too often it is the victim, not the sinner, who reaps the bitter stipend."

Justin found himself wondering if she automatically lumped peers of the realm who were slum landlords into the "sinner" category. If she did, she hid it behind a gracious smile. "Will you join us for the noonday meal, my lord?" she asked, and without waiting for his answer, led him to the chair on Daisy's right and claimed the other vacant place as her own.

Tapping on the edge of her soup bowl with her knife handle, she gained the children's attention. "As you can see, we have a guest today—the Viscount Sanderfield, our landlord." All the bright, young faces turned to Justin; some of the older children even offered cautious smiles.

"And in his honor, our dear Maggie has managed to find a bit of mutton for the soup." Miss Thornhill smiled at the pockmarked woman standing at the foot of the table. "Show them, Maggie."

Reaching into her kettle with a two-pronged fork, Maggie drew forth a chunk of meat the size of a cricket ball. A chorus of "ohs" and "ahs" rippled around the gathered children as she laid it on a small platter, cut it into minute slices and, circling the table, dropped a single piece into each bowl.

Without further ado, Miss Thornhill bowed her head in prayer. "Thank you dear Lord for this bountiful feast and for the joy of sharing it with each other. Amen."

Justin watched the children dip their spoons into the thin,

brown broth, to retrieve their scrap of meat, then beam with pleasure at what was apparently a rare treat. Beside him, Daisy
chewed with solemn concentration.

Remembering the mammoth baron of beef and multitude of
side dishes he'd left virtually untouched the night before as he sat
at his solitary dinner, he found himself wondering if he would
ever again partake of such a lavish meal without suffering pangs
of guilt.

Over Daisy's head, he met a pair of knowing green eyes and realized his astute hostess had somehow read his mind—something
no one else had ever been able to do. It was a disconcerting experience.

With a terrible prophetic clarity, he recalled Reggie's dire
warning, "The hellcat from the stews is not for you—nor for any
man who values his peace of mind." He had the uncomfortable
feeling that Reggie's advice may have been more sound than he'd
credited it at the time.

Not that it mattered. For he had an even more uncomfortable
feeling that the malaise with which he'd been stricken the moment Tess Thornhill walked through his door was one from which
he would never recover.

Chapter Four

"You can't be serious! You agreed to let that officious cripple poke his nose into your business yet another day?" Drew Wentworth's handsome face contorted with rage. He brought his fist down on the table with a force that nearly buckled the sturdy plank—and sent Maggie scurrying to the kitchen with the last of the empty soup bowls.

Tess glanced around her to make certain the children had all gone upstairs for their afternoon naps before answering, "Tuesday next, to be exact."

"Devil take it, woman, have you forgotten the bitter lessons of the past concerning the nobility and their treatment of maidservants . . . and merchant's daughters? Titled rakes like Sanderfield have only one thing in mind when they deal with women of other classes of society—and I can't believe I have to spell it out for you."

"And *I* can't believe the viscount is cut of the same cloth as the men who seduced Bessie Wattling and Laura." Tess scowled at her irate friend. "And even if he were, how pray tell could I refuse to let him complete the inspection of his own building?" It had been a long day. The viscount's visit had drained her of every ounce of energy she possessed. The last thing she needed was this quarrel with Drew.

"He doesn't give that"—Drew snapped his fingers—"for his blasted building. Anyone with eyes in his head could see you were the only thing the lecher was inspecting."

"Lecher?" Tess raised an eyebrow. "That's doing it up a bit brown." She moved to the window to watch the man they were discussing make his clumsy ascent into the garish red-and-gold curricle that struck her as strangely out of keeping with his reserved personality and quiet mode of dress.

"Lord Sanderfield may be attracted to me, but he appears much too shy and sensitive about his unfortunate affliction to be a lecher," she said, marveling at the expertise with which he guided his pair of matched bays into the stream of carts and pedestrians crowding the busy street.

Drew strode across the room to join her at the window. "Then, sweetheart, you are far less observant than I gave you credit for. I was watching from the hall the entire time he was here; believe me, his charming reticence was merely an act to gain your sympathy. The scoundrel was slavering over you like a dog with a particularly meaty bone."

Tess struggled to control the laugh rising in her throat. She could see Drew was deadly serious, but the thought of his peeping at her through a crack in the door painted almost as hilarious a picture as that of spittle dripping off the chin of the dignified viscount.

"You accuse the man unjustly!" she declared. "He was a perfect gentleman at all times. If anyone acted in an ungentlemanly manner, it was you, Drew Wentworth. I do not recall giving you permission to address me as 'sweetheart' either privately or in public. Yet you've done both in the space of an hour."

"Permission long overdue to my way of thinking," Drew grumbled. "How many times must I ask you to marry me before you come to your senses?"

Tess gritted her teeth, thoroughly exasperated with the all-too-familiar turn of conversation. "A better question might be how many times must we have this same discussion before you come to yours? If I've told you once, I've told you a hundred times, I am not the woman for you—nor for any man. You need a wife who will love you in all the ways a woman loves a man. I cannot. I can be your friend—nothing more."

"Nonsense." Drew ran impatient fingers through the lock of straight black hair that had fallen across his brow. "You are obviously a woman of great passion—if only you would let yourself be so. Any man who looks at you can see that—including your 'gentlemanly' viscount. Surely you're not so naive as to think that gleam in his eye was 'friendship.'"

"I saw no gleam," Tess declared, though in truth she had seen it all too clearly.

Drew ignored her protestation. "Mark my words, the next step in his seduction plan will be to shower you with gifts—probably a diamond bracelet or a pair of earrings from Rundell and Bridge. I understand that's the jeweler of choice for titled rakes—and the silly fribbles are all so cut to pattern, they're boringly predictable."

Drew caught her upper arms in his strong fingers. "You need a husband to protect you from such blackguards, and I'm just the man for the job. Hell and damnation, Tess, we were meant for each other. We believe in the same things; we want the same things out of life. There's nothing I couldn't accomplish with you by my side. It's already being talked around I should stand for the House of Commons."

His voice rose to a fever pitch. "Think of the difference I could make in the lives of the downtrodden masses if I had a voice in that august body," he said with a sweeping gesture of his arm.

Tess was accustomed to Drew and his political agitating, but she had never seen anything excite him as much as the thought of gaining recognition as a member of the House. Instinctively, she backed away from his wild gesticulations, but with an agonized groan, he drew her to him and covered her mouth with his.

She suffered his kiss with the same patience she had suffered all the others he'd given her in the years they'd known each other. Not that it was unpleasant; she was much too fond of Drew to ever be repulsed by anything he did. She respected his dedication to bettering the lot of the underprivileged and she loved him like a brother. But as for passion: the closest thing to that emotion she felt was a fervent desire to be done with yet another exercise in futility.

He raised his head and stared down at her. "One of these days you are going to respond to me. It is inevitable; there's not a man alive who kisses with more expertise. I could name you a dozen women who would testify to that truth."

"I don't doubt it for a minute." Tess smiled to herself. Drew had a great many admirable qualities; modesty, however, was not one of them. "You are not the problem, dear friend," she said gently. "I am."

His expressive black brows drew together in a frown. "Devil take it, Tess, why must you be so infernally pigheaded? Why can't you take my word for it that once we're married you will learn to enjoy my lovemaking? Does it mean nothing to you that it was Laura's dearest wish that you and she would one day be true sisters?"

"Laura is dead," Tess said dully. "I cannot marry you to please her, and it is most unfair of you to try to make me feel even more guilty about her than I already do."

With all her strength, she pushed him away and stepped back out of his reach. "Has it never occurred to you that there is something seriously lacking in me? Surely if I were capable of feeling even the slightest passion, I would feel it for you. At the risk of adding to your already monstrous conceit, I freely admit you are the most handsome man of my acquaintance."

"I know that. Then why—"

"You are also my dearest friend."

"Then marry me." Drew's vivid blue eyes searched her face. "Believe me, I have enough passion for both of us."

"Sometimes in the black of night, when I'm aching with loneliness, I confess the idea tempts me. For there is nothing I would like better than to bear a child of my own."

"Then marry me," Drew pleaded again. "Let me give you that child."

Tess shook her head. "Never, dear friend. For I have enough sense to know that such a one-sided arrangement would only end in our hating each other—something I could not bear. Please, Drew, for your own sake, find yourself a whole woman—one who is more than a pretty, empty shell. Make her your wife and the mother of your children."

Long after Drew had thrown up his hands and stalked from the room, Tess stood alone at the window. His bitter parting words rang in her ears: "It's no wonder you're frigid, considering the sanctimonious bastard who fathered you."

Remembering the bewildered look in his eyes, she despised herself for putting it there. What *was* wrong with her? She'd always had more than her share of motherly instincts. Why did she lack the other womanly feelings that all her friends appeared to possess? For lack them she did. It was indifference, not virtue, that kept her an unmarried virgin at the advanced age of five and twenty.

She gripped the window ledge with white-knuckled fingers.

Was Drew right? Had a childhood under her father's domination doomed her to never feel the normal womanly desire for a man?

"Never?" a small voice deep inside her asked, as memories surfaced of the strange fluttering sensation around her heart that Lord Sanderfield's shy smile had prompted. Surely this "passion" the poets and novelists glorified could not be something as delicate and ephemeral as the mere quiver of a bird's wing. Still, it was a sensation she'd never before felt for any man.

A sudden sense of foreboding gripped her. What cruel irony it would be if this soft-spoken viscount—a member of the nobility she despised with every fiber of her being—should be the one man who finally melted the great block of ice that encased her heart.

The first of the viscount's gifts arrived the following morning. Not the expensive baubles from Rundell and Bridge that Drew had prophesied, but a leg of mutton from the Hightower Meat and Poultry Shop and a greengrocer's sack taller than Daisy filled with potatoes, turnips, and carrots. Both were delivered by the groom who had accompanied the viscount on his visit to the stews.

Maggie was in alt. She had never before had such delectable items with which to practice her culinary skills. Tess, on the other hand, felt torn between gratitude and fear that Drew's assessment of the viscount's intentions had been correct. Sanderfield was no fool. He would know she was not the sort of woman to be impressed by diamonds.

The following day the same grinning groom delivered a brace of chickens and a sack of finely milled flour. The chickens were delightfully plump and the flour free of the weevils usually found in that which Maggie purchased at the open market in Seven Dials.

On the third day, a goose, neatly plucked and dressed, and a bushel of crisp apples arrived . . . along with Drew Wentworth, who stopped by just long enough to say, "I told you so."

Enough was enough. The viscount's benevolence was becoming embarrassing. Nor did it help that everyone from Danny to the soup and stew woman was making wagers as to what would be the next gift her titled admirer came up with. Tess decided that despite the obvious benefit to the children of the lavish gifts, she must set Lord Sanderfield straight before the situation got entirely out of hand.

She didn't stop to analyze why it was perfectly acceptable to beg and wheedle every cent she could out of other titled noblemen and rich bankers, but unthinkable to accept much needed food-stuffs from the viscount. She simply labored long and hard over the wording of the brief note she sent him, determined to quash any amorous ideas he might have without unduly antagonizing him before the business of the rent was settled. She was more than pleased with the results:

> "My lord, I thank you most sincerely for your generosity.
> We have already eaten the mutton and the chickens, and I
> shall keep the goose rather than see it go to waste. However,
> for the sake of my good name, which I treasure above all
> things, I must insist you refrain from sending me any more
> such foodstuffs. Please understand and respect my wishes."
> > Yours in good faith,
> > Theodosia Thornhill

The viscount replied by sending her a slab of bacon, two-dozen fresh pullet eggs, and an equally cryptic note:

> "My dear Miss Thornhill, I find myself in the embarrassing
> position of having to inform you that the foodstuffs in ques-
> tion pose no threat to your good name since they were not
> gifts to you personally, but rather donations to your chil-
> dren's home. Be assured that while I have been away from
> England these past seven years, I am not entirely lost to pro-
> priety. In short, should I ever feel so inclined, I can think of
> much more appropriate gifts to give a beautiful, intelligent
> woman than a leg of mutton, two chickens, and a goose."
> > Yours respectfully,
> > Justin Anthony Warre, Viscount Sanderfield

Tess stared in disbelief at the bold, yet scholarly script covering the single sheaf of crested stationery. *Damn and blast!* She couldn't remember when anyone had, with a few well-chosen words, made her feel such an utter fool.

She reread the note and still couldn't decide if she'd been complimented or insulted. She felt certain of one thing only: there was more to the shy viscount than first met the eye.

She sighed. And as if that wasn't disconcerting enough, just thinking about seeing him on Tuesday triggered that inexplicable fluttering in her breast again.

"As I told the duke in the last note I sent him, I grow more worried every day about our new viscount and this brassy do-gooder who has him in her clutches." Wimple offered this telling comment to Pruefrock and Mrs. Pennywacker as the three of them took their evening meal in the small dining room reserved for Viscount Sanderfield's upper servants.

"Why just this morning," he continued, "I happened to be standing outside the door to the blue salon when he told the Earl of Rutledge he planned to pay her another visit come Tuesday."

Pruefrock was heartily sick of listening to Wimple brag of how he'd lately become the trusted confidant of the Duke of Arncott. As if listening at keyholes was something to be proud of. "Squealer" was a better name for the role the toplofty butler played, to Pruefrock's way of thinking.

"The poor lad is downy as a new hatched chick where women are concerned," Mrs. Pennywacker agreed sadly. "That's what comes of stuffing his head with all that bookish nonsense. There's no room left for proper thinking."

She added yet another potato to the three already on her plate and dribbled a generous amount of gravy over the lot. "I maybe shouldn't mention it, but I can't help wondering what the hussy did to persuade Milord he should keep her and all her orphans supplied with better food than you'll find on many a Mayfair table."

"What? What's that you say?" Wimple paused in the act of cutting himself another slice of nicely browned mutton.

"I'm saying the viscount has taken to supplying the Thornhill woman's larder, and that's a fact. For isn't it my own nephew who's delivered as prime a leg of mutton as this one we're eating today, a brace of Hightower's plumpest chickens, and a fine, fat goose—and heaven knows what else to her very door."

"Why haven't I been told of this before? I had no idea the sorry business had gone that far." Wimple popped a piece of mutton into his mouth, washed it down with a healthy swallow of the viscount's finest Burgundy, and gave a satisfied belch. "I dread to think how His Grace will view this latest evidence of his grandson's foolishness."

"If I was you I'd save a worry or two for when the viscount finds out you've been spying on him and throws your bloomin' arse out on the street," Pruefrock muttered under his breath.

"What *are* you mumbling about now, Pruefrock?"

"I'm sayin' the viscount may be smarter than some gives him credit for. One of them quiet ones, he is, but I'd hate to see him riled." Pruefrock cast a meaningful look at the loose-tongued housekeeper and watched her ruddy complexion fade noticeably. "And wot, I asks you, is foolisher about spendin' his blunt to feed a passel of hungry slum brats than pissin' it away in the gamblin' hells like Lord Oliver done?"

"He has a point there," Mrs. Pennywacker admitted. "I'm sorry I spoke up, for now that I think on it, Cook said it was the Thornhill woman who took Bessie Wattling's babe to raise once the poor woman had her head bashed in in some East End alley."

"A commendable act to be sure." Wimple sniffed. "But hardly one to recommend her as *parti* to a viscount. As the Earl of Rutledge so aptly remarked, 'The creature is common as dirt.' "

"There's some as calls her the Angel of the Stews," Pruefrock declared, remembering the glowing account of Tess Thornhill's charitable works he'd heard when he made one of his rare visits to his favorite East End bawdy house.

Wimple chose to ignore him. Laying down his fork, he rose to his feet. "You'll have to excuse me," he said in the lofty tone of voice all the young footmen imitated behind his back. "I must pen a note to the duke concerning a certain Jezebel and her methods of extracting money from our gullible young viscount."

Pruefrock gave a moment's thought to warning the lad that his every move was being reported to his grandfather. He quickly discarded the idea. His was not a daring nature; loyalty to one's employer was all well and good, but a fellow had to think twice before he risked crossing a man with as long an arm and as short a temper as the powerful Duke of Arncott.

Tuesay dawned clear and bitterly cold, with a brisk wind that penetrated even the warmest of greatcoats. Justin briefly contemplated postponing his second visit to the Laura Wentworth Home for Abandoned Children, but some inexplicable sense of urgency made him leave the cozy warmth of his bookroom, and the manuscript he was currently transcribing, to venture onto the chilly, windswept streets.

All across London the feeling stayed with him that the fascinating Miss Thornhill was in serious trouble and desperately needed his help. But by the time he pulled his curricle to a stop before the familiar blue door, he was so thoroughly chilled, he found himself wondering what could have possessed him to make such a trip in weather so cold his breath froze before it could escape his lips. Behind him, John Groom's teeth chattered as noisily as his own and even the bays snorted their protest against the cruel wind buffeting them.

The street was strangely empty and eerily silent. The peddlers and pushcart owners, prostitutes, and flash-house boys who had greeted him with raucous catcalls on his first visit had apparently all sought shelter from the freezing cold.

The street was also surprisingly clean—the usual litter piled neatly against the walls of the dilapidated buildings by the sweeping wind. Even the stench, so overpowering but four days before, had all but disappeared in the face of winter's first icy blast.

"I'll not be long," Justin promised his shivering groom. "I've no choice but to leave you in the curricle, for it would be stolen in a minute if left unguarded on this street. Cover the horses with their blankets and wrap yourself in the fur lap robe," he directed before starting up the stairs toward the blue door.

A disturbingly disheveled Miss Thornhill answered his knock. Her glorious hair hung loose about her shoulders, the buttons of her bright purple gown were all misbuttoned, as if she'd thrown it on in a hurry, and her eyes were red and puffy from crying.

"Oh it's you, my lord," she said with a dampening lack of enthusiasm, as a gust of icy wind nearly whipped the door from her hand. "Whatever are you thinking of to come out in such weather? Surely your inspection could wait another day or two."

She pressed trembling fingers to her lips. "I fear you have made a long, cold trip in vain. For I cannot possibly show you about today. Daisy requires all my attention."

Justin's pulse quickened. "Daisy? What is wrong with Daisy?"

"Her leg." Miss Thornhill's voice broke in a sob. "I awoke this morning to find it dreadfully sore and swollen, and it is all my fault. I should have attended to it when Drew first brought it to my attention. Instead, with one thing and another, I quite forgot about it until I put her to bed that evening."

She caught her breath with another gulping sob. "I cleaned it and applied the salve I always use for cuts and scrapes, but I fear I had waited too long. It hasn't healed as it should, and now the doctor I summoned has sent word that she needs to be bled, but he cannot leave his paying patients to attend a charity case."

Justin limped forward, wrested the door from Miss Thornhill's hand, and closed it firmly. "Where is she? I have some knowledge of medicine. Perhaps I can be of help." *Certainly of more help than a quack who, without ever seeing the child, proposed to subject her to the horrors of bleeding.*

Among other things, his translation of Greek and Roman manuscripts had taught him a great deal about the medical practices of the ancient world—many of which were still being employed in the Asian and African countries he'd visited.

Miss Thornhill looked a bit dubious of his claim, but she led him down the colorful hallway to a small room at the back of the building. "I've gathered all the children in this one room because . . . because we cannot hope to keep the entire building warm in this weather."

Justin had a feeling she'd been about to admit to a lack of firewood before she caught herself. He made a mental note that here was another gift she would find a great deal more useful than the usual baubles a man presented a woman he admired.

A small fire glowed in the fireplace, and with the exception of Daisy, the children were arranged in a semicircle around it, each with a book in hand. Daisy lay on a couch similar to the velvet monstrosities in the entryway, her small form almost lost beneath the blanket covering her. The young pickpocket, Danny, knelt beside her, pressing a damp cloth to her forehead. His thin face looked pinched with worry.

Justin removed his gloves, moved the boy aside, and laid a hand on Daisy's forehead. She was burning with fever and her eyes, overbright and slightly glazed, searched his face in a silent plea for help that tore at his heart.

Gently, he removed the blanket and bandage to examine her leg. It was, as Miss Thornhill had warned, badly swollen and even in the dim light spilling through the room's one window, he could see a narrow finger of red inching its way upward toward the little girl's knee. He heard Miss Thornhill gasp and knew she, too, recognized the telltale sign of serious trouble.

"How long has she been like this?" he asked, careful to keep the shock he felt from his voice.

"The red line wasn't there when I checked her an hour ago."

"But she's been poorly these past two days, now that I think on it." Despair sharpened Danny's voice. "I should've watched her more careful-like, I should've knowd somethin' was wrong."

"As should I," Tess Thornhill added. "But she's grown so much worse in these past few hours, I was taken by surprise." Tears of anguish and remorse welled in her eyes and trailed down her pale cheeks. "And now her wound has gone septic. Dear God, I shall never forgive myself for being so absorbed in my own ruminations, I failed a child who needed me."

Justin could see both woman and boy were tortured with guilt—and fear for this fragile child they loved. He wished he could assure them she would recover but, in all honesty, he could not. Daisy was a very sick little girl. Unless the lethal infection could be stopped before it progressed much farther, she could lose her leg—maybe even her life.

"The area will have to be lanced," he said and watched Miss Thornhill grip the arm of the couch as if her legs had suddenly collapsed beneath her. "But first, I want to return to my town house to collect some healing powders which I brought with me from Greece—with your permission of course." He straightened up and started toward the door. "I must leave immediately. It will take me a good two hours to make it to Mayfair and back, and the child's condition worsens with every passing minute."

"Healing powders—from Greece?"

"From India actually, for it was while on a trip to Bombay that I met the fakir who gave them to me." It had been ages since he'd given a thought to the strange fellow with his burning obsidian eyes and his half-naked body, emaciated from countless religious fasts. Now, with the fate of this child who was so obviously a Warre in his hands, he remembered the holy man's startling words all too well: "These powders will one day mean the difference between life and death for one of your blood, sahib."

"Of what are these powders composed?" Miss Thornhill asked dubiously.

"I can't tell you their composition," he admitted. Nor did he choose to tell her of the strange prophecy concerning them—a prophesy that until this moment he had rejected as so much Hindu mumbo-jumbo. He cleared his throat self-consciously. "All the fakir would say was that they had magical healing power."

"And you believe this?"

Two pairs of eyes, bright with hope, scrutinized him, but Justin couldn't bring himself to be anything but brutally honest. "I am not a man who believes in miracles—nor indeed in anything even remotely metaphysical," he admitted. "But I have witnessed some amazing cures accomplished by such holy men with their herbs and powders. I can only hope I am about to witness another."

He hesitated. "I will say this much. I have found many of the medical practices I've seen in my travels to be a good deal more effective than the infernal bleeding and cupping so popular with our English physicians. The Eastern men of medicine believe that blood is the life force and any loss of it weakens the body's ability to heal itself."

"Makes sense to me." Danny shook his head vehemently. "I've seen them stupid quacks kill more poor coves than they cured, and that's a fact."

"Miss Thornhill?" Viscount Sanderfield turned to Tess and she realized the ultimate decision concerning Daisy's medical care was hers to make.

She winged a small prayer heavenward for the wisdom to make the right one. "I *do* believe in miracles," she said after a moment's thought. "Perhaps your holy man with his magical healing powders is the very thing Daisy needs at this moment. I cannot believe a benevolent God would heap any more calamity on a child who has already known more misery than any human being should be asked to endure."

"Very well then." Justin shoved his fingers back into his gloves and grasped the handle of his stout cane. He had never been a praying man, but he prayed now that he would make it back in time—that the fakir had not been just another wild-eyed fanatic but indeed the healer he claimed to be—that the God Tess Thornhill believed in was truly as charitable as she thought.

"Continue applying cold cloths to her forehead and wrists to keep her fever under control," he said because he could think of nothing else to say.

Tess nodded absently, her anxious gaze riveted to Daisy's fever-flushed face. "I've instructed Maggie to keep a pan of water chilling on the stoop so it will be cold enough to do some good."

"Splendid. Be assured, dear lady, I shall return as fast as humanly possible." Lord Sanderfield turned to Danny. "I'll need your help, son. I'll ride my fastest saddle horse on the way back to save time. But I must rely on you to find a safe, warm place to stable it for the night."

"Don't fret yerself, guvnor. I knows just the place, and once I puts out the word to me cronies, the nag'll be snug as a baby dook in 'is cradle."

"Good lad."

With one of his brief, heart-stopping smiles, the viscount disappeared into the shadowy hall. Moments later, Tess heard the wind-whipped outer door slam behind this unlikely combination of knight errant and mystic that fate had chosen to send her in her hour of need.

Chapter Five

With a muttered expletive, the Duke of Arncott inserted the key which only he possessed into the lock of the door which only he was permitted to enter and strode into the ornate pink-and-gold bedchamber of his mistress—who also happened to be the owner of one of London's most notorious brothels. The night was bitterly cold. The short walk from the discreetly placed stable where he always left his carriage and nags had chilled his aging bones, but the anger coursing through him heated his blood to the boiling point.

As she had every Tuesday and Friday night since he'd purchased the "establishment" in the stews for her some twenty years before, Florabelle Favor greeted him with unbridled eagerness. "Lord luv you, Archie," she squealed, throwing her fleshy white arms around his neck and giving him a smacking kiss, "I'd more'n half given you up on a night like this."

"So I surmised." The duke pushed her aside and strode to the middle of the room. "Where is he, damn his hide?"

"Where is who?"

"The man you're entertaining." He glanced at the decanter and glasses sitting on the bedside table. "And with *my* brandy as well. By God, Flora, this time you've gone too far!"

Sparks ignited in Florabelle's faded blue eyes and a flush stained her plump cheeks. "Who do you think you are, you hawk-nosed old devil—marching in here and accusing me of being a common trollop?" Her generous bosom heaved with indignation. "I've never looked at another man since the day you set me up and well you know it, Archie Warre."

"Then who owns that nag bedded down in my private stable? The damn thing looks familiar; I'm certain I've seen it before."

"How the devil should I know who owns it? I've never set foot inside your private stable."

The duke stubbornly maintained his dark scowl, but he had a suspicion he'd accused her unjustly. Flora was no saint, but neither was she a liar. At least, he'd never caught her lying.

She scowled back at him. "Did you have a lock on the blooming door of your blooming private stable?"

The duke felt a rush of heat spread from his neatly clipped mustache to the tips of his ears. He drew himself up to his full height, which was impressive despite the rheumatism he'd suffered the past few years. "I did not deem it necessary; I never leave my carriage and pair without a groom to guard them."

"Well then, it's probably some young lordling so taken with one of my girls he braved the freezing weather to scratch his itch . . . same as you, ducks."

His Grace recoiled in disgust. This woman who had been under his protection for more years than he cared to admit was beyond vulgar. She had the vocabulary of a dockside sailor and the taste of a gypsy—and she showed no respect whatsoever for his lofty title and position. There was not another soul on earth who would dare call him "Archie" much less "ducks."

Furthermore, now that he took a good look at her in that hideous pink wrapper, she had definitely gone to fat. It was not a pretty sight. Why he had tolerated the annoying creature all these years was beyond him.

Florabelle tossed her hennaed curls—a gesture that might have been appealing in a woman half her age and a few stone lighter. In her present corpulent condition, she resembled nothing so much as a petulant cow.

"Are you going to stand there all night looking like you got a whiff of a fish gone bad?" she demanded. "If so, blow out the candle when you leaves. Personally, I needs my sleep." Without further ado, she removed her wrapper, revealing a pink nightrail that left nothing whatsoever to the duke's imagination.

Plopping her ample hips on the edge of the bed, she regarded him with heavy-lidded eyes. "Of course, if you're determined to go out in the cold, you'd best warm your innards with a bit of brandy first."

The duke could find no argument against that logic. He promptly poured himself a generous glass and tossed it down.

"I hates to give you advice, ducks, you being duke and all," Florabelle purred. "But, if I was you, I'd take off my greatcoat, and maybe my jacket and waistcoat as well, 'cause if you don't, you'll feel twice as cold once you go out again."

That made sense. One of the things about Flora that had always appealed to him was her practical mind. He took her advice, aware that her sleepy gaze followed his every move. Let her look. Damned if he cared. He was still a fine figure of a man, with but a few gray hairs, despite his advanced years.

Then, because he felt like a damned fool standing there in his shirt sleeves while the silly jade ogled him, he lifted the decanter and poured himself another drink.

"You going to drink all that lovely brandy by yourself, ducks?" Florabelle's voice sounded plaintive, but her eyes darkened with the same hungry look she'd turned on him the first time he'd seen her more than twenty years before. She'd been thin as a new willow then—a mere slip of a girl, with the face of an angel and the mouth of a fishwife, who'd taken up the world's oldest profession to keep body and soul together.

He'd been young himself in those days—or at least vigorously middle-aged—newly widowed and in need of a woman to fill the awful emptiness inside him. Flora had filled it with a lusty enthusiasm that had spoiled him for any other woman, and she'd soon become a habit he'd never had the will to break.

He smiled to himself. For all her faults, Flora had her uses. No matter how foul his mood, she was always delighted to see him. He shuddered, recalling that dark night a few months ago when if it hadn't been for Flora—

He poured her a hefty drink and watched her down it in one gulp. There was nothing ladylike about Flora. But neither was she devious and manipulative like the many titled ladies he'd courted in the years since he'd lost his sainted wife. If the truth be known, Flora was not intelligent enough to be devious and manipulative. Maybe it was that comforting thought, as much as his insatiable lust for her lush body, that had kept him faithful to her, in his fashion, all these many long years.

Without another thought, he sat down on the nearest chair and stretched out his legs so she could pull off his boots. He felt no need to apologize for his brief flare of temper. They knew each other too well for such formality. Still, she was a woman—and women liked things put into words.

"In answer to your question, Flora," he said with a patience he seldom bothered displaying, "no, I do not intend to drink alone—nor to let you sleep alone in your nice warm bed."

He favored her with one of his rare smiles. Flora instantly clasped a pudgy hand to her breast, and a glow of satisfaction suffused his being. After all these years, he still had the power to make his mistress's heart skip a beat. How many men his age could make such a boast?

Long after the duke lay snoring contentedly, Florabelle stared into the shadowy depths of the satin canopy above her bed. Why, she wondered, with all the men she'd known, had she chosen to spend the better part of her life with this arrogant, self-satisfied prig who had no more thought for the feelings of the woman he kept as his private whore than he did for the nags he kept in his private stable?

There had been a time when she'd desperately needed his patronage. She needed it no longer—nor indeed that of any man. She was rich as Croesus in her own right. Still, how would the old fool manage to go on if she wasn't around to make him think he was more important than God Almighty? Take that time, for instance, when he'd soaked her bosom with the tears he'd shed for his two grandchildren drowned in a storm off the Dover Coast. Where would he have turned for comfort if not to her?

But then for that matter, what would she do without him after all these years? What would she find to laugh at if she didn't have the pompous duke to tease? Perhaps it was the wicked pleasure she took in watching him cringe when she called him "ducks" that had kept her faithful to him, in her fashion.

Quietly, so as not to disturb him, she slipped from her bed and searched out the burly young Irishman she employed to keep the peace when the visiting lordlings got out of hand.

"Send one of the lads to warn Danny the viscount's nag must be out of the stable before the duke leaves in the morning," she

ordered. It wouldn't do for the old tartar to learn where his heir
had spent this night. The "Angel" had enough on her plate without the duke breathing down her neck.

"Aye, ma'am, I'll see to it right away."

"See that you do." Florabelle smiled to herself. If Danny's
glowing reports of Sanderfield were correct, the viscount was a
much more considerate fellow than his grandfather, and every bit
as rich—just the sort of patron she would have chosen for her
friend, Tess. She planned to see that nothing happened to threaten
the happy connection, for if ever a woman needed a rich patron,
Tess was surely that woman. The softhearted chit had no sense at
all when it came to feathering her own nest.

She glanced up to find the young Irishman still rooted to the
spot and staring her up and down like she was a bonbon he was
about to sink his strong, white teeth into. "Well, what you waiting
for?" she demanded. "I gave you an order. Snap to it!"

"Yes, ma'am. I'm goin'—just as soon as I asks you the question that's burnin' a hole in me brain."

"Which is?"

A cheeky grin spread across his handsome face. "Will you be
receivin' visitors after his dukeship's departed, ma'am? I'm sure
hopin' so, 'cause that pink gown gives me a powerful cravin' for
a bit of your special brand of slap and tickle."

"Devil take it, you forget who you're talking to, boy-o!"
Florabelle raised her collection of chins to an indignant level and
cast the nervy fellow a look as cold as the icy wind howling outside her window. These "bog trotters" were all alike. Give them a
few liberties and right away they thought they had the key to the
strongbox.

"You'll keep a respectful tongue in your mouth, you young
jackanapes," she snapped. "Any 'visiting' you do will be if and
when *I* say so—and don't you never forget it."

But remembering the pretty fellow's undisputed talents between the sheets, she unbent sufficiently to soften her stinging
words with a playful pat on his firm, young buttocks before she
sent him on his way.

Tess had thought the time spent waiting for the viscount to return with his "magic powder" had been the longest two hours of

her life. She was wrong. Compared to the time spent watching
and praying since she'd held Daisy's squirming body while he
lanced the swelling on her leg and applied the poultice made of
that powder, those early hours had fairly raced by.

She'd had such hopes at first. Lord Sanderfield had worked
with an impressive efficiency—first draining the wound of its
dreadful, noxious matter, then applying the foul-smelling poultice. She'd waited breathlessly for some spectacular sign that
the powder was working its miracle. Surely a substance with
magical properties should foam or sizzle or do something other
than simply lie there like a blob of unbaked bread dough.

One hour had stretched into two . . . two into six . . . and on
and on and on until she'd lost all track of time. She'd been
dimly aware that Maggie had given the other children their
suppers and herded them off to bed, dimly aware that when
she'd drooped with weariness, first Lord Sanderfield then
Danny had taken over the task of placing cold cloths on
Daisy's feverish brow.

Midnight had come and gone, as had a gray, cheerless dawn,
and still there was no change in their small patient. Now the
clock on the mantel was striking the hour of eight. Tess held
her head in her hands, too weary and sick at heart to pretend
any longer that she believed in the magic of the viscount's
powders.

She heard a furtive tap at the window shutter and a moment
later Danny scurried from the room, mumbling something
about seeing to the viscount's horse.

Beside her, Sanderfield nodded in his chair—exhausted from
his hell-for-leather ride through the icy streets of London and
his long vigil at Daisy's bedside.

Not since the day she'd learned of Laura's death had Tess
felt so utterly alone and filled with despair. Tears puddled in
her eyes and slid silently down her cheeks. In some inexplicable way, she felt that in failing this helpless child in her care,
she had somehow failed Laura yet again.

All at once, Daisy stirred in her sleep. Her eyes remained
tightly closed, but she pulled her hand from beneath the blanket and popped her thumb into her mouth. Tess held her breath.
Did she just imagine it or was that really a smile that flitted

across the little girl's face? Quickly, she moved to the couch and laid the back of her hand against Daisy's forehead. Dear God in heaven, it was cool. She must have cried out from the sheer exhilaration that swept through her, for the next moment Lord Sanderfield was beside her.

Carefully, he removed Daisy's blanket and gently lifted the edge of the poultice. "There's no apparent suppuration, the red line has receded and the swelling diminished," he declared in a voice hoarse with emotion. "There was magic in the powder after all, just as the fakir claimed."

"Are you saying Daisy is going to be all right, my lord?"

He grinned. "It would appear so."

Justin was never quite sure how it happened, but the next thing he knew Miss Thornhill was in his arms, laughing and crying and hugging him with all her might. Without a second thought, he hugged her back.

Then from the sheer joy of the moment, and because it seemed the natural thing to do, he kissed her trembling pink lips. To his surprise she returned his kiss with an exuberance that more than made up for her obvious lack of expertise. He felt a brief moment of triumph. She was an innocent. Whatever else that Adonis, Drew Wentworth, might be to her, he was not her lover. Then forgetting all else, he abandoned himself to a passionate exploration of her warm, responsive mouth.

Pleasure rippled through him. He felt as if all the sunshine hiding behind the dark clouds over London had suddenly flooded the small room with a light so bright it filled every inch of his being.

Long minutes later, he reluctantly lifted his lips from hers. She stared up at him, her eyes wide with astonishment. "My lord," she gasped, "whatever are we doing?"

Justin viewed her flushed face through a haze of desire. "I believe it is called kissing." Though he knew he was asking for trouble, he cupped her face in his hands and kissed her again— even deeper and more sensually than before. Only when the hunger surging within him hardened his body to where he was certain she must sense his painful arousal, did he force himself to put her from him. "Yes, it was most definitely kissing," he pronounced to cover his embarrassment.

Tess felt oddly bereft when he released his hold on her. He was surprisingly strong—not like a sturdy English oak, but rather with the fluid grace of a willow. It struck her that for such a man to be limited by a crippling infirmity was doubly tragic.

His smile looked a bit strained, as if he, too, were deeply moved by their physical contact. "Under the circumstances, I do believe you might consider calling me Justin from now on," he said gently. "I cannot call you Tess unless you do, you know, and it suits you so much better than Miss Thornhill."

It was such a simple request. Yet, Tess had the strangest feeling that in granting it, she was somehow relinquishing a part of herself to this baffling nobleman—a part she could never again retrieve.

"Justin." The name felt strange on her tongue; the very saying of it made her knees tremble and her pulse pound with the same furor as when his lips had claimed hers. She read the desire slumbering in his amber eyes and for the first time in her life, felt the joy and the power of being a warm, sensuous woman.

She smiled to herself. Drew was right after all; she *was* capable of feeling passion. Like the princess in the fairy tale she had read as a child, she'd only needed the kiss of the proper prince to wake her from her long sleep.

And what an extraordinary talent for kissing this particular prince had shown. There'd been none of that grabbing and groping and mashing his mouth against hers the way Drew did. His touch had been tantalizingly delicate, yet at the same time deeply—there was no other word for it—sensual. She'd had no idea a man could use his lips and his tongue and his hands in such imaginative ways. It occurred to her the viscount was not nearly as shy and retiring as she had first judged him to be.

The thought was a sobering one that instantly burst her euphoric bubble. It was more than possible he could be the rake in disguise that Drew claimed. One thing was certain; he would have to have done a great deal of kissing to have acquired such remarkable skill.

She shivered, remembering the pleasurable sensations his touch had created—sensations so overwhelming, she began to understand how a woman could lose her head over a man who offered such pleasure.

She shivered again. All her life she'd wished she could be a normal, feeling woman. It had never before occurred to her how frighteningly vulnerable such a woman would be.

"Be careful what you wish for, Theodosia. You might get it," her timid little mouse of a mother had once cautioned her. She wondered what Mama would say if she could see the quandary her rebellious daughter had gotten herself into this time.

It took Justin a moment to realize that the look of wonder in Tess's lovely eyes had slowly changed to one of near panic. It took him less than half that time to realize why. He was the culprit and well he knew it. The first touch of her lips had triggered a desire unlike anything he had ever before felt for any woman. From then on he'd acted purely on instinct—kissing her in the passionate, open-mouthed manner Sophia enjoyed, pawing her like she was some bit of Haymarket muslin he'd hired to warm his bed for a few hours.

Too late, he realized he should have restricted himself to simply pressing his lips to hers in a chaste kiss—at least he assumed that was how one was supposed to kiss a lady. The sad truth was his knowledge of women was limited to jades and harlots and his lusty Greek housekeeper. He had only felt safe from the humiliation of rejection with women whose favors he paid for. But how could he tell that to Tess without giving her an even greater disgust of him than she already had?

He ground his teeth in frustration. From the look on her face, he feared he'd managed to convince her he was cut of the same cloth as his profligate brother and the titled rake who had seduced her friend Laura.

"Please, Tess," he began desperately, though he hadn't the slightest idea what he could say that would justify his reprehensible behavior.

As it turned out, he was saved the effort of trying. For at that precise moment, the door burst open and Danny rushed in, closely followed by a grim-faced Drew Wentworth.

"What the hell is going on here?" Wentworth stormed.

"Take your bloody hands off my betrothed, you lecherous cripple, or so help me God, I'll draw your cork."

"And then what happened? Did the cit call you out when he found you with your arms around his betrothed? Or don't cits settle matters of honor in the same manner we gentlemen do?"

Reggie rested his arms on the table and leaned forward, his eyes dancing with laughter. "Pray go on, Justin. I swear I haven't heard anything this entertaining since Lord Belfair caught Prinny with his trousers down in Lady Belfair's dressing room."

Justin was not in the habit of confiding his troubles to anyone. But Reggie wasn't just anyone; he was more a brother to him than Oliver had ever been. However, he was beginning to regret the impulse that had made him seek out his friend at his usual table at White's. It was obvious Reggie viewed the unfortunate fiasco at the Laura Wentworth Home as something akin to a Drury Lane comedy.

"Tess smoothed his ruffled feathers by explaining we were simply congratulating each other on Daisy's recovery," he said tersely.

"Tess? So you and the virago from the stews are already on a first-name basis!" Reggie raised an eyebrow. "Which makes me wonder, were you simply congratulating each other on the child's recovery, or is there more to the story than you're divulging, my shy friend?" He chuckled. "Perchance I should refer to you as my sly friend from now on."

"Devil take it, Reggie, I'm sorry I ever broached the subject. I can see you consider it all a monstrous joke."

"While you consider it—what? A tragedy?" Reggie sobered. "Come now, Justin, you can't have been so foolish as to form a serious attachment to the woman."

Justin stared morosely at his untouched dinner. "I can and I have," he stated simply. He raised his eyes to meet Reggie's incredulous stare. "I want her as I've never wanted any other woman. She is the most glorious, vibrant, unconventional creature imaginable. She couldn't bore me if she tried—something every other woman I've ever known has managed to do within minutes of meeting her."

"I should have known." Reggie groaned. "Of all the women on whom you could have fixed your interest, why must it be Terrible Tess Thornhill?"

"I have it on good authority she is called the Angel of the Stews by those who know her well," Justin said reprovingly. "A much more appropriate name for a lady with a heart as large as the nave of St. Paul's Cathedral."

Reggie rolled his eyes heavenward. "I can see you're not to be persuaded from your foolish passion." Polishing off the last of his meal, he signaled the waiter to bring his usual brandy. "Very well then," he said when the waiter departed, "since you are lost to reason, what are you going to do about the cit?"

"Do?"

"Not that I approve, for I don't. But, if nothing else, it is heartening to see you interested in something other than those moldy old documents of yours. However, it is rather obvious that if you want the woman, you are going to have to fight for her."

"Fight for her? Are you mad? What have I to offer a beautiful, intelligent woman like Tess? And don't tell me a title and wealth. I am foolish enough to want a woman to love me for myself despite my deformity. I will settle for nothing less."

Reggie took a healthy sip of his brandy. "I can understand that. I've spent a lifetime searching for a woman who could recognize the handsome devil hiding behind this ugly physiognomy of mine, but that is neither here nor there. The question at the moment is how did the lady you find so desirable respond when you kissed her?"

"How did you know I kissed her?"

"A lucky guess." A grin spread across Reggie's homely face, momentarily giving him the appearance of a lascivious gargoyle. "So, how *did* she respond?"

"To my surprise, she kissed me back." Justin smiled reminiscently. "Rather enthusiastically, I must say, despite the fact that I lost my head and kissed her somewhat more . . . more ardently than I believe is customary when dealing with a lady."

"Hmmm. Interesting. Then one must assume that either this particular 'lady' is not given to honoring her commitments or that engagements are not considered as binding by the lower classes as by the nobility."

Justin frowned. "I don't think I care much for your assumptions. What is your point?"

"My point is she must have liked your 'too ardent kiss.' From what I've seen of the volatile Miss Thornhill, I suspect she would have blackened both your eyes if she didn't."

"By George you're right!" Justin felt as if an anvil had just been lifted off his shoulders. "Why didn't *I* think of that?"

"Haven't you heard, men in love—or lust—are not noted for their clear thinking." Reggie drained the last of his brandy and studied Justin speculatively. "So, now that we have established that the lady is not entirely indifferent to you, what are your plans for her should you manage to cut out this cit to whom she is apparently engaged?"

Justin's momentary elation quickly subsided. "I have no plans. I haven't thought that far ahead."

"There is always marriage."

"How could I consider offering for her? I wouldn't fit into her way of life and she would find mine insupportable."

"Then you plan to make her your mistress?"

"Of course not. I could never bring myself to insult her by offering her carte blanche."

"I see. In short, you cannot see how you can logically have her, yet you cannot envision living without her." Reggie raised an eyebrow. "Offhand, I would say you have a problem."

"Don't I bloody well know it!" Justin shoved his plate of food aside, braced his elbows on the table, and leaned his chin on his hands. "I'm just certain of one thing. Wentworth is not the man for her! She mothers him, for God's sake. Scolds him out of his tantrums as if he were a naughty little boy—which is precisely what he acts like most of the time. She already has a dozen children in her care; why would she want to take on another?"

Reggie nodded. "Ah, I begin to understand. Your main objective at the moment is merely to save a woman you greatly admire from a fate worse than death."

"That's it precisely. You couldn't have put it better." Justin beamed, feeling more at ease with himself than he had since that fateful moment when Drew Wentworth had walked in on Tess and him. He wondered if any man had ever had a truer or wiser friend than good old Reggie. With a few concise words, he had put the entire situation into perspective.

"Very commendable," Reggie said dryly. "I wish you success. I have always had a soft spot in my heart for crusaders. I suspect I may have been born in the wrong century."

Justin shrugged off his cynical friend's facetious comment and with a gusto he hadn't thought possible but a few minutes before, tucked into his now cold roast beef. In between bites, he admitted, "I was dreading returning to inspect Daisy's wound tomorrow, as I'd promised. But now I find myself eager to do so."

"And I find myself eager to accompany you." Reggie raised a hand to forestall Justin's objections. "Don't, I beg you, refuse me. The Little Season is winding down. There's not a single respectable lady around with whom to set up a flirt, and my mistress grows more boring with every passing day. The idea of your jousting with a handsome cit for the favors of Terrible Tess Thornhill is the first thing to pique my interest in months."

Chapter Six

Tess paced the floor of the common room, too nervous over Justin's pending visit to stay still. What must he think of her, kissing a near stranger with such abandon? She, herself, could come up with no logical explanation for her passionate response to the touch of his lips on hers—except that kissing Justin had seemed as easy and natural as drawing a breath.

Yet, even as she acknowledged her inexplicable bond with him, she recognized it for the illusion it was. She knew nothing about him except that he was an unlikely combination of shy recluse and accomplished roué whose kiss had given her the first hint of her own latent sensuality.

She groaned, remembering every humiliating detail of what followed on that fateful Wednesday morning. As if her own uninhibited behavior wasn't enough to give Justin a thorough disgust of her, Drew had had to burst on the scene with his claim that she was his betrothed. From the look of utter amazement she'd spied on the viscount's face, she had to conclude he'd believed Drew without question. So, of course, he must also believe her to be the most conscienceless and deceitful of flirts.

Well, there was nothing she could do about that now except grit her teeth and bluff her way through the next couple of hours as best she could. There was no defending her own actions and she had a feeling that if she tried to explain away Drew's insane jealousy, she would end up making an even greater fool of herself than she already had.

She reminded herself that Justin's opinion of her as a woman did not signify; theirs was a purely business relationship involving her tenancy of his building. Then why, she wondered, did the ache in her heart intensify each time she remembered the bleak expression in his eyes when he'd taken his leave of her?

She resumed her pacing, ending up beside the window that looked out on the street just as a familiar blue barouche drew up to the curb. She groaned. Oh no! Of all times for Florabelle Favor to make one of her rare visits, why must she pick this morning? If Justin had any doubts about his tenant's loose morals, he would surely dismiss them if he found her serving tea to one of London's most notorious bawdy-house madams.

No sooner had the traitorous thought entered her head than she felt a deep sense of shame. Florabelle had been too good a friend and too generous a patron of the children's home to be turned away because a peer of the realm was expected. Let her noble landlord think what he wanted! Chances were he'd already drawn his conclusions as to the profession of the home's benefactor from the colorful furnishings she'd donated.

Florabelle was still making her precarious way up the slippery steps when Tess greeted her at the door. Covered from head to toe in a hooded sable cape that many a *ton* matron would have given her husband's fortune to possess, the aging bird of paradise still managed to appear more vulgar than elegant.

"How nice to see you," Tess said and realized she really meant it. Though she heartily disapproved of the way Florabelle made her living, she couldn't help but like the crusty owner of The Silver Slipper. Whatever else she might be, Florabelle Favor was a certified original who could always be counted on to do the unexpected.

Tess smiled warmly. "Come have a cup of tea and tell me what brings you out on a cold morning like this."

"Morning!" Florabelle grumbled. "Feels more like the middle of the night to me. Haven't been up this early in twenty years." She crossed the threshold, stopped to catch her breath, and got straight to the point as usual. "You said if ever I needed a favor, I was to ask you."

"A favor?" Tess gulped, afraid to ask what favor a bawdy-house madam could need of her. Not that it mattered. Whatever it was, she could scarcely refuse any request that was not completely outrageous. Without Florabelle's generous help, she would have had to close her children's home long ago, and this was the first time her benefactor had ever asked anything in return.

"There's a young woman waiting in my carriage," Florabelle said, still panting from her exertion. "One of my Irish bully boys found her wandering down Haymarket Street this morning. Seems she'd been staying at some hotel nearby till her money run out and they tossed her into the street. So, he brung her to me, thinking she'd be a fine addition to my house. But I'd take it kindly if you'd hire her instead. From what Danny tells me, you could use a little more help now that you have a full dozen orphans beneath your roof."

Tess gaped at the older woman, utterly taken aback by her startling suggestion. There was no denying the children were becoming more than she could handle, but she would never have thought to look for the help she needed in a brothel.

Florabelle frowned at her hesitation. "If you're worried the chit's not respectable, don't be. Consuela's a lady if ever I seen one, and proud as a duchess to boot."

"Consuela?" Tess echoed. "She's Spanish?"

"That she is. And a real looker too. I admit, just for a minute or two, I was tempted to try talking her into taking up the 'profession.' Lord knows every highflier in London would be lining up at my door once the word got round I had a beauty like her in my house." Florabelle gave a heartfelt sigh. "Trouble is she'd most likely faint dead away first time some drunken lordling laid a hand on her. And anyways, a brothel's no place for a baby—not even a high-class brothel like The Slipper."

Tess gasped. "Good heavens! Are you saying she has a baby?"

"Yes indeed. A boy child no more'n three or four months old and kind of sickly-looking, if you asks me. Which is another reason I'm hoping you can find room for her. I know very well she's got to eat proper so's she can nurse the little fellow, and it's not like she can find work as a seamstress or a lady's maid, is it? I doubt fine Spanish ladies is taught such trades any more than fine English ladies is."

There was no arguing the logic of Florabelle's assumption. Tess had firsthand knowledge of the kind of education the daughters of the English nobility received, since her father's great wealth had given her entry to Miss Haversham's Academy for

Young Ladies on the outskirts of Bath. She and her titled class-mates were taught to wield a watercolor brush, ply an embroidery needle, and perform a few simple compositions on a pianoforte—all skills necessary to become the wives of affluent men, but certainly not designed to prepare them to support themselves in trade.

"The poor woman must have been absolutely terrified when she found herself alone and penniless in a city like London," she agreed sadly. "But where is her family? Why aren't they helping her? And what is she doing in England in the first place?"

"All questions I was dying to ask, Tess. But I'm not one to poke my nose in another's business and she didn't offer no answers on her own." Florabelle shrugged. "Truth is I don't have to have none to see she needs help."

"Of course you don't. Nor do I." Tess had known the outcome of this conversation from the instant Florabelle had mentioned the baby. She could never bring herself to deny refuge to a helpless woman and child. But how she was supposed to pay another employee, much less feed and clothe her and her baby, was beyond her. She was already hard put to manage the pittance she paid Maggie and Danny.

"Don't worry about the cost," Florabelle said, as if reading her mind. "I'll pay the chit's stipend and whatever expense she and her babe cause you. Wouldn't have it any other way, for I know you're already rowing upstream where money's concerned. Just promise me you won't let on where the blunt come from. I suspect the poor little thing's had to swallow enough of her pride as is; no sense making her choke on it."

Another wave of self-disgust swept through Tess when she remembered how loath she'd been to let Justin know a notorious bawdy-house madam was her friend and benefactor. "Once again you prove what a generous-hearted person you are," she said contritely.

"Humbug!" Florabelle tossed her head, sending her hennaed curls writhing like so many vermillion serpents. "I'm an evil old woman and well I know it. But not so evil I'd take pleasure in aiding in the ruination of an innocent. The girls who work in my house know which side of the sky the sun comes up on long before they come to me." She studied Tess through narrowed eyes. "It's agreed then?"

"Agreed," Tess said firmly.

Florabelle gave a satisfied nod, stuck her head out the door, and whistled through her teeth. Instantly, her burly, redheaded groom threw open the door of the carriage and a young woman stepped out. She wore neither gloves nor bonnet, but she carried a beaded reticule and was dressed in a dark gray pelisse which, while the height of fashion, looked somewhat the worse for wear.

Tess's first thought was that Florabelle hadn't exaggerated in the least when she'd called Consuela beautiful. She was, in fact, the most exquisite creature imaginable. Huge, startlingly blue eyes dominated a delicate heart-shaped face, their sooty lashes echoing the rich blue-black of her hair. Her lips were full and softly pink, her skin the color of rich cream, her bearing regal.

She looked shockingly young—more like an elegant child than the young mother Florabelle had described. But the proud tilt of her head and the small, blanket-wrapped bundle in her arms proclaimed her the "fine Spanish lady" who had found herself homeless and destitute in a foreign land. Tess's heart instantly went out to her.

"This here's Miss Thornhill," Florabelle said, ushering her shivering charge into the entry hall. "She's looking for someone to help her take care of a houseful of orphans and she's willing to give you a try."

"*Madre de Dios*," the Spanish girl breathed, crossing herself reverently. Her lovely eyes sought Tess's with a look of such profound gratitude, Tess found herself wanting desperately to declare it was directed toward the wrong person. Florabelle's warning frown stopped her. Instead she simply said, "I shall be most grateful for your help."

Consuela's lips parted in a shy smile. "*Gracias*, Mees Thornhill," she murmured in heavily accented English.

"Well that's that then." Florabelle's sigh of relief broke the uncomfortable silence that had settled over their small group once Consuela's immediate future was arranged. "Now I'll take you up on that cup of tea, Tess, though Lord knows I'd welcome something stronger if you should happen to have it. This early-morning rising takes its toll of a body."

Tess shook her head. "I'm sorry. Tea will have to suffice. We can take it in the common room, since the children are busy at their lessons in the salon." She smiled companionably at Consuela, certain a nice hot cup of tea and a comfortable chat would dispel any lingering uneasiness the girl might have about taking a position on the staff of the Laura Wentworth Home.

"This way," she said, indicating the door leading to the common room. But before they could reach it, the outside door burst open, revealing a wild-eyed Danny. "He's 'ere, just like I warned you 'ed be," he announced, leveling an accusing look at Florabelle. "Pulling up in front this very minute, 'e is, and with some fancy-lookin' cove sittin' beside 'im. Why'd you 'ave to go on the prowl in the daytime, you crazy old cat? You're goin' to ruin all me plans!"

"Danny! What in the world?" Tess stared at the boy's livid face, as shock at his incredible rudeness wiped everything else from her mind. "Who is here? And what are you thinking of, speaking to my guest in such a manner?"

"It's your fine young lordling, dearie. Danny told me all about him." Florabelle's painted brows drew together in a scowl. "And don't cut up at the lad, for he's dead right. I'd no business dawdling around here once I'd gotten Consuela set up. God only knows what kind of offer Sanderfield will come up with if he finds you drinking tea with the likes of me."

Two bright spots of color flamed in Consuela's pale cheeks, and Tess suddenly recalled her own qualms about just such a situation. "I doubt my landlord will raise or lower my rent one iota based on whom I invite to tea," she said quickly to mask her feeling of guilt.

Florabelle rolled her eyes. "Hear that, Danny? Lord luv us, the woman's got no more sense than God give a lamppost."

"That ain't the kind of offer we're talkin' about," Danny explained in the same patient tone of voice Tess, herself, used when conversing with one of the slower-witted children. "In case you missed noticin' it, his lordship goes goggly-eyed every time he looks at you, and it sure ain't your rent wots on 'is mind."

Consuela's eyes grew round as teacups. With a startled gasp, she clutched her baby a little tighter.

Tess felt a rush of heat suffuse her cheeks. "Really, Danny!"

She fixed him with a quelling look. "I'm afraid we are going to have to have a serious discussion about your perception of the viscount's role in my life, young man!"

"Now don't get on your highhorse, Tess. The lad's just thinking of your welfare, same as me." Florabelle pointed toward the outside door. "Run, Danny, fast as your legs'll carry you. Tell my coachman to pull round to the alley. I'll leave by the back door before his lordship has a chance to see me."

"You'll do no such thing," Tess protested. "And I never want to hear another word out of either of you about an 'offer' from Viscount Sanderfield. Even if I was hoping for one—which I most certainly am not—wealthy noblemen do not make offers of marriage to mere merchants' daughters."

"Marriage!" Florabelle and Danny exclaimed in unison. "Who said anything about marrying him?"

"Just like I said—no more sense than God give a lamppost," Florabelle muttered. "Well it's high time you started to smarten up, Tess Thornhill. Five and twenty is a bit long of tooth to be looking down your nose at the idea of nabbing a generous, good-hearted patron like the viscount." Without further ado, she gathered her luxurious fur about her and disappeared down the hall toward the rear of the building.

Danny promptly scurried in the opposite direction. "Amen to that," he agreed as he headed for the door leading to the street. "And the sooner we has that 'serious discussion' the better if you asks me. I'll be mighty interested in hearin' why a woman wots smart as a perfesser about everythin' else is so bleedin' clothheaded when it comes to settin' herself up proper with a gent."

Tess stared after him in utter disbelief. What was there about her that led the people closest to her to believe she would ever consider becoming any man's mistress? She had chalked Drew's ugly insinuations up to jealousy and frustration over his inability to make her bend to his will. But to what could she attribute the fact that both Danny and Florabelle obviously believed she should be angling for Justin's patronage?

She shook her fist at the departing boy. "I do not need to be 'set up' as some wealthy nobleman's plaything," she declared. "I am my own woman and proud of it."

Danny didn't hear her angry proclamation. He'd already rushed

out the door and slammed it behind him before she could get the
first word out of her mouth.

She was still muttering to herself when a soft mewling sound
like that of a newborn kitten—or a baby—alerted her to the fact
that she was not alone. Good heavens! She'd left her new employee standing in the drafty entryway all this time—and with a
sickly baby in her arms. To say nothing of subjecting the poor girl
to the embarrassing imbroglio with Danny and Florabelle. A fine
introduction to her new home!

She turned to Consuela to apologize for the tasteless display
she'd just witnessed and found, to her dismay, the Spanish girl
had grown noticeably pale. "Are you quite all right?" she asked
anxiously.

"I am fine," Consuela said, looking anything but.

Alarmed, Tess studied the girl's blanched face. "Good heavens! I never thought to ask. When did you last have a meal?"

"I . . . I cannot remember," Consuela murmured, her huge eyes
alarmingly vague. Her bloodless lips continued to move but no
sound came forth except a faint moan as she pitched forward.
Tess had just enough presence of mind to snatch the baby from
her arms as she collapsed to the cold stone floor in a crumpled
heap.

The bitter cold that had made Justin's previous trip into the
stews a nightmare of frost-bitten fingers and ice-encrusted lashes
had given way to a slightly more moderate temperature. Life in
the East End of London had returned to normal. If anything, the
carts piled with used clothing, tattered quilts, and tin pots were
move prevalent, the vendors hawking their wares even louder of
voice and their customers more odoriferous after spending two
days huddled against the cold behind closed doors.

Yet, no one could deny that the city was still in the grip of winter. Children were not yet playing in the streets and the adults
who were out and about were bundled up in whatever garments
they could lay their hands on in an attempt to keep warm. For the
wind had a bite to it that reddened Justin's ears and nose and penetrated the folds of his greatcoat, rendering him more than happy
to catch sight of the familiar blue door of the Laura Wentworth
Home for Abandoned Children.

"We're here at last," he announced to Reggie, who was shivering noticeably despite his heavy clothing. Guiding his matched pair past a slow-moving vegetable cart and around a used boot stall, Justin brought them to a halt a few feet behind a gaudy blue barouche that occupied the spot where he had parked his curricle two days earlier. He looked up just in time to see Danny come barreling down the steps of the Laura Wentworth Home, slide across a patch of ice, and careen into the side of the barouche.

A furtive conversation ensued between the former pickpocket, the coachman, and the groom of said vehicle, which ended with the coachman cracking the whip over his horses and making a hasty exit into the alley separating the Laura Wentworth Home from the building next to it.

"Now what was that all about?" Justin wondered aloud as Danny sauntered toward him.

Handing his reins to his groom, Justin dismounted. "Good morning, Danny. How goes it with you?"

"Could be worse," the boy said, casting a wary glance toward Reggie. "Daisy's doin' fine and that's the main thing far as Tess and me's concerned."

Justin smiled. "Just the kind of news I'd been hoping for." He waited until Reggie had descended from the passenger's side of the curricle, then said, "May I present my friend, the Earl of Rutledge." He clapped Danny on the shoulder. "And this, Reggie is—"

"Your new building manager you were telling me about," Reggie interjected. "Happy to meet you, lad."

"Likewise, guvnor," Danny replied, swelling with obvious pride at the use of his new title by a member of the *ton*.

"Which reminds me"—Justin reached into the pocket of his greatcoat and drew forth a neatly folded piece of paper— "I had my secretary draw up an employment contract. I'd appreciate your looking it over and affixing your signature if the terms are agreeable."

"I'll have to do some thinking on that one." Danny backed up a step, a dubious frown replacing his heretofore friendly expression. "What's a signachoor?"

"I'll need you to sign your name—or make your mark—so the

contract is legal," Justin explained, managing to keep a straight face.

"Oh, that! I don't need to make no mark; I can sign me name proper as any man," Danny declared proudly, hopping back onto the curb to avoid a collision with a soup and stew cart. "Tess showed me how. She's a rare one for learnin', she is. Like to drive me crazy with her everlastin' readin' and writin'. But I can see now it's got its use when it comes to dealin' with toffs."

"Indeed it has," Justin agreed gravely.

With equal gravity, Danny doffed his cap. "I'll be proud to sign me name to your contract, guvnor, seein' as how you and me has already agreed we trusts each other."

"Very well then, we'll take care of that bit of business after I've had a look at Daisy's leg. I assume Tess has pen and ink she can lend us."

"Yessir, she has that, but not much else, if you takes my meanin'." A thoughtful frown creased Danny's freckled brow. "I hates to say it, but the truth is she ain't the smartest woman alive when it comes to lookin' out fer herself. Her friends has to look out for her 'cause she spends so much time worryin' about what everybody else needs, she forgets about wot she needs."

He looked Justin straight in the eye. "But you seen that right off, didn't you, guvnor! Sendin' her mutton and chickens and such every day was usin' the old noodle. Long as she believed the presents was for the children she couldn't throw 'em back in your face like she done all them fancy gewgaws them other toffs tried to give her." Danny beamed with approval. "I know'd you was a smart one first time I laid eyes on you. Yessir. His lordship's the kind of toff even Tess would take to is what I told me cronies."

Reggie chuckled. "I do believe you forgot to mention the 'mutton and chickens and such,' " he murmured in Justin's ear.

Justin ignored him. "I've enjoyed our little talk, Danny," he said self-consciously. "But I believe Tess is expecting me and I, for one, am ready to seek shelter from the cold. The sunny clime of Greece has spoiled me for such weather as this." So saying, he limped forward and with the help of his cane, began climbing the icy stairs, with Reggie close behind him.

Danny pounded up the stairs after them. "Wait up! There's somethin' you needs to know before you sees Tess." He passed

Justin and stopped on the step above him. "It's like this, guvnor. What with Daisy's leg and all, you and me has gotten to be friends—and I've never been one to look the other way when one of me friends was bein' hoodwinked."

Justin felt a sudden chill that had little to do with the November weather. Irrational as it might be, he found he'd rather not know if Tess was deceiving him in some way. Apparently there was more truth than fiction to Reggie's claim that men in love were devoid of good sense. "Forget it, Danny," he said impatiently, attempting to brush the boy aside. "You're not my keeper."

"Hear the lad out, Justin." Reggie caught his arm in a viselike grip. "What he says may be important."

"Aye, it is that if the wind's blowin' the way I think it is." Danny cleared his throat. "What that blighter Wentworth said on Wednesday mornin' weren't true. Tess is too much of a lady to call him a bald-faced liar in front of a gent like you, but she called him that and plenty more once you left. I know, 'cause I was standin' out in the hall listenin'."

A look of satisfaction crossed his pinched young face. "Read him up one side and down the other, she did. Told him right out she was no man's be . . . be . . . you know, that word he said."

"Betrothed?" Justin managed to squeeze past lips that felt as frozen as the ice on the steps beneath his feet.

"That's the one." Danny grinned triumphantly. "I guess he thinks 'cause he's known her longer'n anyone else, he's got dibs on her. But it ain't so. You can kiss her anytime you wants—providin' she wants it too, of course." A devilish smile crossed his thin, freckled face. "Just thought you'd like to know where things stands, guvnor," he said as he turned to run up the rest of the stairs.

Justin felt such a rush of elation, he was tempted to cast his cane aside and race the boy to the blue door—until he caught a glimpse of Reggie's knowing grin. "Good God!" he groaned. "Am I so transparent, my infatuation with Tess is obvious even to a boy of thirteen?"

"Perhaps to this particular boy, but don't make the mistake of equating this child of the slums with the green lads we were at his age," Reggie warned. "He may have the body of a thirteen-year-old boy, but his mind is that of a thirty-year-old man who has seen more of the seamy side of life than you and I together can boast. Furthermore, it's obvious the clever fellow agrees with your assessment of the handsome cit—and equally obvious he has chosen you as the knight in shining armor to rescue his lady from the villain's clutches."

His familiar laugh joined the myriad sounds of the street. "I prophesied this mission of yours would be just the thing to alleviate my boredom. And by George I was right! The situation grows more intriguing by the minute!"

"I'm happy to know you find my activities so entertaining," Justin said somewhat peevishly. He was beginning to tire of Reggie's thinly veiled cynicism, as well as his persistently humorous outlook on life. The man seemed incapable of a serious thought. Even the Peninsular War had had its comedic moments to hear the Earl of Rutledge tell it.

He cringed, imagining how Tess's gaudy furnishings would strike a man of Reggie's disposition. The face on the god Pan alone should be enough to provide him with uninterrupted laughter for the next fortnight.

With gloomy resignation, Justin followed Danny through the open doorway of the Laura Wentworth Home, only to stop short at the sight that met his eyes. He blinked and looked again, but there was no doubt about it: There was Tess, kneeling beside the prostrate figure of a young woman, apparently attempting to staunch the trickle of blood seeping from a wound near the woman's temple with a square of white linen.

"What the devil!" Justin exclaimed, pushing past Danny, only to have a grim-faced Reggie shove him aside an instant later with a force that nearly sent him sprawling. "Lady Camden!" Reggie cried, his voice fraught with an emotion Justin had never thought to hear his jovial friend display.

As Justin watched, Reggie dropped to his haunches beside the unconscious woman and faced Tess across her limp body. "Would you be good enough to explain to me, Miss Thornhill," he said with unmistakable menace, "why the Countess of Camden lies bleeding and unconscious on the floor of this godforsaken tenement in the heart of the London stews?"

Chapter Seven

Godforsaken tenement! Tess didn't know if she was more incensed by the insult to her children's home or by the earl's threatening tone of voice.

She was sorely tempted to inform him that but for the grace of a kindhearted bawdy-house madam, Consuela could have ended up in a place far more disreputable than a home for abandoned children. But, of course, she couldn't bring herself to cause the poor countess such cruel embarrassment. As Florabelle had so aptly put it, Consuela had already "had to swallow enough of her pride."

Instead she declared coldly, "I am but newly acquainted with the lady. I was not aware she was a member of the nobility when I offered her and her child sanctuary. But had I known, I hope I would have had the decency to do so despite her unsavory connections."

"Bravo, Tess!" Justin choked with laughter.

Tess pretended to ignore him, though in truth, his encouraging words made her heart sing. Rising to her feet, she stared down her nose at his insolent friend. "As to why the Countess of . . . Camden, was it . . . is, at the moment, lying on my floor, the answer is simple: She fainted from hunger."

The earl's eyes narrowed. "The devil you say! That, madam, is something I find difficult to believe. I am aware her husband died at Salamanca, but his family is one of the wealthiest in all of England. Why in God's name should his wife faint from hunger no more than an hour's drive from their London town house?"

Tess shrugged. "That, my lord, is something you will have to ask her."

"But not before you offer Miss Thornhill an apology for your insufferable rudeness, Reggie. Whatever the circumstances, she would have no reason to lie about the countess."

Out of the corner of her eye, Tess saw Justin limp forward to stand beside her like a belligerent guardian angel. She cast him a grateful smile. If nothing else, this business with Consuela had eased the embarrassment of their first meeting since they'd shared that brief moment of passion on Wednesday.

The earl swept an angry glance in Justin's direction, then mumbled something Tess assumed was the demanded apology. Once again his gaze dropped to Consuela's still form and a look so fraught with anxiety crossed his face, Tess instantly forgave him his rude comment. Instinct told her this homely giant harbored far more tender feelings for the beautiful countess than those of a casual acquaintance—a fact that only added to the mystery surrounding the lady.

Quickly, she retrieved the sleeping baby from the nearby couch on which she'd placed him when his mother fainted. A mistake, she realized a moment later when he opened his tiny mouth and let her know he did not appreciate being awakened from his peaceful slumber.

With a nod toward the open door on her right, she called out to be heard over the infant's cries, "If you would be kind enough to carry Consuela to the sofa in the common room, my lord, I'll find some sal volatile. I'm certain that will bring her around."

The earl instantly leaped to do her bidding, but the look on his face told her he was highly skeptical of her diagnosis. Tess took pity on him. "She's not badly hurt, you know," she continued in a loud voice as she followed close behind him. "I've tended enough victims of local street fights to recognize a serious head wound when I see one. Believe me, the countess merely received a minor bump when she collapsed to the floor. I think what she needs most is a bowl of hot, nourishing soup."

She propped the screaming infant against her shoulder and briskly patted his back, hoping his complaint stemmed from something as simple as a bubble of gas in his little stomach. His screams merely accelerated to a more deafening pitch. For a baby who was purported to be sickly, Consuela's son certainly had a healthy pair of lungs.

Tess looked for Danny to relieve her of her charge, but he had conveniently disappeared at the first sign of trouble. Danny was no fool. In desperation, she marched across the room to where Justin stood just inside the doorway. "Sorry, I've no choice. His mother needs me more than he does," she said and thrust the wailing infant into his arms. The baby promptly stopped crying, gave a contented gurgle, and nestled into Justin's neatly tied cravat.

Shaking her head in amazement, Tess hurried toward the kitchen for a bowl of the soup Maggie had prepared for the children's noonday meal. What was there about Justin that made children of all ages instantly trust him—and normally sane women lose their heads over him?

She shivered, gripped by a disturbing premonition that the gentle, soft-spoken viscount could turn out to be a far greater danger to her peace of mind—and her heart—than if he had been the unprincipled rake she'd first believed him to be.

Consuela had regained consciousness by the time Tess returned to the common room followed by Maggie bearing a tray containing a bowl of soup, a chunk of bread, and a vial of sal volatile. The Spanish girl was sitting up, propped against the arm of the couch, her baby asleep in her arms. She looked wan and fragile and, at the same time, more breathtakingly beautiful than any of the madonnas in the impressive collection of religious paintings Tess's father had spent a lifetime accruing.

As she watched from the doorway, the Earl of Rutledge knelt beside the couch on which the Spanish girl reclined and discreetly arranged the hem of her cloak to cover a dainty, stocking-clad ankle. "Dear lady, what could you have been thinking of to venture into a cesspool of sin and corruption like the London stews?" he inquired softly.

Consuela regarded him with obvious puzzlement. "Do I know you, sir?"

"I was a senior officer on Wellington's staff and your husband's direct superior, my lady."

Her finely arched black brows drew together in a frown. "It seems so long ago." She sighed. "Did you know *mi querido* died at Salamanca?"

Reggie's ruddy complexion paled noticeably. "I was there, my lady. Camden was a gallant officer—a true hero. The charge he led may well have turned the tide of battle."

"But what good will that do me?" Consuela's soft pink lips trembled and her luminous blue eyes filled with tears. "I do not understand war."

A look of profound tenderness softened the earl's craggy features. "I doubt anyone does, my lady—least of all a soldier like myself."

Instinctively, Tess glanced at Justin to judge his reaction to the beautiful countess, and found the expression on his face every bit as idiotic as that on the earl's. In truth, with his mouth hanging slack and his eyes round as a cricket ball, he looked as if he were the one suffering from a blow on the head.

Pain, sharp as a knife blade, slashed through her. It was not that she was jealous of the admiration the beautiful Spanish girl elicited. God forbid. She had never had a jealous bone in her body. She simply found it a trifle disillusioning that Justin could kiss one woman silly on Wednesday, then slaver over another on Friday. It appeared Drew had been right after all; the Viscount Sanderfield was no different from the rest of his noble breed. All of which, she sternly reminded herself, meant absolutely nothing to her.

Gritting her teeth, she marched into the room, lifted the baby out of Consuela's arms, and deposited him at the foot of the sofa. Then relieving Maggie of the tray, she placed it on Consuela's lap. "See that she finishes every drop of soup," she ordered the earl. "The viscount and I have another patient to attend to."

She turned to Justin. "I assume you are still interested in examining Daisy's leg, my lord?"

"What's that you say? Daisy? Oh, yes of course." Justin gathered his scattered wits and followed Tess's militant form down the drafty hall. How, he wondered, had he triggered the lovely firebrand's temper this time? From the tilt of her chin and the rigid set of her shoulders, he suspected he was about to be treated to another of her glorious tongue-lashings. He chuckled to himself. What a magnificent woman! Life was never dull around Tess Thornhill.

But what could he have done that displeased her—other than ignore her while he gaped at Reggie and the Countess of Camden. Well, he could scarcely be faulted for that. The sudden change in his care-for-nothing friend had completely astounded him.

He could see nothing in the Spanish girl to inspire an intelligent man like Reggie to make such a blithering idiot of himself. True, she was pretty enough in an insipid sort of way, but she simply faded into the background once a vibrant beauty like Tess came on the scene.

There was more here than met the eye. He knew his friend too well to believe he had suddenly lost his head and his heart over the beautiful countess.

Tess came to an abrupt halt outside a closed door at the far end of the hall and turned to face him. "I hated to interrupt your daydream of the charming countess, my lord, but Daisy has been waiting all morning to see you."

Her voice shocked him into instant attention—not because of its tone, though it was certainly sharp enough to slice his ears off his head—but rather because he could scarcely believe the words she'd uttered.

Your daydream of the charming countess. Unbelievable as it might seem, Tess wasn't just angry; she was jealous. He felt his heart leap in his chest. This beautiful, witty, warmhearted woman was actually jealous of his supposed admiration for another woman. Reggie had been right; she *was* attracted to him.

Suddenly he felt six feet tall and handsome as a Greek god. He felt like kicking up his heels and shouting to the heavens. Shouting hell! He felt like casting aside his cane and dancing a jig, or better yet escorting Tess to one of those lavish balls to which the hostesses of the *ton* were always inviting him. He smiled at his own idiocy. Of all the fantasies he could indulge in, that was surely the one least likely to occur.

Still, what a lovely fantasy it was. He closed his eyes, imagining what it would be like to take Tess in his arms and waltz around a vast ballroom—four perfect feet skimming effortlessly across the floor, two perfectly matched bodies moving as one to the rhythm of the intoxicating music. What could heaven offer that would compare to such an earthly paradise?

"If you please, my lord, I would like to get on with this business of examining Daisy's leg. You may have all the time in the world; I do not!"

Justin's eyes popped open. So, they were back to "my lord" again, were they? Tess really was spark-spitting mad. He couldn't remember when anything had delighted him more. "Would you deny a man his daydreams, Tess?" he teased.

"It is not my place to deny you anything, my lord—so long as it does not involve me."

"Ah, but there's the rub, Sweet Tess. For it does. I have a perverse nature, you see. I don't doubt most men would find a dark-haired beauty with exquisite azure eyes to be the woman of their dreams—especially if she were small and sweet-natured and helpless. There is something very appealing to the average man about a beautiful damsel in distress. It certainly seemed to appeal to my friend, Reggie. I found the sight of him making such a bufflehead of himself so fascinating, I couldn't take my eyes off him."

"How interesting, my lord." Tess's words were laced with skepticism, but the fleeting look of relief that crossed her face triggered a streak of rakish daring in Justin totally foreign to his naturally reserved nature. He moved forward, effectively pinning her against the closed door at her back. "Now I, on the other hand, lean more toward strong, independent ladies of the blond persuasion—ladies with fiery tempers and, dare I say it, a penchant for lascivious Greek gods."

Tess's eyes widened. "What an outrageous thing to say."

Justin chuckled. "Not nearly as outrageous as what I'm about to do." Transferring his cane to his left hand, he cupped her chin with his right and captured her lips in a long, deeply satisfying kiss that ended only when they were both gasping for breath.

Tess pressed herself against the dark, heavily scarred wood of the door, her golden halo of curls and cherry-red gown vivid splashes of color in the shadowy hallway. Her eyes were glazed with the lingering passion of their kiss, her lips moist and softly parted. Justin found himself wondering if there had ever before been a face as beautiful or as endearing as that of this woman he loved.

The thought shocked him; the sudden realization of the depth of his feelings for Tess shocked him even more. His logical brain instantly protested that it was not possible to love a woman he had known such a short time. But his illogical heart acknowledged that the center of his universe had just shifted to where the moon and the stars now revolved around a pair of emerald eyes and a glorious head of honey-gold hair.

Tess licked the tip of her tongue over her kiss-swollen lower lip. "I hope you realize you cannot keep doing this."

"Doing what?" Idly, he twisted a stray tendril of her hair around his finger and brushed it behind one small, perfect ear.

"You cannot kiss me whenever you happen to feel like it, my lord."

"But of course I can." With the tip of his forefinger he traced the delicate arch of her right eyebrow. "I have Danny's permission to kiss you whenever and wherever I want—so long as you want it too, of course."

"Danny! That rascal! What kind of bird-witted nonsense has he been prattling now?"

Justin smiled enigmatically. "Not nonsense, Sweet Tess. The unvarnished truth—and an extremely helpful suggestion as well."

Justin had expected sparks to fly as a result of his provocative remark. Instead, a worried frown creased Tess's brow. "I have a good idea what that suggestion was," she said grimly. "I have already had words with him about it, but I see I will have to be a good deal more stern in the future."

She avoided Justin's eyes, obviously embarrassed. "You must remember, Danny is a product of the London stews. In his world, morality is based on one thing only—survival. I've come to understand that world in the past five years. I've seen firsthand the endless, soul-degrading poverty that leaves no time to think of anything but filling an empty stomach or warming a shivering body."

She raised her chin in the proud gesture Justin had seen so often in the past two weeks. "But I tell you this, my lord. While I cannot fault the moral code of the inhabitants of this 'cesspool of sin and corruption' in which I live, I will never accept that code as my own."

Justin searched her troubled face, wondering what in the world she thought Danny had said to him. He racked his brain to say something to diffuse the anxiety his teasing remark had triggered in her. "Don't sell the lad short," he said finally. "He is devoted to you—fanatically loyal, in fact. He only wants what is best for you."

"I know that," she said wearily. "But his best is a far cry from mine."

Justin scowled, utterly perplexed by the strange turn their conversation had taken. "Are my kisses so repugnant to you then that you feel you must chastise the lad for condoning them?" he asked softly.

"If there is one thing you are not, my lord, it is dense. So please do not insult me by pretending you think we are merely discussing something as simple as your kisses."

Simple? Justin felt strangely affronted. "I'm afraid I've lost track of exactly what we *are* discussing," he admitted uneasily. "But I would still like an answer to my question. Do you find my kisses repugnant?"

Tess pressed herself even more firmly against the door, as if to put another inch or two between them. Instinctively, he moved back a step to give her the space she desired. From the troubled look in her eyes, he suspected her natural reticence was waging war with her unremitting honesty. As he'd known it would, the honesty won.

"I cannot deny I enjoy your kisses," she admitted finally. "But I think you may have misinterpreted my reaction to them. I think it only fair to tell you that there is nothing you could ever do or say that would induce me to become your mistress."

Justin gasped, more startled than shocked by her amazing frankness. He should have known his lovely hoyden would do the unexpected. He wondered if she knew what a rare treasure she was; he wondered if he would ever be able to talk himself into returning to the quiet, reclusive life with which he'd been content before he met her.

But treasure or not, it would never do to give Tess Thornhill the upper hand. With a flair for drama he'd never before suspected he possessed, he cocked his head as if pondering a weighty question. "Have I somehow missed something in the course of our fascinating conversation?" he asked innocently.

"Missed something?" She looked as perplexed as he had felt but moments before.

Choking back his laughter, he fixed her with an earnest gaze. "At the risk of offending you, Sweet Tess, I am afraid I must admit I honestly do not recall offering you a position as my mistress."

He'd done it to her again. Or rather she'd done it to herself—with his help. He appeared to take delight in besting her at every turn, yet managed to do it in such a charming way she was never certain if he'd been laughing at her or with her. Even now, after committing the most unpardonable gaffe of her life, she felt more inclined to remember it with a chuckle than to crawl away in shame—and all because of the twinkle she'd spied in Justin's eyes when he'd delivered his shocking set-down.

But why had he taken to calling her "Sweet Tess"? She had no illusions about herself; she had never been sweet. Not even as a child. She couldn't remember a time when she hadn't rebelled against authority—when she hadn't questioned what those around her blindly accepted.

Mama had thrown up her hands in despair at her independent ways; Papa had called her a "child of the devil" and laid his razor strop across her backside so often, it was a wonder she had any hide left. Even Drew, who professed to love her, had declared her pigheaded and exasperating.

So why did Justin call her "Sweet Tess"? And why did her heart do flip-flops when he said the words? Hearts were such illogical things. Of all the men in the world, why should the Viscount Sanderfield be the one man to whom hers responded? Didn't the silly thing know rebellious slum dwellers had nothing in common with peers of the realm?

But then she found everything about Justin confusing. She could never second-guess him as she did most other people. Even now, watching him examine Daisy's leg and bandage it with such quiet efficiency, she could scarcely believe he was the same man who just moments before had kissed her with a passion she felt certain no gentleman ever displayed for a lady—then calmly informed her she was mistaken in her belief he wanted her to become his mistress.

"So, guvnor, ain't our little patient doin' fine?" A familiar voice interrupted her disturbing rumination. She looked up to find Danny in the doorway of the salon, a cock-of-the-walk expression on his freckled face. She gave him her sternest "I'll talk to you later, young man" scowl—a threat that didn't dim in the least the conspiratorial smile he shared with Justin.

Tess frowned. Why did she get the feeling the two of them had joined forces against her in some nefarious plot? Once again she found herself wondering what it was Danny had told Justin to make him look so satisfied with himself.

Finished with bandaging Daisy's leg, Justin sat down beside her on the small couch and lifted her onto his lap. Daisy immediately snuggled against his chest, the same contented look on her face that Consuela's baby son had worn.

Tess felt a familiar tug at her heart as she registered the unabashed affection between Justin and his small look-alike. If she had ever doubted he was a uniquely compassionate man, she relinquished that doubt now. Only such a man could inspire unwavering trust in a child who had witnessed the unspeakable horrors Daisy had in her short life.

"Daisy likes you, guvnor." Danny smiled benignly at the tender scene before him, but Tess detected a hint of envy in the boy's voice. He had had so little love in his life, it was only natural he would feel threatened by any rival for Daisy's affection.

To his credit, he quickly returned to his usual cheerful self. "I got a present for you, guvnor," he said, crossing to the small table where he spent each evening drawing on the sheets of butcher paper Tess had inveigled from a local merchant. "It ain't much, but Tess and me is mighty grateful for wot you done for Daisy and there ain't nothin' else we could give a rich bloke like you."

Tess had forgotten the drawing of Daisy that Danny planned to give Justin. The boy had anguished over it for hours—wondering if a man like the viscount would scoff at such a poor thing as a drawing on a piece of butcher paper. Tess had assured him Justin would find the drawing delightful; she hoped to heaven she'd judged right.

"A present for me?" Justin felt both pleased and embarrassed at being the recipient of an unexpected gift. If the truth be known, he'd received so few gifts in his life, he scarcely knew how to act.

Lifting Daisy from his lap, he set her down beside him on the couch and accepted the tube of paper the boy held out. He could feel Danny's eyes on him as he carefully unrolled the tube. A slight tic at the corner of the boy's mouth warned him how important his reaction to the gift was to the young giver. Feeling oddly touched by the boy's eagerness, he determined that whatever it might be, he would make certain he showed proper appreciation.

"Well, what do we have here?" he asked, spreading the square of coarse-grained paper on his lap. But in the next instant he knew he'd have no need to fake a pleased response to the pen-and-ink drawing that met his astonished gaze.

He felt his breath catch in his throat. It was a remarkable likeness of Daisy. True, the technique lacked the polish one might expect of a professional artist. But the talented amateur, whoever he might be, had perfectly caught the little girl's expression. It was all there. The delicate bone structure, the haunted look in her huge eyes, the softly vulnerable mouth that had been silenced by cruelty too monstrous for her young mind to fathom.

"What a remarkable drawing! But it isn't signed. Who is the artist? He must know Daisy extremely well." Justin raised his eyes to search Danny's face. "Surely no stranger could portray her with such profound sensitivity."

"It weren't no stranger." Danny chortled with unrestrained glee. "I drawed it meself."

Justin stared at the grinning boy, literally speechless with surprise. "That is absolutely amazing," he said finally. "You are a very talented young man, and I cannot begin to thank you enough for sharing that talent with me. I shall treasure this wonderful drawing forever. In fact, I'll send it to a framer this very afternoon so I can have it hung in the bookroom where I spend most of my days."

Danny turned to Tess, a triumphant look on his bright young face. "What'd I tell you? I knowd all along he'd like it."

Tess didn't have the heart to remind him of the anxious hours he'd paced the floor pondering whether or not to offer Justin his gift. "You should sign your drawing for the viscount, Danny," she said gravely. "In the lower right-hand corner. All good artists sign their work."

"Might as well since I got to sign the guvnor's contract anyways," he agreed, bristling with importance.

"Contract? What contract?"

"I believe I already mentioned I planned to make Danny my building manager." Justin shrugged. "This piece of paper will just make it legal."

Danny made a great ceremony of affixing his signature to both pieces of paper, then proudly handed them to Justin. But once that was accomplished, he began shifting restlessly from one foot to the other, as if eager to be off on some mysterious errand of his own. Tess had no doubt that "errand" would entail some tall bragging about his triumphs to his less fortunate cronies.

"Well, I gots to be going," he said at last, "and whilst I'm at it, I'll take Daisy back to the schoolroom so's she can soak up some more learnin'." He grinned. "That way she'll have plenty to say when she finally gets around to talkin'." With that, he swept Daisy up in his arms and dashed for the open door, leaving Tess and Justin alone.

Instantly, an uncomfortable silence descended on the small room. Tess sat on one end of the sofa, staring at her hands; Justin sat on the other end, staring at the drawing spread across his knees with such intensity, she began to wonder if he were even aware of her presence.

She supposed she owed him some kind of apology—for what exactly she wasn't certain—but she had rushed her fences and flatly refused an offer he hadn't yet made. Probably never intended to make. Irrationally the thought depressed her, since she'd never in a million years consider accepting such an insulting proposition. Another example of her perverse nature, she supposed.

Another few moments of the oppressive silence, and she was game to try anything to relieve the tension building within her. "My lord—" she began hesitantly. His gaze remained riveted on the drawing, almost as if he hadn't heard her. Why was he making this so difficult?

"Justin—" she tried a new approach, although she'd vowed earlier to maintain a strictly formal dialogue between them.

At the sound of his name, he raised his head and looked at her with eyes so glazed with pain, she knew at once what was wrong. Danny's little drawing may have skillfully depicted Daisy, but it was obvious it had also reminded Justin of the beloved sister he'd lost.

"Except for the sadness in her eyes, the child in this picture could be my sister, Anne, as I remember her at Daisy's age," he said bleakly.

Without thinking, Tess dropped to her knees before him— everything forgotten except the urgent need to comfort him. "Oh, Justin, I am so deeply sorry. I never thought to cause you pain when I urged Danny to give you that drawing."

Justin stared into Tess's tear-drenched eyes and something deep inside him blossomed like a flower that long deprived of the sun, first feels its life-giving rays. No woman had ever cried for him before; no woman had ever sensed the terrible loneliness that was as much a part of him as his arms and legs and the grotesque lump of flesh and bone he called his left foot.

He ached to tell this wonderful, caring woman that he wanted her more than he had ever wanted anything else on the face of the earth—that her courage and honesty and warmth had spread light into all the dark and dreary corners of his life.

It was too soon. A fortnight only. She would think him a madman—or worse. She would think him a liar and a rake—a debaucher of innocents like his brother Oliver had been.

So, he merely cupped her tearstained face in his two hands and placed a chaste kiss on her smooth forehead. "I came here today empty-handed, Sweet Tess," he said softly. "I leave with the two most precious gifts I have ever been given—Danny's drawing and your compassion."

Chapter Eight

Justin could never remember seeing Reggie in as grim a mood as he was on the drive from the stews back to Mayfair. Apparently the Countess of Camden had divulged enough of her troubles during the time he'd sat with her to make him realize she was in truly desperate straits.

Reggie started relating those troubles the minute the carriage got underway and Justin listened with half a mind—the other half on his own dilemma. His startling discovery that he was deeply and irrevocably in love with Tess Thornhill had shocked him into realizing he was going to have to do some serious thinking about what part he hoped to convince her to play in his future—indeed, what he, himself, intended to do with that future.

Not that he had much chance of talking an independent woman like Tess into doing anything she didn't want to do, but a fellow should at least know his own mind—maybe even have a goal he was aiming for. Up until now he'd simply taken life a day at a time, content with dealing the best he could with whatever problems that day produced—even if they were as monumental as inheriting a title he didn't want and a great deal of money and property he didn't need. But he would be three and thirty on his next birthday; he could no longer justify such a casual attitude.

But this was not the time for such weighty decisions. Reggie obviously needed to vent his frustration over the plight of the beautiful Spanish widow and, as his friend, Justin was obliged to listen.

"Start at the beginning again," he said. "I confess my mind was wandering. I fear I missed a good deal of what you said."

"I said that thieving younger brother of Percy Strathmore's had the gall to close the door in Lady Camden's face when she arrived at the family town house carrying the rightful earl in her arms." The earl slammed his massive fist against the carriage frame with a force that sent the high-spirited matched bays into a head-tossing, high-stepping frenzy that threatened to overturn the curricle or at the very least, throw it into the path of a passing hackney coach.

"Stubble it, for God's sake," Justin grumbled, struggling to bring the frightened nags under control. "Killing us won't solve the countess's problems."

"Sorry, old sod." Reggie waited until Justin had the horses successfully quieted before he continued. "I'm just so damned angry about the injustice done the widow of a fellow officer."

"I can understand that," Justin said, looking over his shoulder to make certain his groom was still clinging safely to the bar at the back of the carriage. "Especially if he was the hero of Salamanca you described to his widow."

"He was." Reggie frowned. "Though oddly enough, Camden was the careful sort when he was single. Only after he married did he turn into the kind of reckless daredevil heroes are made of."

He stared into space for a long, silent moment. "Truth is, I never liked him much. He was too handsome, too glib, too much of everything I could never be, I suppose. Hell, you must remember him from Oxford."

Justin shook his head. "No, can't say I do . . . but wait a minute. Was he that dashing fellow who was sent down for smuggling one of the local tavern wenches into his chamber?"

"The same." Reggie shrugged. "Always was a devil with the ladies. Rumor was he'd tumbled half the women in Spain—and all the while professing to be madly in love with his childhood sweetheart, the Duke of Rutherford's daughter. To hear him tell it, they were pledged to marry once the war was over. You can imagine how surprised we all were when he eloped with the Conde de Alvarez's only daughter."

Reggie's smile lacked its usual humor. "Of course we found out soon enough why he was caught in parson's mousetrap. The lady was breeding. Though how he'd managed to get her alone long enough to—well, you know—is beyond me. Never saw her without her dragon of a duenna close behind."

He frowned. "I'll say one thing for him; he didn't shirk his duty to the Spanish lady he'd seduced, as a lot of our fellows did. The man was an enigma in more ways than one."

"How so?"

"He was the last man on earth I'd have expected to volunteer for The Forlorn Hope."

"The Forlorn Hope? That's a new term to me."

"It's what we called the squads who stormed the enemy defenses before a battle so we could gauge if there were any weak spots in the French fire. Only men desperate for a battlefield promotion volunteered; they were assured one if, by some miracle, they survived."

"And you're wondering what prompted a man of wealth and title, like the Earl of Camden, to volunteer," Justin guessed.

Two grim lines bracketed Reggie's mouth. "More than that, I'm wondering why *I* didn't refuse his request. As his superior officer, I could have—if for no other reason than that he was a married man with a child on the way. But I didn't."

He closed his eyes as if reliving some remembered horror. "God help me, I stood on a knoll beside Wellington and watched the poor fool get himself blown to kingdom come."

Justin cast a worried glance in Reggie's direction before guiding the nags around a slow-moving freight wagon. The note of anguish in his friend's voice was something new. He wondered how many other bitter memories were hidden behind the hail-fellow-well-met exterior Reggie showed the world.

"The fact that you witnessed Camden's death doesn't make you responsible for it," he declared firmly.

"So I've told myself time and again. Then why do I still wake from nightmares soaked in my own sweat and sick with the same shame I felt that godawful day."

Reggie rubbed his hand over his eyes. "I've never told anyone this, but I searched for his widow before I left the Peninsula. Never found a trace—just a rumor the conde had disowned her when she married Camden. The blighter was happy enough to have Englishmen die to save his precious

Spain from Bonaparte, but he apparently didn't want one as a son-in-law."

Reggie's eyes gleamed with a holy fervor. "Finding her like this, I can't help thinking the Almighty's given me a chance to right the wrong I let happen at Salamanca—and right it I will if it's the last thing I ever do. I'm just sorry I had to ride off today and leave her in that disreputable tenement."

"The Laura Wentworth Home is not exactly a den of iniquity," Justin said dryly.

"The devil you say! Did you take a good look at the wallpaper in that so-called common room?"

"It is actually a rather lovely meadow once you get past the god Pan. I have it on good authority the children love it."

"It's something straight out of a French bordello and well you know it. What's more, that red velvet sofa looks suspiciously like one that used to be in Florabelle Favor's bawdy house." Reggie grimaced. "Imagine how I felt conversing with the countess on the damn thing when for all I knew, I'd had one of Florabelle's strumpets on my lap the last time I sat on it."

Florabelle Favor. Justin vaguely remembered Tess mentioning that a local entrepreneur by that name was her benefactor. He chuckled. So, the minx *had* furnished her children's home with castoffs from a bordello. He wondered what other rules of Polite Society she'd dared flaunt for the sake of her orphans.

He decided it was time to change the subject. The less Reggie, or anyone else, knew about how Tess Thornhill kept the wolf from her door, the better.

"We've strayed from our discussion of the countess and her problems," he said. "I, for one, would be interested in knowing how this younger brother you mentioned managed to bar the mother of the rightful heir from the family town house."

Reggie immediately rose to the bait. "The very question I asked her. Believe it or not, the pawky fellow actually had his brother's papist marriage annulled by an uncle who's an archbishop in the Church of England."

"Which, of course, made the countess's child a bastard and the brother the heir to the title." Justin shook his head in disgust. "I don't know why I find that surprising. Our history reeks with the monstrous things we English have done to gain our titles." He shrugged. "I guess that's that then. You can't fight the Church of England."

"Maybe not, but I can see the countess takes her rightful place in the London social world—and I will too, just as soon as I get her properly settled at my mother's place."

"You're planning to involve your mother in the countess's problems? Are you sure that's wise?" Justin had met the Dowager Countess of Rutledge on several occasions. Somehow, he couldn't imagine a high stickler like her befriending a Spanish girl with the scandal of an annulled marriage clinging to her skirts.

"Mother's the logical one to bring it about," Reggie declared. "She's a powerful figure in London society. How else could she have fired off those two bran-faced sisters of mine and gotten them leg shackled in their first Season?"

A satisfied smile spread across his face. "Once my mother gives her stamp of approval to the countess, she'll be accepted everywhere—maybe even find herself another wealthy husband."

Justin raised an eyebrow. "Could it be you see yourself in that role?"

"Good God no! I've no stomach for married life—and even if I had, I doubt such a beauty would give an ugly fellow like me a second glance. I'll be more than content to settle for a few nights of peaceful slumber."

Reggie drummed his fingers impatiently on the metal carriage frame. "I'll pop over to the old girl's place tonight and break the news to her that she's about to have house guests. Then I hope you'll see your way clear to accompanying me when I gather up the countess and her son. It would make it easier all around, with your knowing Miss Thornhill so well."

Justin started to refuse, then thought better of it. He could see Reggie was deadly serious about this crusade on which he'd embarked. The least he could do was lend a hand. "I'll be busy the next two or three days on urgent business of my own," he declared. "I plan to discharge my man-of-affairs and must interview applicants to replace him. But once I've accomplished that—and paid a brief visit to the Royal Academy—I'll be happy to accompany you on your mission of mercy."

"The Royal Academy?" Reggie's brows met in a puzzled frown. "Didn't know you had an interest in art."

Justin guided his curricle to a stop before Reggie's Brook Street town house. "As a matter of fact I haven't," he admitted. "But I believe I may be about to develop one."

As if the day hadn't been eventful enough, Justin was met at the door of his town house by a decidedly smug-looking Wimple, who informed him his grandfather awaited him in the bookroom. It had been a good month since his last encounter with the duke—not long enough by half to erase the memory of the barely concealed animosity the old man had displayed for him.

Why, of all places, must their meeting take place in the bookroom—the one room in the pretentious town house Justin felt truly belonged to him. He wondered if it would ever again seem the same cozy refuge after today. With grim resignation, he limped down the hall and opened the heavy oak-paneled door.

The duke was standing with his back to the fireplace, evidently warming his backside. He fixed Justin with a jaundiced eye. "Well, sir, what do you have to say for yourself?"

"On what subject, Your Grace?"

"On the subject of this ill-bred creature you're currently consorting with in such a blatant manner, it has become common gossip in every drawing room in Mayfair. What else?"

Justin felt a surge of white-hot anger at the insulting reference to Tess. He had, until this day, managed to refrain from answering his grandfather in kind out of respect for his venerable age. The vicious old bigot was welcome to denigrate him all he wanted—but an attack on the woman he loved was something else.

"I have met no ill-bred creatures since returning to England, with the possible exception of the gaggle of debutantes you and my mother chose to parade before me," he said coldly. "I assure you, I have not consorted with a single one of them."

"Damn it, sir, you will keep a civil tongue in your head if you know what's good for you." An angry flush suffused the duke's autocratic face. "I have it from a reliable source that you are openly subsidizing this crazy do-gooder who is the laugh-ingstock of all London. Did you think it would go unnoticed that a groom from this town house was delivering all manner of foodstuffs to your paramour's establishment?"

"I assume you are referring to Miss Thornhill, who rents one of the tenement buildings I recently inherited. I assure you she is not my paramour. She is, in fact, a woman for whom I have the greatest respect."

"She's a madwoman—disowned by her own father for her peculiarities, and he no better than a merchant for all his money." The duke gave an indignant sniff. "And where is it written in the creature's rental contract that you should supply her with her daily sustenance? Willard Drebs knows of no such paragraph. What he does know is that you have stopped him from raising the rent on a property that is grossly undervalued. Do you deny that, sir?"

"I do not. In fact, I plan to instruct him tomorrow to decrease it by half—shortly before I discharge him. I will tolerate no employee who cannot keep my affairs confidential."

The duke's flush darkened to the color of a fine port wine. "By God, you forget to whom you speak, sir. In case it has slipped your mind, I am not only the Duke of Arncott; I am the patriarch of the Warre family. Any business of the family is *my* business."

"I beg to differ with you, Your Grace. The dukedom and the properties pertaining to it are *your* province. I am the Viscount Sanderfield. Any properties held by that title are administered by me."

Justin limped to the desk at which he normally worked on his translations and sat down in his familiar chair—something he would ordinarily never have done when the duke was standing. It was a rather childish gesture of defiance, he admitted, but one that felt particularly apropos at the moment.

The look of rage that crossed the duke's face left no doubt he was aware of the implied insult. "It is obvious you have no con-cept of how to go on as a gentleman of title and wealth," he said indignantly.

Justin shrugged. "That is probably true. I did not choose to inherit the title; it was thrust upon me. Ergo, I shall simply have to do the best I can."

"Your best is not good enough, sir. For one thing, you apparently know nothing about conducting a proper affair. If you must take your pleasure with this madcap merchant's daughter, have the goodness to be discreet about it. I have had the same mistress for twenty years, and not a soul in London is the wiser for it."

Justin doubted that very much, but that was neither here nor there. He was beyond angry over this pointless discussion. A vast weariness had set in that robbed him of both the desire and the energy to quarrel further with his grandfather. One had to care to quarrel with vigor and the truth was he had long since stopped caring that he could never win the duke's approval.

"I have already told you Miss Thornhill is not my mistress," he said quietly but distinctly. "As for the foodstuffs I have had delivered to her"—surreptitiously, he crossed his fingers—"they are not for her, but rather for those in her care. She has turned the tenement into a home for abandoned children—an enterprise which depends on the largesse of the more fortunate since it shows no profit."

"Humpf! This home, as you term it, is obviously the whim of an eccentric busybody. Those children belong in the Lambs Field Foundling Home with the rest of the slum brats."

"Slum brats like this one?" Justin said, unrolling Danny's drawing of Daisy.

His grandfather's ruddy countenance immediately paled to a sickly gray, and before Justin's very eyes the haughty aristocrat changed into a tired old man. "How came you by this drawing of Anne as a child?" he demanded in a voice hoarse with pain.

Justin instantly regretted his cruel action. It was common knowledge that Anne had been the duke's favorite grandchild. He should have realized the terrible grief the old man hid behind his autocratic exterior. "It is not Anne," he said softly. "Daisy is one of the children in Miss Thornhill's care. I have good reason to believe she is Oliver's by-blow."

The duke sat down abruptly in one of the chairs facing the desk, the drawing still clutched in his shaking hands. He stared at it for a long, silent moment. "I see it now. The eyes are different."

Justin nodded. "Anne's were always full of laughter; Daisy has had little to laugh about in her short life."

"Still I would have it."

"I cannot part with it, Grandfather. It was a gift to me. A very personal gift. But I shall ask the boy who drew it to do another."

The duke rose to his feet. "I will pay him, of course."

"Of course."

Without another word, the crusty old aristocrat turned on his heel and strode toward the door.

"Good-bye, Grandfather," Justin said to his rigid back.

"Humpf!"

He watched the duke open the door and step into the hall, and some devil inside him made him call out, "One more thing before you leave—"

The duke didn't turn his head; he did, however, hesitate.

"In case it has slipped your mind, Grandfather, my name is not Sir, as you are wont to call me. It is Justin. I would very much appreciate your using it if you should have occasion to address me in the future."

It was not, Tess felt certain, that Consuela meant to be difficult. On the contrary, she was the most biddable young woman imaginable. One might even say childlike in her eagerness to please. And therein lay the problem. Dealing with the Countess of Camden was very much like dealing with one of the children—one of the slower-witted, more helpless children.

Take the matter of the care of her baby, for instance. Justin and the Earl of Rutledge had no sooner departed for Mayfair than Tess deduced, from the smell of things, that the baby was long overdue for a change of nappies, and said as much to his mother.

Consuela's lovely eyes grew wide with horror. "But you cannot expect *me* to change a nappy!" she wailed. "The wet nurse I brought with me from Spain took care of such things."

"Where is the wet nurse now?" Tess asked, with a worried glance at Maggie, who hovered nearby. A change of nappies for the poor little scrap presented no problem; the chief function of the wet nurse was another thing entirely.

"I do not know." Consuela withdrew a handkerchief from the cuff of her sleeve and dabbed at her brimming eyes. "My money was all gone, so I gave her my diamond earrings to sell. But I fear she got lost. I waited and waited but she never came back."

She fingered the enameled pendant nestled between her breasts. "I am glad I didn't give her my miniature of my dear Percy. How would I remember him if I couldn't see his face?"

Out of the corner of her eye, Tess caught Maggie's dumbfounded expression. With all the former lady's maid had seen of life, she would find it difficult to believe anyone could be so stupidly naive.

"It must be hours since the wet nurse left. How have you managed to feed the baby?" Tess asked gently. Consuela searched through her reticule and came up with a well-suckled sugar teat.

"Good God, girl. He can't live long on that!" Maggie snatched up the smelly baby as if he were in mortal danger. "I'll bathe him. Then I'll make a milky gruel and spoon it down him till I can rig up a way for him to suckle some milk." She raked the tearful young countess with a fulminating look. "There ought to be a law against children breeding babies."

It was the longest speech Tess had ever heard her taciturn assistant make—and the most impassioned. Maggie's own baby had died at birth three years earlier, shortly after she'd arrived half-starved at Tess's door. A lesser woman might have let her grief destroy her; Maggie had chosen instead to lavish her love on the motherless children who found sanctuary in the Laura Wentworth Home.

Those first few revealing moments with Consuela set the pattern for her involvement with her baby. She seemed perfectly content to let Tess and Maggie take over his care, leaving her free to play with him, much as a child might play with a doll.

Still, with all her shortcomings as a mother, Tess found it difficult to resent the lovely Spanish girl who had been thrust upon her. Consuela was too sweet-natured, too pathetically eager to do whatever was asked of her. It was just so difficult to find anything she was capable of doing. With each passing hour, it became more apparent the beautiful countess was a woman of shockingly limited intelligence.

By the end of the third day with her new "employee" under-foot, Tess's nerves were in shreds and her temper so short, she found herself snapping at Maggie for things that would not have bothered her in the least before Consuela's arrival. Maggie bore it all in stoic silence, as if aware that Tess could no more vent her frustration on the hapless countess than on one of the children in her care. By tacit agreement, the two women simply left the lovely woman-child to her own devices while they performed the myriad tasks required to keep the home running efficiently.

"But what in the world am I going to do with her?" Tess asked as Maggie and she shared a late-night pot of tea. "We can't go on like this forever."

For once, her pragmatic assistant failed to come up with a single practical suggestion.

Justin settled back against the squabs of Reggie's elegant closed carriage and resigned himself to listening to yet another chapter in the saga of the Countess of Camden. It had been three long days since he'd seen Tess and he had so much to tell her, he would have preferred to visit her on his own—but he had made a solemn promise to support Reggie's efforts to aid the unfortunate Spanish girl.

A glance at his traveling companion warned him that Reggie was not in his usual jovial mood. He waited for an explanation. When none was forthcoming, he took it upon himself to initiate the conversation. "I take it from your grim expression that things have not gone exactly as you planned."

Reggie's only reply was a deep, unintelligible growl and a blank stare at the bouquet of roses he'd apparently purchased from a Mayfair florist.

Justin tried again. "What happened? Did your mother decline to sponsor the countess's entrance into London society?"

"Mother was in a sticky spot," Reggie said defensively. "As it turned out, she and the Dowager Countess of Camden are bosom bows, and the dowager is backing her younger son's claim to the title. It appears the old besom has a horror of a foreigner and a papist inheriting—even if it is her own grandson."

A bitter smile crossed his face. "Though she didn't come right out and say it, I gathered Mother agreed with her."

Justin felt it prudent to refrain from comment on that telling bit of information. He studied his friend's stiff profile. "I'm sorry your plans have gone awry. I know you had your heart set on sponsoring the countess."

"Damned right I did, and I've not given up yet. As the saying goes, there are more ways than one to skin a cat." A dark flush stained Reggie's angular features. "I've given the matter a great deal of thought these past three days. Since none of my aunts would dare act without Mother's approval, there's but one thing left to do." He took a deep breath. "I will court the lady myself. I may not be the answer to a maiden's prayer, but I'm richer than God and she'd have even more prestige as the Countess of Rutledge than as Camden's widow."

"You can't be serious!" Justin gasped. "You can't marry a woman simply because you've talked yourself into believing you could have prevented her husband's death."

"I have to marry someday if only to produce an heir—as my mother keeps reminding me. It might as well be now."

"I doubt this alliance is what your mother had in mind."

"My mother's opinion is not what matters here," Reggie declared. "The countess is everything any man could desire. She's beautiful and shy and sweet-natured and she's obviously a devoted mother. By George, now that I think on it, I believe I'm halfway in love with her already."

"If you're not, I'm certain you'll talk yourself into it," Justin said dryly. "It appears to be something you've gotten quite adept at."

He regarded the man who was closer to him than his own brother for a long, measured moment. "If you honestly believe she is the woman with whom you wish to spend the rest of your life, then I shall be the first to wish you happy if she accepts your suit. But think carefully, my friend, before you embark on a course from which there is no escape."

"I'm not a fool, Justin. I'm well aware that marriage is a lifetime commitment, and I've no more wish than you for the meaningless kind of union that's common to the *ton*. I promise you I won't rush my fences. I'll call on the lady a few times to see how we rub along together. Then, if I think we can make a match of it, I'll tender my offer."

Reggie's smile seemed genuine, his words reassuring. Then why, Justin wondered, had the odd feeling of uneasiness that had plagued him the past few days suddenly accelerated into a full-fledged premonition of impending disaster?

Chapter Nine

To Justin's surprise, it was Danny who answered his knock on the blue door. "Lord luv you, guvnor, I was hopin' you'd turn up today. Maybe you can talk some sense into the crazy woman." With a brief nod toward Reggie, he stepped aside so the two noblemen could enter.

Justin didn't bother pretending ignorance as to what "crazy woman" Danny had in mind. "What is Tess up to now?" he asked warily.

"It's not her wots up to it this time. It's that bleedin' do-gooder, Wentworth, and she thinks she has to go along with him to make up for that fallin' out I told you about. Not that I ain't for better'n the lot of the downtrodden, bein' one meself, but stirrin' people up like Wentworth does only causes trouble. Sooner or later somebody's goin' to get hurt at one of those blasted meetings of his and I don't want it to be Tess."

His thin young face contorted into a sneer. "Lord Amighty, it ain't like the bloomin' slaughter 'ouse is in the stews. Who gives a rat's ass what 'appens in the South End of London, I asks you."

Justin clapped a hand on the boy's thin shoulder. "What slaughterhouse? What the devil are you talking about?"

"Ask 'er 'ighness," Danny said, pointing down the hall to where Tess was emerging from one of the doors, dressed in the same bonnet and pelisse she'd worn that first day when she'd arrived at Justin's town house.

Her eyes widened at the sight of the gathering in her entryway. "Justin! My Lord Rutledge! I didn't expect you." She sounded a bit breathless. "I was just leaving."

"So Danny informed us." Justin scowled. "What's this about your attending some kind of protest meeting at a slaughterhouse?"

Tess leveled an accusing look on Danny. "My friend Drew
Wentworth has organized a rally to demand decent wages and
working conditions for the women who toil in London's stock-
yards," she explained. "I feel I should support him in his endeavor."

"Female butchers! Good Lord! Never heard of such a thing."
The Earl of Rutledge gaped at her as if she had declared that
Satan and the denizens of hell were doing London's butchering.

"I doubt many people have. According to Drew they're like
great, dumb draft horses—laboring in the most hideous of conditions, and totally unaware of the world outside the slaughterhouse
and the gin cellars surrounding it. The women to whom he's spoken didn't even know England had a king, much less a regent and
a parliament."

Loyalty forbade her adding that she suspected a great deal of
Drew's interest in the illiterate amazons was due to the support he
hoped to gain for his bid for a seat in the House of Commons.
Whatever Drew's ulterior motives might be, he was undeniably a
force for good where the city's poor were concerned.

"Who will take care of the children if you leave?" Justin's
voice held an accusatory note.

"Maggie is perfectly capable of handling things while I'm
gone."

"And the countess is here as well, I presume," the Earl of Rutledge suggested.

"Hah!" Danny mumbled. "Fat lot of help she'll be."

Justin cast him an odd look but made no comment. "Tell me,
Tess, just how do you propose to cross over to the South End?"
he asked quietly.

"In a bloomin' 'ackney coach, that's 'ow," Danny answered for
her. "Tell 'er it ain't safe, guvnor. She won't listen to me."

The scowl Justin had worn for the past few minutes darkened
noticeably. "Danny's right, you know. God only knows what per-
ils a woman alone could face on such a journey. Was this falling
out you had with Wentworth so severe, you feel you must risk
your safety to atone for your part in it?"

Danny again! Tess found herself wondering just how much of
her personal life he had divulged to the viscount. She turned on

the boy. "Since when have you been appointed town crier?" she demanded.

"Now, Tess, the lad is only thinking of your welfare," Justin chided, his remonstration amazingly similar to that which Florabelle Favor had made but a few days prior. "If you won't listen to reason," he continued, "I've no choice but to accompany you."

Tess stared at the elegantly garbed viscount in disbelief. "You will do no such thing. You would be completely out of your element in such a place—and futhermore, my lord, you are not my keeper."

"Better yet, with the earl's permission, I'll convey you there in his carriage," Justin said, ignoring her protest. "That way, I can put the time to good use since there are a couple of matters I need to discuss with you."

The earl made an expansive gesture. "My carriage is yours, old boy, and I shall put *my* time to good use renewing my acquaintance with the Countess of Camden."

Before Tess could object further, she found herself firmly in Justin's grip, hustled down the steps and into the waiting carriage. "This is ridiculous," she said, struggling to free herself as he gave directions to the earl's coachman. "What kind of reception do you think we'll get arriving at a rally such as this in a carriage bearing an earl's lozenge?"

Again Justin ignored her. Settling himself on the squabs opposite her, he rested his cane against the window frame and perused her with a self-satisfied expression that made Tess grit her teeth in frustration.

"Now as to those matters I wish to discuss with you," he began as soon as the carriage got underway. "First, there is Danny and his undeniable artistic talent. The boy should have training; it would be a shame to waste such potential."

"So I have always thought," Tess agreed, momentarily forgetting her indignation at Justin's high-handed treatment of her. "But I haven't the slightest idea how one would go about obtaining such training."

Justin cleared his throat self-consciously. "It so happens I had occasion to visit the Royal Academy yesterday. I carried Danny's sketch of Daisy with me and Lord Applewhite, who heads the selection committee, agreed with me that the crude little portrait showed more raw talent and more insight into human nature than many of their most prominently displayed pieces. He has agreed to help me find an artist willing to take the boy on as a pupil—providing Danny is willing to submit himself to the rigid discipline of apprenticeship."

"Oh, Justin, how can I ever thank you enough! Of course he will welcome the chance to be an artist's apprentice. His drawing is the most important thing in his life. Imagine what it will be like for him to work in watercolors and oils."

"I'm afraid it will be some time before he is ready for those mediums. But it is a beginning. Applewhite has promised to get back to me once his work with the annual competition is completed. I'll make certain he does."

Justin looked into Tess's eyes and frowned. "What's wrong? Why are you looking at me with that odd expression on your face?"

"I'm thinking you're the kindest man I have ever known," Tess said softly. "Something I never expected to hear myself say to a titled nobleman."

A flush of embarrassment spread across Justin's chiseled features. "Yes, well, I daresay our mutual acquaintance, Willard Drebs, would disagree with you on that score. The second thing I have to tell you is that I have discharged him as my man-of-affairs. Upon checking with my other tenants, I found yours was not the only rent he'd raised—and neglected to enter in the books."

"Hah! I always knew he was an unscrupulous blackguard. You could hire someone off the street who would do a better job for you than that thief."

"Perhaps so, but I chose instead to advertise in the *Times* and am quite content with the man I found to replace him." Justin cleared his throat. "There's more—I have instructed my new man to cut your rent in half."

Tess felt a twinge of conscience, wondering if she had pled her case a little too vigorously. "I certainly don't expect you to be that generous," she demurred. "The rent I was originally paying was a fair one."

Before she could say more, Justin raised a silencing hand. "Let us call it my contribution to the welfare of your orphaned children—in particular one whom we both have good reason to believe is closely related to me." He paused. "For the time being, I believe Daisy is happiest where she is, but when she grows older, I should like to make other arrangements for her."

Tess felt tears of gratitude and relief spring to her eyes. She turned to stare out the window, unable to meet Justin's earnest gaze. "Again, I find myself unable to find a way to properly thank you," she murmured.

"I'm certain that with a bit of thought I can come up with something," he said, the laughter in his voice mitigating his suggestive words.

Tess flushed and he sobered instantly. "But back to the subject of abandoned children. My grandfather mentioned a place called Lambs Field Foundling Home in a context that piqued my interest. Can you tell me anything about it?"

The question took Tess by surprise. "What do you want to know?"

"Is it a good institution? I understand it receives financial support from a great many of London's wealthiest men."

Tess thought for a moment. "The mavens of charity extol its virtues. I, myself, think it both good and bad. Good in that before it came into being in the last century, there was no help whatsoever for the abandoned children of London. Bad in that the children within its walls receive nothing but the most basic care from an overworked and underpaid staff. As a result, the mortality rate is shockingly high."

She shrugged. "Still, there are those who survive. Danny, for example. He was a Lambs Field basket baby, which is why we celebrate his birthday in August. He's not sure of the year in which he was born, but he's fairly certain he was a summer babe."

"How so?"

"There's a large basket on the steps of the foundling home. Unwanted babies are left in it—generally late at night—to be collected each morning. Few of the very young ones survive the ordeal in the winter." She turned her head lest she betray the sudden pain that gripped her. Laura's baby had been born in January.

"Good God!" Justin gasped. "Surely something can be done to change such a barbaric system."

"Have you any idea how many unwanted babies are born each year in London?" Tess asked. "They number in the thousands. Except for the few who find refuge in homes such as mine, they either end up at Lambs Field or in the Thames."

She registered the horror in Justin's eyes, and some wicked imp deep inside her spurred her on to further satisfy the wealthy viscount's curiosity as to the fate of the unwanted offspring of the poor.

"I guess the thing I hold most against the administrators of Lambs Field is that they are blind to the need of properly screening the people who adopt the children under their protection. Anyone can apply for a child. Farmers come to London looking for cheap labor, chimney sweeps take the smallest ones for human scrub brushes, mill owners and workhouse managers use them in ways you wouldn't want to know."

"And this could have been Daisy's fate!" Justin's voice sounded hoarse with shock.

"Oh, I doubt that. She is much too pretty a child to be wasted in mill work. She would probably have ended up in one of those houses in Seven Dials where wealthy perverts take their sexual pleasures with small children. Surely you've heard the old wives' tale that sexual intercourse with a child of ten or under will cure the French pox. It doesn't, of course. Merely condemns the child to the same horrible death."

Tess managed a humorless smile. "When you think on it, Danny was very lucky. The man who 'adopted' him when he was but four years old was a flash-house owner. His only interest was in the money the boy could bring in once he taught him to be a cutpurse."

"Enough!" Justin raised his hands before his face as if warding off a blow. And indeed he felt as if he had sustained a mortal wound to his spirit. He'd gained some vague idea of life in the stews from his visits to Tess, but her graphic description of the fate of London's unwanted children had shocked him deeply.

"No wonder you and your friend, Wentworth, have dedicated your lives to bettering the lot of the poor," he said humbly.

Though it galled him to admit it, he found he had gained a grudging respect for the man who was his rival for Tess's heart.

The balance of their trip to the South End was accomplished in silence. Justin could think of a dozen questions he wanted to ask about London's unfortunates; he wasn't certain he could bear to hear the answers. Luckily, Tess appeared to have said all she planned to on the subject.

At long last they arrived at their destination. Tess wasn't sure what she'd expected, but her first sight of the vast slaughter-house was a shock. Doors ten feet wide and twice as high stood open despite the chilly weather, and even before the coachman brought the carriage to a halt the stench of blood and rotting entrails assaulted her nostrils. Her stomach roiled, and from the look on Justin's face, his was reacting in the same way. Only her pride kept her from begging him to take her home.

"Good Lord, look at that," Justin said as he helped her from the carriage. "It's enough to turn one off flesh eating."

Tess swallowed the bile rising in her throat and turned to stare at the blood dripping from hundreds of carcasses hung from the great overhead racks. "If not that, I think the butchers will do it." She pointed to the open area to the left of the carcasses, where twenty or so gigantic women in filthy, blood-splattered smocks were gathered around Drew and another man. Both men were taller than average, but they were dwarfed by the amazons—many of whom had their meat cleavers in hand.

"Good heavens, have you ever seen anything like them?" she whispered, her gaze locked on the huge woman nearest her.

"Never!" With a shudder, Justin drew Tess close to his side just as Drew spotted her. "You came!" Drew mouthed, but his smile instantly soured when his gaze slid to Justin. Tess frowned at him, hoping he would get the message that she found his childish jealousy disgusting.

Justin touched her arm. "Who is that strange-looking fellow with Wentworth?" he asked.

"It must be his friend, Michael Diehl—the one who's urging him to stand for the House of Commons." Tess took another look at the pasty, ferret-faced fellow, and an instant feeling of repulsion swept through her. It was as if the pale stranger ex-

uded an aura of evil so powerful, its chilly tentacles reached out
to contaminate everyone near him.

She shivered, wondering what Drew saw in him. But, of
course, she knew. Anyone who flattered Drew was his friend,
and Diehl's hints of a political future were the ultimate flattery.

As she watched, Drew climbed onto a makeshift platform
and launched into the speech she'd heard him give at a dozen
such rallies. "Human dignity is vital to the spirit of all men and
women," he intoned. "Yet it is the very thing most often denied
the poor by those who consider themselves their betters."

One of the amazons promptly translated his words into the
strange, guttural dialect Tess heard spoken all around her. The
stolid, bovine faces of the women remained impassive. Human
dignity did not appear to be high on their list of priorities.

Drew's voice rose a decibel. "It is this magnificent spirit, this
innate democracy of purpose of the men and women who live
by their honest toil which terrifies the idle nobility and the
greedy merchant class."

Mortified, Tess realized he was staring at Justin, as if sin-
gling him out as a representative of such vile oppressors. Raising his fist above his head, he shouted, "Stand with me against
these grasping tyrants—"

A loud commotion sent Tess's head swiveling toward the entrance through which Justin and she had passed just moments
before. Fifteen or twenty more women, every bit as huge and
blood-splattered as the first group, filled the doorway. The only
difference she could see in this group was that instead of meat
cleavers, they carried long, lethal-looking knives.

At the same moment, the leader of the first group hopped
onto the platform with surprising agility for a woman her size,
grasped Drew by his cravat, and hauled him up until his feet
dangled six inches off the floor.

Tess held her breath as a deathly silence fell on the gathering. "Does ee think to have them stand wi ee same as us, little
man?" she asked, jerking her head toward the newcomers.

"Of course," Drew gasped, his face turning an ugly purple.

"No!" the amazon bellowed, dropping him like a sack of
potatoes. "Girls as kills and skins and whacks legs off cattle
don't never stand wi girls as guts hogs!"

"So much for the democracy of spirit," Justin whispered in Tess's ear. "I have seen enough. We are getting out of here while we still can." Taking a firm grip on her arm, he herded her through a nearby side door.

Tess struggled to free herself. "But what about Drew? We can't just leave him in the midst of all those barbaric creatures with their cleavers and skinning knives," she protested, as behind them a deafening roar exploded from the throats of cattle skinners and hog gutters alike. She glanced behind her but already Drew and his friend, Diehl, were lost to sight in the maze of massive sweat-soaked bodies.

"Not to worry," Justin assured her as he hastened her into the waiting carriage. "Those great, hulking creatures might tear each other apart, but I doubt they'll harm a 'little man.' "

With a few hurried instructions to the coachman, he climbed in behind her, and a moment later the carriage lurched forward.

Tess collapsed onto the seat and straightened her bonnet, which had been pushed askew during their hasty flight. "I am so sorry Drew's rally turned into such a disaster," she lamented. "The poor dear means well, but he does have the worst luck with these meetings he organizes. Something always goes wrong."

She glanced at Justin and realized he was choking with silent laughter. "It wasn't funny," she protested. "It was a terrible affront to his dignity." She looked at Justin again and despite herself, burst out laughing. "He sets such store by dignity," she choked, "and how was he to know that girls who kill and skin and whack the legs off cattle would feel it beneath *their* dignity to associate with girls who gutted hogs?"

"If he had an ounce of sense, he should have," Justin said. "Human nature being what it is, I, myself, am not the least bit surprised to learn that the great unwashed cling to their prejudices and pecking orders with the same tenacity as the most illustrious members of the *ton*."

A wicked grin spread across his face, and as if on cue, the two of them simultaneously started laughing with the same uncontrollable hilarity they'd shared a fortnight earlier over the lascivious god Pan. What was there about this nobleman, Tess wondered, that brought out the hoyden in her in the most unlikely of situations?

She reached into her reticule for a handkerchief to wipe her brimming eyes. At the same moment, the front wheels of the carriage bounced into a deep rut in the road, and without warning, she found herself catapulted forward, to land on her knees at Justin's feet.

His eyes widened. Grasping her upper arms in his strong fingers, he simply stared at her for a long moment as if mesmerized by her touch. Then his gaze lowered to her lips and an instant later his warm, moist mouth followed suit.

The kiss was brief and incredibly sweet—laced with laughter and passion and some deeper, more mysterious element she could not quite define. "Once again I find myself kneeling at your feet," she murmured, feeling herself redden with embarrassment.

"That can be easily rectified," he quipped, lifting her onto his lap as easily as if she weighed but a feather.

"You go too far, my lord," she protested, struggling in his arms. "This is most improper."

"Most improper, indeed." Justin kissed her again. Deeply. Sensually. Possessively. Then, as if momentarily satisfied, he relaxed his hold on her.

"Come now, Sweet Tess, confess," he said as she scrambled back to her own seat. "Haven't you secretly longed to do something risqué—even wicked—as long as the person with whom you did it was comfortably safe?"

He chuckled at the confusion he read in her eyes. He was beginning to understand this intriguing woman he loved. She was a living, breathing contradiction—rebelling against her rigid, evangelical upbringing with her unconventional ways, yet adhering to her own code of conduct as strictly as the most modest Methodist maiden. She was like a beautiful, exotic bird bravely flapping its wings inside a cage it dare not exit. The thought made him ache with tenderness.

"You know me too well," she admitted with the disarming frankness he found so delightful. "But how dare you have the audacity to describe yourself as 'comfortably safe.' You are the most dangerous man I have ever had the misfortune to know."

"You find me dangerous?" Justin's eyes widened and once again the sly smile crept across his face. "How intriguing."

"I do indeed," Tess declared. "It is positively frightening to think how often you've managed to prevail when we've had a difference of opinion."

She frowned. "But enough is enough, my lord. You'll not find me so biddable in the future."

Justin laughed. "Using the word 'biddable' to describe you is tantamount to applying the term 'frugal' to our noble Regent. Surely you know by now, sweet hellion, that your stubborn perversity is the very thing I love best about you."

He wasn't sure which of them was more shocked by the words he'd carelessly blurted out. For the first time since he'd met her, Tess appeared utterly speechless—and his own traitorous tongue seemed tied in knots now that it had wrought its mischief.

With sinking heart, he watched her huddle in a corner of the carriage as far away from him as she could get without climbing out the window. He'd obviously embarrassed her; he'd certainly embarrassed himself.

He made a few halfhearted attempts at polite conversation; she would have none of it. His unfortunate remark had effectively ended all the easy rapport he'd managed to build between them.

He took some comfort in the fact that she considered him "dangerous." It was certainly more interesting a term than "dull" or "quiet" or "reclusive," which were the ones usually applied to him. He basked for a moment in the novelty of it—until he remembered she'd called that pompous prig, Wentworth, a "poor dear" and grieved mightily over his failed rally. Then all that was left to him was a bitter regret for his own stupidity—and a long, hellish ride in which to torture himself with visions of the many ways Tess might find to comfort the disappointed rabble-rouser.

Justin hadn't actually said he loved *her*, Tess reminded herself. He'd said he loved her stubborn perversity in much the same tone of voice she might claim she loved strawberries and clotted cream. It had been a casual remark; nothing more.

Then why had she acted such a fool? Why had the word "love" conjured up fantasies of his strong arms holding her and his warm lips pressed to hers, his quick mind challenging her as none other ever had and his generous heart beating only for her? When, she wondered, had she begun to think of him as the noblest of men? More to the point, why had she let that impossible illusion render her as wide-eyed and speechless as the greenest of schoolroom chits?

A woman five and twenty, who had seen as much of the world as she had, should have more control over her emotions. Yet, a good two hours later, she'd still been hard put to gather her wits sufficiently to bid him a proper farewell when he and the earl left for Mayfair, for by then she'd known all too well what her trouble was. Without realizing it, she'd been slowly but surely falling in love with the Viscount Sanderfield.

She sighed. Not that anything could come of such an impossible love. From the befuddled look on his face when he took his leave of her, she had to assume it would be a long time before her noble landlord made the mistake of knocking at her door again.

Well, what was done was done, she decided in her usual practical manner. There was nothing for it but to bury her feelings deep inside her aching heart and get on with her life.

As if waking from a dream, she looked around her, surprised to find the other occupants of the home involved in their normal activities—just as if nothing earthshaking had happened. Danny was already working on the drawing of Daisy which Justin had commissioned him to do before he'd made his hasty departure, Maggie was rocking Consuela's baby to the tune of one of her ancient Irish cradlesongs, the children were busy at their sums.

Even Consuela had found something to occupy her time—namely arranging the roses the earl had brought her. Tess registered the fact that she was arranging them in the pitcher that normally contained the children's milk, but held her tongue, grateful that the girl had finally shown a talent for something other than making a nuisance of herself.

"Did you enjoy your visit with the Earl of Rutledge?" she asked, curious as to what the lovely dimwit and the haughty aristocrat could have found to talk about for the more than two hours they'd been closeted together in the common room.

The Spanish girl shook her glossy black head. "I could not think of anything to say to him. It was most unpleasant sitting so long in silence." She shrugged. "He did not mind, of course. He said he could spend a lifetime just looking at me because I am so beautiful."

Tess stared at Consuela, afraid to believe her ears. Could the earl be the solution to this problem she'd inherited from Florabelle? It was almost too much to hope that he could be so blinded by the girl's beauty, he couldn't see she had the intellect of a seven-year-old.

Maybe he simply didn't care about her mental deficiencies. Maybe to a man like him, mere beauty was enough. Tess's gloomy spirits brightened noticeably at the thought. It made sense. She'd been warned time and again by her teachers at Miss Haversham's Academy that the last thing a man wanted in a wife was too much intelligence.

The more she thought of it, the more perfect a solution it seemed. She thoroughly disliked the haughty, caustic-tongued earl, and she bitterly resented the fact that he made no effort to hide his disgust of her beloved children's home. If any man deserved to be saddled with Consuela, he was certainly that man.

"Do you think the earl is . . . interested in you?" she asked cautiously.

Consuela placed the pitcher of roses on a small gilt-trimmed table and stepped back to admire her handiwork. She smiled. "Oh, yes. All men are interested in me."

Tess felt strangely humbled by the younger woman's supreme self-confidence. What Consuela lacked in intelligence, she more than made up for with feminine charm and intuition—traits Tess feared were sorely lacking in her own makeup. "Do you think you could ever be interested in the earl?" she asked and waited for the answer with baited breath.

Consuela's eyes widened with something akin to horror. "I could never love a man who looks so much like *El Conde's* horse," she said indignantly. At the mention of her father, her lovely blue eyes filled with tears.

"I cannot help but laugh whenever I see the earl," she added, quickly brushing away the moisture with the back of her hand. "I dread to think what *El Conde* would say if he knew I had sat with him all afternoon. He hates all Englishmen. He would particularly hate one who looked like his horse."

She snuffled noisily. "Still, I believe I must marry again since my dear Percy's brother is so cruel to me—and I know no other man in England save the earl." She sighed. "He is kind, I think, and very rich—and how else shall I ever get another new gown or bonnet unless I marry a rich man?" Raising the hem of her gown, she peered at her feet. "And my slippers are quite worn out."

"A gown and a pair of slippers are not the most compelling reasons I can think of to marry," Tess said more sternly than she intended. Her conscience was beginning to nag her. Even the horrid earl deserved better than this.

More tears welled in the Spanish girl's eyes and slid down her cheeks. When it came to watering pots, Consuela took second place to no one. "That is easy for you to say, Mees Thornhill," she sobbed. "You are strong and fearless. I am not. The earl is right. This is not the proper place for me."

She made a sweeping gesture which included the red velvet sofa, the leering god, and the group of noisy, laughing children gathered around the table for their evening meal. "He says I am too . . . too—"

"Sensitive?" Tess suggested.

"Yes, that is the word. My *ingles* is not so good." Tears gathered in her beautiful eyes. "I do not wish to hurt your feelings, dear Mees Thornhill. You have been so very kind. But now that I think on it, I do believe that when the horse-faced earl makes his offer, I shall be obliged to accept."

"I have made up my mind," Reggie announced as Justin and he lunched together at White's a week after Justin's ill-fated visit to the slaughterhouse. "I've called on the countess every afternoon for the past seven days and the more I've seen of her, the more I've become convinced she's the woman for me."

He smiled, apparently recalling their pleasant times together. "She has the sweetest nature imaginable. Why, she actually bursts into laughter the minute I walk into the room. And the shy little darling is not at all like the silly, chattering magpies my mother keeps dangling beneath my nose. There have been times this past week when we have simply sat together in companionable silence for the full hour of my visit."

"She sounds a paragon."

"She is, Justin, she is. I've never before felt this way about any woman." His eyes gleamed with the same holy fervor as when he'd first spotted the countess lying on the floor of Tess's entryway.

"I have never thought I'd be one to make old bones, but suddenly I want to live forever." He laughed self-consciously. "And conversely, I know I could gladly lay down my life for that sweet little woman tomorrow and die a happy man."

"Let us hope it doesn't come to that, dear friend," Justin said fervently. Though, if the truth be known, a feeling deep in his gut warned him that the step Reggie was about to take might very well amount to the same thing in the long run.

Chapter Ten

It was not yet noon and already Consuela paced the common room, impatient for the Earl of Rutledge's daily visit. "I feel certain today is the day he will make his offer," she confided to Tess. She lifted her skirt to show her right foot. "I certainly hope so. As you can see, my slippers will not last much longer."

Tess jabbed her needle into the thick woolen stocking she was darning and somehow managed to refrain from comment. She had made a point of observing the earl closely the past week and decided he was really not such a bad sort of fellow—for a nobleman. Now her conscience not only nagged her; it reminded her she would have to live the rest of her life with the guilt of knowing that her silence had contributed to the poor man's misery. For miserable he would be if he had to contend with the flea-brained countess on a daily basis.

"What is the time, Mees Thornhill?" Consuela asked, tapping an impatient tattoo on the windowpane with her forefinger.

"It is exactly five minutes since you last asked and still three hours until the earl arrives," Tess replied. "I suggest you find something to do to help you pass the time."

"But what?" Consuela asked petulantly. "I am so bored and I cannot bear to wait for anything."

Tess jabbed again at the hapless stocking. The baby lay sleeping beside her in the crib Danny had procured from a local peddler in exchange for a drawing of his young wife. But it seemed a shame to wake the dear little fellow simply to provide a toy for his mother to play with. She glanced at the bouquet of roses adorning a small gilt table nearby and had a sudden inspiration. "Why don't you rearrange the flowers the earl brought you yesterday? The bouquet is never so perfect it cannot be improved."

Consuela's face lighted up. "Of course. Why did I not think of that?" Within moments, the Spanish girl was happily employed separating the full-blown blossoms from the buds and snipping minute particles from the ends of the stems.

A quiet hour passed, in which Consuela hummed happily to herself. Tess, on the other hand, spent more time soul-searching than darning and came to the sad conclusion that she was probably not as decent a person as she had always considered herself to be. For, conscience not withstanding, she simply could not face dealing with Consuela forever. If the Earl of Rutledge was foolish enough to want to take the lovely dimwit off her hands, she would keep her counsel and offer the poor man her blessing.

The sound of a heavy carriage rolling across the cobblestones sent Consuela dashing to the window. "It is only a hired coach," she moaned. "And the man stepping from it is certainly not the earl. Why he almost looks like . . . but, of course, he cannot be." She pressed her nose to the glass. "*Madre de Dios* it is . . . *El Conde!*"

Tess looked up from her darning. "Your father? Are you certain?" Consuela didn't bother to answer; she was already running toward the entry hall. Tess barely had time to put her sewing aside when the Spanish girl returned with a tall, black-haired man whom she shyly introduced as her father.

It was easy to see from whom the girl had inherited her spectacular looks. The Conde de Alvarez was without a doubt the most handsome man Tess had ever seen. Silver threaded his ebony hair, but his finely chiseled features were as youthful and unlined as a man half his age.

Still his eyes were what captured Tess's immediate attention. Like chips of pale blue ice, they surveyed her with a glacial contempt that left no doubt in her mind what he thought of her, of her children's home, and probably of England in general.

"Leave us, Mees Thornhill," he commanded. "I wish to speak to my daughter alone."

Tess's hackles rose. Who did this arrogant Spaniard think he was, ordering her about in her own home. "You may take your father to the small salon at the end of the hall, Consuela," she said, and calmly picked up her sewing.

The count made her an insultingly curt bow, then spun on his heel and strode down the hall toward the designated salon with Consuela at his heels, but not before Tess glimpsed the flash of anger in his pale eyes. Less than half an hour later he returned, executed another curt bow, and declared, "My daughter will apprise you of the decision I have made concerning her future. I shall await her in my carriage."

Consuela's cheeks were unusually pale and her eyes reddened from weeping. She stood before Tess, hands clasped behind her back like a schoolgirl about to address her headmistress. "El Conde has graciously forgiven my foolish behavior," she recited in a flat, singsong voice. "He says he knows Lord Camden was an evil man who preyed on my innocence and persuaded me to elope with him. But now Lord Camden is dead and I can return home. El Conde says all will be as before because no one will dare speak against the daughter of one of the most powerful men in Spain."

"And how do you feel about it, Consuela? Do you want to go back to Spain?"

An expression of profound relief brightened Consuela's sober countenance. "Oh, yes, Mees Thornhill. I dream every night of the sunshine and the flowers and my own beautiful room in El Conde's house. I find your England to be very—"

"Dreary," Tess finished for her. In truth she'd found it a bit dreary herself this past week. Justin had apparently washed his hands of her once he'd settled the matter of her rent, and she could hardly blame him, considering her idiotic behavior on the drive back from the slaughterhouse.

She smiled at Consuela, her own relief at this unexpected turn of events so overwhelming, she felt positively dizzy. It was the perfect solution to the dilemma she'd found herself in. Without raising a finger, she was rid of her impossible "employee" and the Earl of Rutledge was spared a lifetime of bondage to an eternal child.

Too honest to pretend she would miss the girl, Tess settled for, "Maggie won't know what to do with herself without the baby to fuss over."

Consuela's eyes widened in what looked like genuine surprise. "But surely you must know I cannot take the baby of Lord Camden to Spain, Mees Thornhill. El Conde has forbidden it. He says no one will forget my mistake if the baby is there to remind them."

Tess couldn't believe her ears. Her first thought was that not even the tyrannical Conde de Alvarez could be so cruel as to separate a mother from her child. But remembering he had never even asked to see his grandson, she realized the depth of his hatred for Lord Camden was such that he would go to any length to erase the last trace of the Englishman who had dared usurp his power over his daughter.

"All things considered, you are probably right about the baby," she admitted reluctantly.

"I know I am, Mees Thornhill. El Conde is a man of great kindness, but I do not think he would be kind to the son of Lord Camden."

It was the first intelligent thing Tess had ever heard Consuela say—and the saddest. She could not even begin to envision what the child's life would be like under the thumb of the hate-filled tyrant.

"You will keep the baby then, Mees Thornhill." It was not a question. Consuela held out a thick sheaf of pound notes. "El Conde said I should give you this money to pay for his keep."

Tess refused to acknowledge the offering. She felt sickened with disgust at the callous attitude of the simpleminded countess and her autocratic father. Turning her back on Consuela and her sheaf of pound notes, she picked up the baby and cuddled him—instinctively offering him the love denied him by those of his own blood.

"Good-bye then, Mees Thornhill," Consuela ventured between sobs. "Please do not hate me."

Tess didn't answer. Instead, she buried her nose in the baby's silken curls.

She heard the outer door slam and a moment later the rattle of carriage wheels on the cobblestones. It was done then; the incredible saga of the Countess of Camden was over at last. The baby slept on, oblivious to the fact that the child-woman who had given him life had just abandoned him to the care of strangers.

Gently, Tess returned him to his crib and went in search of Maggie to tell her the astonishing news. As she passed the small gilt table where Consuela had spent the morning arranging her flowers, she spied the bundle of pound notes among the scattered blossoms. Atop them lay a heavy gold chain from which hung the miniature of Lord Percy Strathmore, the late Earl of Camden.

To Justin's surprise, it was Tess herself who answered Reggie's knock at the blue door. "Good afternoon, my lord. I've been expecting you," she said, though she looked anything but happy at the prospect of his visit.

Her gaze slid past Reggie's tall form and a look crossed her face that sent Justin's heart leaping in his breast. "Justin! I had no idea . . . I mean I never hoped. But thank heavens you've come."

Justin instantly forgot the tension that had existed between them when last they'd parted. Pushing past Reggie, he stepped into the entry hall. "What is it, Tess? What's wrong?"

She cast a nervous glance, first at Reggie then at the colorful nosegay he carried. "It's Consuela. She's gone."

"Gone? Gone where?" Reggie's eyes narrowed menacingly. "I warn you, madam, if any harm has come to the countess . . ."

Justin expected Tess's volatile temper to flare at Reggie's implied threat but, strangely enough, the look she gave him conveyed more sympathy than indignation. "Consuela has gone home to Spain with her father," she said quietly. "But come let us go into the common room where we can sit down, and I promise you I shall answer any questions you may have."

At first glance the room looked empty, but a soft, mewling sound indicated there was at least one occupant. Reggie's head shot up like a hound at bay. With a muttered expletive, he strode toward the small wooden cradle at the far end of the room. "What kind of taradiddle are you spinning us, Miss Thornhill?" he demanded. "How can the countess be gone when her young son lies here before us?"

Tess studied the distraught face of the earl, wondering which would be kinder—to soften the truth and salvage some of his pride or be brutally honest and let him see how lucky he was to have escaped the effects of his own bad judgment. She chose the latter. "The Conde de Alvarez demanded she leave her baby behind. He claimed that with the child around to remind them, the Spanish nobility would never forget Consuela had made the mistake of eloping with an Englishman."

"The devil you say! What kind of man would willfully separate a mother from her child?" The earl stared down at the sleeping infant. "And what kind of mother would submit to such a dictate?"

"The answer to your first question is a cruel, unfeeling tyrant," Tess said bitterly. She hesitated, racking her brain for the proper wording before she continued. "The answer to the second, I believe you already know, my lord, if you will but search your memory of this past week. Surely, with all the time you spent with her, you must have come to realize that Consuela was not a woman at all—but rather a slow-witted child masquerading in the body of a woman. The baby was never more than a toy to her, and as anyone who has raised children will tell you, a child is easily parted from a toy by a promise of a new delight."

"But—but she was such a charming little creature," the earl stammered.

"Of course she was, my lord, and you were kindness itself when it seemed she had no one else to turn to." Tess sighed audibly. "I know it was not always easy for you. A man of your intelligence must have wondered why she so often laughed for no apparent reason; must have recognized that her long silences stemmed, not from shyness, but from lack of wit."

She hesitated, wondering how far she dare go with this "truth" she was imparting to the earl. She exchanged a glance with Justin and gained the impression he was urging her on. "Lord Strathmore's death on the Peninsula was a terrible tragedy," she said finally. "But I have to believe that his life would have been equally as tragic. What man in his right mind could endure a lifetime of being shackled to a wife with the mental capacities of a seven-year-old?"

The earl opened his mouth to protest again, then apparently thought better of it. As Tess watched, the expression on his long, angular face made a painful transition from disbelief to doubt to dawning realization. He would hate her for forcing him to see how he'd been taken in by a beautiful face, but better that than to let him grieve the rest of his life for a woman who never really existed.

"I don't suppose she left any message for me."

"No, my lord. Consuela's only thought was of returning to Spain. She was not one to think of two things at one time, you know."

"You have made your point, Miss Thornhill." The earl's cynical smile looked a bit thin around the edges. "I am not entirely a fool. I realize you did so for my own good and I may someday thank you for it, but I find I am not quite capable of doing so today."

He dropped the nosegay onto the roses that still lay scattered on the table where Consuela had left them. "If you will excuse me, I believe I shall wait in the carriage while the viscount completes his visit." With a graceful bow and a mumbled "Your servant, ma'am," the Earl of Rutledge quit the room.

Tess pressed her trembling fingers to her mouth. "Oh dear," she murmured, "I'm afraid I went too far, as usual."

"Not at all." Justin shook his head emphatically. "You said exactly what needed to be said and in the most tactful of ways. I am grateful you had the wisdom to see that unless Reggie was made to realize the truth about the countess, he would have grieved deeply for the loss of the perfect woman he imagined her to be. A bruised self-esteem will heal a great deal quicker than a broken heart."

"Still it cannot be a pleasant experience for such a proud man. I regret I had to be the instrument to wound his pride," Tess said, avoiding Justin's steady gaze. Now that the business with the earl was completed and the two of them were left alone, the self-consciousness she'd experienced on the day of their visit to the slaughterhouse returned in full measure.

As if reading her mind, Justin said, "I have rehearsed all week how to apologize for embarrassing you with my precipitous declaration of love when last we met. But now I am faced with a new dilemma, for I've discovered something else about you to love. Your remarkable compassion."

Tess stared at him. Speechless. Afraid to believe what she was hearing. Luckily the baby chose that moment to wake with his usual lusty demand for attention. She quickly crossed to the cradle and picked him up. "Shush, little one," she crooned, "all is well." A deep, aching tenderness welled inside her for the tiny scrap of humanity abandoned by those who should have loved and cherished him.

"I just realized after she'd gone that Consuela never called him anything but 'the baby,' " she said more to herself than to Justin. "I don't think she ever got around to naming him. So I shall name him." She thought for a moment. "David. David Strathmore—a strong name for a lad who will need to be strong enough to survive the cruel fate dealt him." She dropped a kiss on the baby's silken curls. "And he will survive. For I shall teach him to be so wise and so independent, no one will ever be able to hurt him again."

She raised her head to find Justin watching her, a bemused look on his face. She cleared her throat. "Why are you staring at me like that?"

"How can I help it? Have you any idea how beautiful you look with that babe in your arms?" A look of such tenderness crossed his face, she felt as if her knees were melting beneath her. "You should have babies of your own, Sweet Tess, on whom to lavish that great store of love you harbor within you."

The sincerity in his voice forbade her being anything but honest with him. "It has always been my greatest wish," she admitted, "but one I believed could never come true."

"Why?"

"Because a child should be born of love and until very recently I believed I was incapable of loving any man," she said without thinking. Instantly, she realized what she had admitted with her revealing statement. To make things worse, she felt a hot flush creep up her throat and into her cheeks.

Justin picked up on it immediately. "But now you feel differently? Dare I ask why?" His eyes held that wicked twinkle Tess had come to know so well, leaving her no doubt he had guessed the reason for her change of mind. Her cheeks flamed even hotter.

Justin laughed softly, joyfully. "We will talk of this tomorrow, Sweet Tess, when I have had time to formulate certain plans I have in mind for the future—plans I believe you will find most interesting. For I, too, have had a change of mind and heart, my love."

He caught her hand in his and drew her to him. "Now, regrettably, I must leave you to help poor Reggie lick his wounds—as he has so often done for me in the past. But not before I have my good-bye kiss."

This kiss was different from all the others they had shared. More deeply passionate, yet somehow tender as well. It was as if, with their mutual admissions of love, they had crossed a new threshold of intimacy where every touch created an exciting magic that drew them ever closer.

Lost in the wonder of the kiss, Tess was suddenly jolted back to reality by the sound of angry voices just outside the door of the common room. She stepped out of Justin's arms just as Drew burst through the open door. "What the devil is going on here?" he shouted, glaring at Justin and Tess with such venom, she shivered in spite of herself.

Justin, on the other hand, greeted his rival with an airy "Good afternoon to you, too, Wentworth. Lovely day for the middle of November."

Tess was his. She had as much as confessed she loved him, and there was nothing the pompous cit could do about it. He could almost feel sorry for the bothersome fellow. Almost, but not quite. With a final show of nonchalance, he raised his lady's hand to his lips and staring deep into her eyes, whispered, "Until tomorrow, my love."

Danny was waiting for him by the outer door, fury stamped across his thin, young face. He and Wentworth had obviously had words and the boy was still fuming over the outcome.

Justin stopped a few feet from him. "What's the matter, lad? You look like you lost your best friend."

"It could come to that the way things is going," Danny grumbled. "That fool, Wentworth, has hatched up another of his bleedin' meetings for Friday next and he's talked Tess into attendin'. I don't like it, guvnor. Don't like it at all. This one's different from the others. Bigger and more dangerous."

A familiar sense of foreboding gripped Justin. A sixth sense that in the past had never failed to be a reliable barometer of things to come. Anxiously, he studied Danny's troubled face. "What kind of meeting, and why do you deem it dangerous?"

"Him and his friend, Diehl, has come up with this idea of gettin' together all the soldiers wot fought with Wellington on the Peninsula to protest the way they been treated since the war ended. Just another one of their schemes to get folks to know Wentworth so's he can stand for the bleedin' 'ouse of Commons, if you asks me.

"Though Lord knows them poor devils wot gave their all for good old England has got plenty to complain about. Starvin' in the streets they is. Even them wot 'as all their arms and legs can't find work. There's not a day passes Tess don't feed a half dozen of the rag and tatters wot comes beggin' at her door, and even old

Florabelle Favor has set up a soup kitchen in the alley back of her bawdy house."

Justin stared at the boy in disbelief. "I had no idea times were that bad."

"Well, they is. Not that you rich toffs livin' in Mayfair would know it. But them of us as lives in St. Giles and Shoreditch and Lime House knows it all too well." Danny clenched his fists in obvious frustration. "It ain't that I'm against tryin' to talk them loose fish at Whitehall into doin' somethin' for the poor blokes. But gettin' hundreds of hungry men together at one time is askin' for trouble. Hungry men is desperate men, and desperate men can turn ugly just like that." He snapped his fingers. "Gorblimey, guvnor, I wish you'd try your hand at talkin' Tess out of attendin' this particular meetin'."

Justin frowned thoughtfully. "I doubt there's anyone on earth could talk our Tess out of doing something once she's set her mind to it. But I can promise you this much. I will make certain I accompany her—insist she ride in my town coach, in fact, so that if there is trouble, I can get her away to safety."

He put an arm around the boy's narrow shoulders. "Don't worry, Danny. I won't let anything happen to Tess. I love her too, you know."

Reggie was hunkered down in one corner of the carriage, the picture of misery, when Justin joined him. He had apparently drained the flask of brandy he always kept in the door pocket, for it lay empty on the seat beside him.

"Go ahead and say it. I know you're thinking it—and God knows I deserve it."

"Say what?" Justin settled onto the squab opposite the morose earl and braced his cane against the window wall.

"That I made a blither . . . blithering idiot of myself." Reggie spoke slowly and precisely but the words still came out somewhat slurred.

"If you erred, my friend, it was on the side of kindness and you need feel no shame in that. I am just grateful that fate was kind enough to spare you the fruits of that error."

Reggie grimaced. "I keep thinking about what your Miss Thornhill said—you know, that 'no man in his right mind could endure a lifetime shackled to a wife with the mental capacities of a seven-year-old.' Do you think that Camden might have . . . that he could have volunteered for the Forlorn Hope because . . ."

"We'll never know and I, for one, do not care to speculate, for I would lose all respect for him if I thought he'd taken the coward's way out. A man is honor bound to provide for his offspring, however he begat them."

"Well, now that's a novel point of view for a nobleman." Reggie regarded Justin through half-closed eyes. "Next thing I know you'll be rising in the House of Lords to support that radical, Maclendon, and his bill to abolish child labor."

"I might very well do that and more," Justin agreed. "I've seen firsthand the ragged, hollow-eyed children of the poor on my visits to the stews these past few weeks. They haunt my dreams. For the first time in my life, I've begun to realize that a title and wealth could be powerful tools to further a just cause when in the right hands."

"Devil take it, Justin. You're beginning to sound like a raving do-gooder. It's that Thornhill woman; she's bewitched you. Mind you, I admit she's as close to a saint as I'm liable to meet in this life. I don't know another woman who would accept responsibility for that poor little tyke of Camden's without so much as a whimper. But think, man, what can come of this infatuation of yours? You're the future Duke of Arncott. What kind of duchess would your eccentric lady-love make?"

"The only kind I'd ever want. And don't bother telling me my grandfather won't approve of her. The old tyrant will never approve of me either, so what does it matter? Tess is the woman I love and I mean to have her as my wife."

"Somehow that statement has a familiar ring to it." Reggie's laugh was tinged with cynicism. "Never fear, old friend, I shall stand by you no matter what—as you've stood by me in my lunacy. But I fear any scandal I might have caused by allying myself to the ostracized countess will look like a stroll down a country lane compared to the furor you'll raise in the *ton* when you announce you plan to wed Terrible Tess Thornhill."

Chapter Eleven

"**Y**ou let that lecher kiss you!" Drew Wentworth strode through the door of the common room, his handsome features contorted with rage. "Don't bother to deny it; I have only to look at your face to know exactly what has been going on behind my back."

Startled, Tess looked up to find the man she had long considered her dearest friend towering over her. Her lovely euphoria vanished like a puff of smoke in a windstorm. "I have no intention of denying Justin kissed me—or that I kissed him," she said coldly. "But as for my doing so behind your back, I fail to see how you can justify that contention. You have no claim whatsoever on me, Drew Wentworth; what I do is none of your business."

Drew paled noticeably. "I claim the rights of your oldest friend, as well as those of a man who has made you an honest offer of marriage—which, I venture to say, is something you'll never receive from that titled lecher who's sniffing around you."

"Lecher," Tess fumed. "That's twice you've used that ugly term to describe Justin—and without any reason whatsoever. He is the most forthright and honorable of men, as well as the most reasonable. I cannot imagine him flying into a fit of childish jealousy such as you are presently displaying."

"Honorable? Bah! If the pawky fellow has voiced any 'honorable intentions' toward you, my foolish friend, you may be certain they are lies. And as for forthright, surely not even you are so naive as to believe he intends to make a merchant's daughter from the London stews his duchess. Think of the scandal that would create in the *ton*."

"For your information, Justin is a viscount, not a duke, and he made a point of telling me it is a title he never wanted—but was forced to accept because of the tragic death of his older brother."

"That may be, but the fact remains that Justin Warre is not only the Viscount Sanderfield; he is also the only grandson of the Duke of Arncott, and as such stands to inherit the title when the old man dies."

Drew gave a bark of cynical laughter. "I see that interesting bit of information comes as a surprise to you. Doesn't it strike you as rather odd that such a forthright and honorable man would withhold it from you?"

"We have never had occasion to discuss the subject," Tess declared in a surprisingly calm voice, considering the shock waves reverberating through her as a result of Drew's startling revelation.

Drew raised a skeptical eyebrow. "Perhaps he was planning to apprise you of his true status in the ranks of the English nobility when he made you an offer. Let me see, what sort of offer could a woman of your class expect from a future duke? A lucrative business, perhaps, such as the one the present duke set up for your friend, Florabelle Favor."

"How dare you!" Tess's palm struck Drew's cheek with such force it sent him reeling backward.

He braced himself against the sturdy table, a sheepish look on his face. "I apologize for that last remark," he said humbly. "It was uncalled for." Gingerly he rubbed his reddening cheek. "You are right, of course. I am jealous of your incomprehensible infatuation with a man who represents everything you and I have good reason to despise. I love you, Tess. I could not bear to see you hurt—and hurt you will be if you continue on this reckless course."

"You've made your point, Drew. Now leave it be."

"But, Tess—"

"Leave it while I can still call you friend," Tess said wearily. "I have always considered petty jealousy one of the most despicable of human traits. I would never have equated it with you. But you have been literally consumed by it since the moment Justin came on scene."

"It is not only jealousy that consumes me—but fear as well, Tess. Fear for you. I watched, helpless, while another unscrupulous nobleman destroyed my sister. They are all cut of the same cloth, whether or not you want to admit it. I only hope you come to your senses before history repeats itself."

Drew clenched his fists in frustration. "I wish to God I had never heard the name Justin Warre," he said bitterly. "And I prophesy the day will come when you will wish the same."

Left to his own devices, an exclusive men's club was the last place on earth Justin would have chosen to spend a chilly November evening—particularly this November evening. He would have much preferred to hole up in his own cozy book room to dream of the life he planned to share with Tess. But he'd made up his mind to devote the next few hours to shoring up Reggie's crumbling self-esteem, and his homely friend was more at home in White's than in any other place in London.

From the very beginning, the evening bid fair to be an unqualified success. The Earl of Rutledge was a popular member of the club and he had been missed in the fortnight he'd been courting the countess. One by one the men in the dining room and at the gaming tables came by to tell him so and to make the acquaintance of the new Viscount Sanderfield.

Reggie blossomed under the regard of his peers. With each passing minute, he became more like the jovial, quick-witted fellow Justin was accustomed to—discarding his recent, lovesick persona as carelessly as he might discard a topcoat cut in last season's style. Justin shook his head in amazement. For a man who claimed to have been sorely wounded in the game of love, Reggie was certainly making a rapid recovery. He tried to imagine how he would face a life in which Tess was no longer a part, but the very idea was so unthinkable he could scarcely fathom it.

The evening seemed interminable to Justin. All that kept him from packing it in was his realization that White's had been a good choice of venue to begin Reggie's healing process. The sanctum sanctorum of London's privileged aristocrats was undeniably the earl's natural milieu. Under Justin's watchful eye, he tucked into his perfectly cooked beefsteak with the gusto of a man long deprived of sustenance, consumed a quantity of the club's fine brandy that would have laid a lesser man low, and spent the next three hours cheerfully losing a small fortune to the powerful Tory leader, Lord Ingraham, in a game of hazard.

"By George, what more could any man ask of life than this?" he asked, gazing around him with bleary goodwill. He lowered his voice to a hoarse whisper for Justin's ears only. "To think I nearly gave it all up for . . ." He shivered. "A close call, my friend. A close call. Best you think carefully before you forge your own leg shackles."

"That I will," Justin agreed, knowing it was pointless to argue with a man in his cups. But the truth was he had always found the life of a wealthy man-about-town exceedingly shallow and boring. Whatever challenges marriage to his passionate do-gooder might offer, he was certain of one thing: life with Tess would never be boring.

Lord Ingraham laid down his cards and gathered up his winnings. "I've instructed the doorman to have my carriage brought round," he remarked casually. "Can I drop you and Sanderfield somewhere, Rutledge? I feel it's the least I can do after relieving you of so much of your money." His smile was friendly, but his eyes were chips of pale blue ice that sent shivers down Justin's back. Despite his charming manner, there was something about the man that made one wonder if there wasn't a grain of truth in the ugly rumor of how he'd attained his political prominence.

"What say you, Reggie, shall we call it a night?" Justin asked hopefully. "I, for one, am ready for my bed."

"And I am ready for any bed but my own. I don't know about you, my friend, but I'm in the mood to celebrate." Reggie's cheeks were flushed and his words slurred, but the hand that raised his glass was steady as a rock. "To freedom," he declared and downed a healthy swig of brandy. "Another drink or two with my friends, then I'll toddle on down to Covent Garden to see what kind of merchandise is available for a night's romp."

A few weeks earlier, Justin might have considered joining him. It had been a long time since he'd last lain with Sophia in his cheerful little house in Athens. But the days of satisfying his physical needs with mindless fornication were over. Only one woman could satisfy him physically, emotionally, and spiritually now, and he would wait for the moment when she was truly his.

"So, it is good night then, my friend. Enjoy your night of celebration, but take care." Justin briefly laid a hand on Reggie's shoulder, then walked with Lord Ingraham through the adjoining anteroom.

Accepting his greatcoat and high crowned beaver from the doorman, he exited White's to find that the earlier rain had given way to a thin, chilling fog that swirled like a dancer's skirt around the torches at the base of the shallow stairs. "Devil take it," Ingraham exclaimed, "my bones are getting too old for this miserable weather." Together, he and Justin hastened toward the inviting warmth of the waiting carriage, but just as they reached the door, a figure stepped out of the shadows.

"A word, my lord, if you please. It is most urgent." The low, silky voice sounded oddly menacing despite the seemingly innocuous words. Startled, Justin turned his head in time to glimpse the speaker's face before he slipped back into the surrounding darkness. There was no doubt about it; he was the ferret-faced fellow who, but a few days before, had stood beside Wentworth at the slaughterhouse.

"Wait in the carriage, Sanderfield, if you please. I'll be but a moment. I've a mare about to foal in my mews and my head groom has brought me word of her progress." Lord Ingraham's lie was so glibly told, Justin would have believed him without question if he hadn't recognized the "groom" who waited on the perimeter of the pool of light cast by the torch.

Justin moved as slowly as possible toward the carriage, hoping to overhear the furtive conversation behind him, but the few words he could distinguish told him nothing of the business they transacted. He asked himself what a political rabble-rouser could have in common with a member of the King's Privy Council. A moment later he glimpsed a quick exchange of money between Lord Ingraham and his "groom" and suddenly the answer to that question was all too obvious. There was truth to the rumor he'd heard about a government spy in Wentworth's organization—and Ferret-Face was that spy.

Was the rest of the rumor true as well? Were the spy and Lord Ingraham even now plotting the arrest of the leaders of the upcoming rally? It would seem the only logical explanation to this odd scenario.

The sense of foreboding that had gripped him since Danny confessed his fear for Tess immediately accelerated tenfold. Somehow he must convince her to stay away from Wentworth's ill-fated rally.

"And Wentworth himself? What will you do about him?" a nagging little voice deep in his head asked. Justin had no illusions as to how much consideration the surly cit would give him were the roles reversed. But for Tess's sake—and that of his own honor—he felt obliged to warn the troublesome fellow he could find himself clapped into Newgate Prison if he persisted in this rally of his, no matter how just the cause.

Justin looked up as Lord Ingraham entered the carriage, an undeniable gleam of triumph in his icy eyes. "I take it all is well . . . with the mare," he said dryly.

"Couldn't be better," Ingraham quipped, his smug smile grating on Justin's nerves like a nail drawn across a slate. "Suffice it to say we have everything under control."

Justin slumped despondently against the comfortable squabs of Ingraham's elegant town coach. Hell and damnation! Tomorrow was to have been the day he asked Tess to become his wife. Now he must deal with this bumblebroth instead. It was almost as if Wentworth had jinxed him. One way or another, the miserable fellow always managed to cast his murky shadow over every moment Justin shared with Tess.

Tess rose from her bed an hour later than usual the morning after Consuela's departure. Her throat felt parched and her head throbbed with the annoying persistence of a carpenter pounding nails into a block of wood. Sleepless nights could do that to one, and she had spent the entire night tossing and turning, reliving the shock of learning that Justin would one day be the Duke of Arncott.

Or rather, she admitted bitterly, the shock of knowing he had withheld the information from her. In the short time she'd known him, he had persuaded her to believe in him so wholeheartedly, she had been totally unprepared to learn there was a crack in the shining armor of her fairy-tale knight. But the crack was there and widening by the minute. Doubt fed upon doubt until everything he'd ever said or done seemed suspicious. If he had lied to her, by omission, about that all important fact, how many other untruths, or half-truths had he told her?

More important, what did he hope to gain by concealing his true identity? Did he judge her such a ninny she would believe she could be more to him than a mere paramour if he were just a viscount? If so, he'd been clever in the extreme. His unexpected declaration of love had been a brilliant stroke. For a few brief moments she had actually dared to dream impossible dreams of their future together. She had even managed to forget his title and wealth—remembering only that he was the one man whose kisses had awakened her to her potential as a woman.

His kisses. She groaned, remembering the magic he'd created just by touching his lips to hers. Had she been so bewitched by the man she had lost all power of reason? Anyone but the most naive fool should have recognized the expertise behind that magic. Anyone but that same fool should have realized that Drew was right: The charming viscount was anything but the shy, good-natured fellow he purported to be—a demeanor that, in itself, was another subtle kind of lie.

Yet, was it? A memory surfaced of the night he'd kept vigil by Daisy's bed and his unrestrained joy when the powders worked their magic on the sick little girl—and another of how touched he'd been by Danny's drawing. These were not the actions of an evil man. If it were not for the one monstrous deception she had caught him in, she would believe him the most honorable and most sensitive of men.

Even now, after all Drew had said about him, she found it hard to believe Justin's kindness and generosity were prompted by ulterior motives. It made no sense. If he was simply seeking a mistress, there must be a dozen willing ladies of his own class far more clever and beautiful than she. Unless. She had a thought. Could it be she piqued his interest because a woman of another class of society offered a new kind of challenge? She'd heard it said it was the chase that intrigued a rake. Certainly the blackguard who had destroyed poor Laura had pursued her avidly up until the moment she surrendered to him—then discarded her without a backward glance.

Tess shuddered, remembering how Justin had mesmerized her with his shy smile, his wicked humor, his tantalizing kisses. The man was a sorcerer. If Drew's revelation hadn't broken the spell, it would have been only a matter of time before she offered herself to Justin like a lamb for the slaughter.

Well, what was done was done. The fact that she'd acted the fool didn't excuse her from pulling herself together and going on with her life. With grim determination, she did up the buttons on her favorite scarlet dress, bathed her face in the bowl of tepid water Maggie had left on her dressing table, and twisted her heavy hair into a prim knot at her nape. Except for her unusual pallor, the face she viewed in the mirror looked very much like her own everyday face—something she found rather amazing considering the turmoil still raging inside her head.

Her excruciating headache persisted all morning, fueled by the knowledge that Justin had promised to return today to discuss "his plans for the future." She had a fairly good idea what those plans might entail, and for the first time in her life she wondered if she would have the strength to follow her own convictions and resist whatever temptation he offered.

"Are you going to mope around here all day like a dog that's lost its last bone?" Maggie's voice was brusque and a scowl darkened her normally placid face. "Because if you are, you may as well save me the trouble of taking the children for their walk. I have other things I could be doing."

Tess pressed her fingers to her aching temples. "Of course. I'm sorry. I know you've taken them the past two days and it is my turn."

Maggie's scowl deepened. "There's something you should know before you go. I meant to talk to you about it last evening, but I could see you had enough on your plate as it was." She hesitated, obviously gathering her wits. "There was a carriage pulled up to the curb across the street when I took the children out yesterday—a fancy black one with a coachman and one of those things on the door like the viscount has on his."

"A nobleman's lozenge," Tess said.

"Right. A real fancy one it was, too, like the owner was maybe some earl or duke."

Tess shrugged. "That's not too surprising. It is a well-known fact that a great many of London's titled gentlemen come to the stews seeking the kinds of pleasures Mayfair doesn't offer," she said bitterly, thinking of one particular titled gentleman who had apparently done that very thing. "The fellow was probably looking for Florabelle's house and took the wrong turn."

"He was looking for something all right, but it wasn't Florabelle's place." Maggie looked around her to make sure there was no one within earshot before continuing. "I think he was one of those sons-of-Satan who use little children for their evil purposes."

Tess gasped. "That is a very serious accusation. What, pray tell, made you come to that conclusion?"

"What else could I think? The carriage followed us for a good part of our walk—creeping along beside us just the width of the street away. Whoever was in it never showed himself, but I could see him peeking at us through a slit in the window curtain, and all the while the nose-in-the-air coachman never looked to right nor left. I tell you, it fair made my skin crawl."

"Good Lord!" Tess felt her own skin crawl just thinking of some deviant stalking her children. She hurried to the window and peered up and down the street to make certain no such bogeyman lay in wait for her innocents today. The street was clear of all but its usual seedy occupants, and she had long ago lost all fear of them. Still, she took the precaution of persuading Danny to accompany her just in case.

"Be careful," Maggie cautioned as Tess, Danny, and the children set out a short time later. "There are alleyways where a carriage could hide," she whispered for Tess's ears alone. "Not that I think the fiend would dare try snatching one of the children in broad daylight."

"He'd better not!" Tess fingered the small pistol she had slipped into the pocket of her pelisse. It had been a gift from Drew the day she opened her children's home. He'd insisted she learn how to defend herself if she planned to take up residence in one of London's most notorious districts. Once again, she found herself thankful for Drew's loyal friendship.

"I don't know why I needs to take a walk. I already run me legs off today fetchin' and carryin'," Danny grumbled. Tess had thought it best to keep the information Maggie had relayed from him. There was no point upsetting him when the chances were they'd seen the last of the mysterious black carriage.

"Everyone can use a little fresh air and exercise this time of year," Tess declared. And indeed, her headache had subsided noticeably soon after she'd stepped outside. A pale November sun added a bit of brightness to the dreary street, the children chattered noisily and even little Daisy wore a happy smile because she had Danny's hand to cling to. By the time they'd traversed the first block, Tess felt almost cheerful.

Then they turned a corner and she saw it. Just as Maggie had described it. Black and menacing, the elegant town coach waited like a great, evil spider for its innocent prey to draw near. Surreptitiously Tess clutched the handle of her pistol as she directed Danny to pick up the pace.

They drew abreast of the carriage and instantly the coachman gave a flick of his whip over the heads of the matched grays. The carriage slowly inched forward at the same pace as the children. Out of the corner of her eye, Tess saw a slight movement of the window curtain. Whoever was inside was obviously positioning himself to get a better look at the covey of rosy-cheeked youngsters enjoying their morning walk.

Tess stared in horror at the sinister-looking vehicle. It was as if the black carriage and its occupant represented all the sins she had come to associate with the titled aristocracy. This same deviate who preyed on the helpless children of the poor was probably a respected husband and father in his own world—and who among his peers would believe her if she publicly exposed him for the monster he turned into once he entered the stews?

She could see Danny casting covert glances in the direction of the carriage, and a few hundred feet farther on he brought their little procession to a sudden halt. "Devil take it, what's that old buzzard up to now?" he exclaimed, openly staring at the ominous-looking equipage.

Tess grasped his arm. "You know who that carriage belongs to?"

"Of course I knows. Weren't more'n a week ago I seen it and that cow-handed coachman cozied down in the stable behind Florabelle's place."

"He's one of Florabelle's customers?"

"In a way of speakin', I suppose. Rumor has it the old girl's been under the protection of the Dook of Arncott for more'n twenty years."

Tess swung the boy around to face her. "Good heavens, Danny, are you saying that carriage belongs to the Duke of Arncott?"

Danny pulled out of her grasp. "That's right. Have you gone deaf or somethin' all of a sudden? But beats me what kind of game the old boy's playin' now. You never know with the toffs; far as I can tell they're all an odd bunch of ducks—except our friend, the viscount, of course."

The Duke of Arncott. Justin's grandfather! Anger, swift and hot, raced through Tess. First Justin had laid siege to her heart as if he were Wellington and she some Peninsula stronghold he'd vowed to conquer; now his grandfather stalked her precious children. Were the Warres all as mad as poor old King George? Did they think her incapable of defending herself against such tyranny because she was a woman and a commoner? If so, they both had another think coming!

She would deal with Justin later, once she'd heard what he had to say for himself. Right now the object of her indignation sat the width of a street away. "Mind the children," she ordered Danny. "I am going to have a few words with His Grace, the Duke of Arncott."

Danny's eyes nearly popped from his head. " 'old on, you crazy woman," he sputtered. "There's rules about such things. Folks like us don't have words with a bleedin' dook!"

"Oh, no?" Tess reached into her pocket and gripped the handle of her pistol. "Well, you just stand there and watch me, my lad. Because the rules are about to be changed."

Chapter Twelve

"My friend, Tess, done what?" Florabelle Favor rose from the depths of her rumpled bed and stared at her unexpected guest through sleep-glazed eyes. It was neither Tuesday nor Friday and unless she was sorely mistaken, it was still the south side of noon. Then why had the Duke of Arncott just burst through her door like a crazed bull charging a red flag?

"You heard me," the duke said, pacing back and forth across her colorful Axminster carpet like a caged animal. "The harridan forced her way into my carriage and threatened me. Me! The Duke of Arncott."

"Threatened you with what, ducks?"

"A pistol, damn it. Bold as brass, she yanked open the door of my carriage, demanded to know what I was doing in the stews, and threatened to put a bullet between my eyes unless she liked my answer. She'd have done it too if my coachman hadn't come to my rescue." The duke ceased his pacing long enough to remove a handkerchief from his pocket and mop his perspiring brow. "I've half a mind to call the watch and level charges against the silly bitch."

"And wouldn't that make a juicy bit of scandal for the readers of the *Times*!" Florabelle reached for the peignoir that lay across the foot of her bed and jammed her swollen feet into a pair of well-worn slippers. Settling her ample bulk on the nearest chair, she studied the duke with a jaundiced eye. "Tell me, ducks, just what was it you done to rile Tess so? I know her. She's a lady through and through. She wouldn't threaten you without good reason."

"A lady! Hah! Maybe by your standards, madam." The duke resumed his pacing. "By mine she is a hoyden with the tongue of a fishwife and the mannerisms of a wild-eyed termagant."

"That's doing it a bit brown, Archie."

"Nevertheless, I fail to understand what my idiot grandson sees in the woman."

"Aha! Just as I thought. You was checking out Lord Justin's lady love, wasn't you? And Tess took offense at your snooping. Can't say I blame her."

"I was doing nothing of the sort," the duke declared in his loftiest tone. "If you must know, I thought to quietly and unobtrusively observe the children in her care. One in particular, actually. A little girl who bears a striking resemblance to my beloved granddaughter at that age."

"Little Daisy, Lord Oliver's by-blow," Florabelle said without hesitation.

"You know about the child?"

"I makes it my business to know such things." Florabelle frowned. "And just how was you going about this 'observing' of yours?"

"In the only way possible, of course. From the window of my carriage."

Florabelle rolled her eyes heavenward. "Don't tell me you was following Tess and the children on their morning walk."

"Well, yes." The duke mopped his brow again. "What other time would they be available for scrutiny?"

"Holy Mother of God, no wonder she took after you with a gun, you silly old fool. She probably thought you was some deviate looking to take his sport with one of her brood. You're lucky she didn't shoot first and ask questions later. She's like a lioness with her cubs where those children of hers are concerned."

Florabelle looked up to find a sudden tinge of sickly gray had given a strange, muddy tone to the duke's usually ruddy complexion. For the first time she could remember, he looked every one of his sixty-nine years. "Come sit down, ducks," she said. "I'll pour you a brandy. You look like you could use one."

The duke obeyed her summons without question. His confrontation with Tess had obviously taken its toll of him, and she could see the realization of what a fool he'd made of himself was beginning to sink in.

She poured him a healthy portion of brandy, watched him down it, and poured him another. "Now, Archie," she said, once he'd settled back in his chair, "just what is your interest in Daisy, besides observing her from afar, that is?"

"I have no interest other than that of a lonely old man who grieves for the granddaughter he loved more than any other living being." The duke held his head in his hands. "I am not mad, Flora; I know this child of the slums is not my little Anne, but she is so like her, I thought if only I could talk with her, hear her laugh . . . perhaps it would ease some of the pain that binds my heart like a band of iron."

"Oh, Archie." Never in all the years she had known him had Florabelle come so close to feeling real compassion for the impossible autocrat who was her protector. This softening of the heart was a dangerous weakness—one she could ill afford. "If you'd bothered to ask me, I could have told you that you could not possibly talk with Daisy. For the simple reason she's a dummy—can't make a sound," she said cruelly and watched the duke flinch as if she had struck him. "Come to think of it, I never hear her laugh neither, but I guess that's to be expected considering she'd been beaten half to death when she was left on Tess's doorstep."

The duke stared at her with bleak, shock-filled eyes and she felt another stab of pity for him. She quickly shook the feeling off. It was none of her concern that he was particularly low in spirits at the moment; it was, however, a golden opportunity to wheedle what she wanted from the old fool. And what she wanted was his approval of his grandson's alliance with Tess Thornhill. She owed the Angel a favor after burdening her with that useless twit, Consuela. Her ears were still ringing from the dressing down Danny had given her over that bit of misjudgment.

"You needn't worry your head about your granddaughter's look-alike," she continued companionably. "Tess don't care that Daisy's 'different.' She loves her same as she loves all the other little bruised and battered scraps she's taken in. The woman's got a heart as big as Astley's Amphitheater and Covent Garden combined."

She could see she had the duke's reluctant attention. With her usual ruthless determination, she drove her point home. "You was wondering what Lord Justin saw in Tess. I'd say her generous heart what allows her to love them as isn't perfect by other folk's standards is probably the thing he admires most. It must be mighty comforting for a man with a gimpy foot like his to find such a woman."

The spots of color in the duke's pale cheeks and the haunted look on his gaunt face told her that her vicious little verbal darts had hit a sensitive spot. If ever a time was right to strike the fatal blow, that time was now.

She bestowed a toothy smile on her hapless victim. "My friend, Danny, and me thinks Tess is the best thing that could happen to a fellow like the viscount. At first we was just hoping he'd take her under his protection—set her up in a pretty little house in Chelsea or some such place and provide her with the money to hire the help she needs to run her children's home. For she'd never give that up for no man.

"But lately we've changed our minds. Tess is a lady. She'd never stand still for a slip on the shoulder. If the viscount wants her, he'll just have to marry her proper-like, and according to Danny, he wants her so much his tongue is practically dragging on the ground."

The duke instantly came to full attention. "My grandson, the future Duke of Arncott, marry that vulgar commoner," he sputtered. "Never! I won't allow it."

"I doubt you'll have much to say about it, ducks." Florabelle's smile broadened into a satisfied grin. "From what I hear, the viscount is rich as a nabob in his own right. He don't need your say-so, and you'll only end up losing your last remaining grandchild if you try to stand in his way."

The duke seemed to wilt before her very eyes. It was a pitiful sight, one that not even a heart as hardened as Florabelle's could withstand. She sought to comfort him in the only way she understood. A shrug of her plump shoulders sent gown and peignoir alike sliding downward in a manner that could only be construed as a tantalizing promise of things to come.

"Let the young viscount choose his own *parti*, Archie. He knows what he needs in a woman," she purred. "Never met the fellow myself, him not being one for taking his pleasure in a grinding house. But from what I hear from my friend, Danny, he has a better head on his shoulders than most of the young blades of the *ton*." She was tempted to add that he was twice the man his rakehell brother, Oliver, had been, but it was bad luck to speak ill of the dead.

She leaned forward to clasp the duke's hand, and her gown slipped another inch or two. "Think on it, my love," she whispered seductively. "Don't waste your time worrying about something you can't change. A man your age needs all his energy to conduct his own affairs properly."

To Tess's dismay, Drew was waiting in the common room when she and the children returned from their walk. Her greeting to him was less than enthusiastic. She was not in the mood to quarrel with the man she had once called friend, and lately quarreling appeared to be their only means of communication.

The truth was, she had not yet recovered from her upsetting confrontation with the Duke of Arncott. He had been nothing like she'd expected. Oh, he'd been haughty enough, but she suspected that beneath his arrogant exterior, he was just a lonely old man who was guilty of nothing more sinister than a wish to glimpse the child who reminded him of the granddaughter he'd so tragically lost. Much as she hated to admit it, threatening Justin's grandfather with a loaded pistol had not been one of her more brilliant ideas.

"What brings you out on a Sunday morning?" she asked as Drew helped her out of her pelisse. "Nothing too serious, I trust. I slept very poorly last night and I have a beastly headache."

"Poor darling." Drew's hands lingered longer than necessary on her shoulders. She tried to step away, but he pulled her back against him until the back of her head rested against his chest. "I bitterly regret my part in bringing on your headache, Tess, but for your own good, certain things needed to be said."

Tess wrenched loose of his embrace and moved to stand on the opposite side of the table. "I told you yesterday I didn't wish to discuss it," she said in a voice sharpened by exasperation. "I am of the same mind today."

"As am I, sweetheart. I have never been one to dwell on the mistakes of the past. Each day is a new beginning."

"Well, what with one thing and another, this particular day has begun rather badly, so unless you have a specific reason for your visit, I must ask you to excuse me. The only thing that appeals to me at the moment is a quiet lie-down in a dark room with a damp cloth on my head."

"Poor darling," Drew said once more, looking properly sympathetic. "As a matter of fact, I do have a specific reason for being here, but I'll state it quickly so you can rest before it's time to see to the children's noon meal."

As if proving he meant what he said, he promptly drew on his new York tan gloves and picked up his curled beaver. Drew was always dressed in the height of fashion; he allowed no one but the exalted Weston to tailor his garments. In truth, at this particular moment, he looked more like a member of the Mayfair set than Justin ever had.

He favored Tess with his most charming smile. "When I told Michael Diehl you planned to attend Friday's rally, he was ecstatic. He feels my relationship with you will be a definite asset when I declare for a seat in the House of Commons."

The smug look on his face grated on Tess's already frayed nerves. It bore all the earmarks of the male animal which, having successfully vanquished its rival, lays claim to the female. All that was missing was the pawing of the ground and the triumphant bellow. "You have no relationship with me except that of a friend, Drew Wentworth—and lately you've strained the bounds of that," she snapped.

"Michael has arranged for you to sit on the platform with the families of the other leaders of the rally," Drew continued, ignoring her barb.

"I think not. Such an arrangement would be most inappropriate. Besides, I shall have Danny with me. I prefer to stand with him in the general audience."

Drew's handsome face contorted with anger. "Must you always be so aggravating? Just for once, relax and let wiser heads make your choices for you."

Tess gritted her teeth. "By 'wiser heads' I assume you mean men. No thank you. That is the last piece of advice I would consider taking. Every unhappiness I have ever known has been at the hands of men."

"I told you Michael has already made the seating arrangements. You will place me in a most embarrassing position if you refuse the courtesy he has extended you."

Tess's temper flared. Nothing set her off like having some man try to arrange her life for her. "That, my friend, is your problem—not mine," she said. "You should have asked my permission before offering my services to the cause."

"Devil take it, Tess, enough is enough!" Tossing his hat aside, Drew strode forward and clasped her in his arms so quickly he caught her totally unawares. "Stubborn little fool," he muttered. "Why do you continue to fight the inevitable? You are mine, Tess. Mine! The man does not live who can take you from me." With a groan, he claimed her lips in a rough, demanding kiss.

At first Tess was too surprised to struggle; when she had her wits about her, she still offered no resistance. It occurred to her that now might be the time to determine once and for all if one man's kisses were so different from another's. The test was still in progress when she decided the results were conclusive. Drew's lips created none of the magic she had come to expect from Justin's. She sighed. Sad to say, it appeared she was destined to be a one-man woman with a dangerous proclivity for falling in love with the wrong man.

Finally, just when she was certain her lungs would collapse from lack of air, Drew raised his head to stare down at her with blazing eyes. "Now will you admit we are destined for each other?"

Tess blinked, wondering why mashing his mouth against hers until her lips were numb should lead him to that amazing conclusion.

"Excellent question, Wentworth. I confess I am as curious as you to hear the lady's answer." The glacial intonation in the familiar voice sent chills slithering down Tess's spine. Over Drew's shoulder she met Justin's coldly assessing eyes. Leaning heavily on his stout cane, he stood in the open doorway. How long he had been there, she had no idea. But the rage and disgust she read on his face indicated it had been long enough to witness the kiss Drew and she had shared.

Tess's heart thumped so loudly in her breast, she felt certain the two men now facing each other across the width of the common room must surely hear it. "I didn't hear your knock, my lord," she said to cover her embarrassment.

"I didn't knock because the door stood open." Justin's unyielding gaze sought Tess's with chilling intensity. "Foolishly I took that as an invitation to enter. I apologize for my unwarranted assumption."

"As well you should, Sanderfield. What the devil are you doing back here so soon anyway? I cannot believe a daily inspection of your slum properties is warranted, and I am certain Tess does not appreciate such close scrutiny." Drew's voice sounded thin and childishly petulant. Tess couldn't remember when she'd come closer to despising him.

"It was my understanding that Miss Thornhill and I had agreed to a private discussion this afternoon. I see now I was mistaken in that also," Justin said stiffly, his gaze still locked with Tess's.

Not even his Mediterranean tan could hide his pallor, and the bruised look in his expressive eyes ripped a hole in Tess's battered heart. Her fierce independence evaporated like steam from a cooling kettle. She longed to do nothing more than fling herself into Justin's arms and tell him she would listen to anything he had to say; she would be anything he wished her to be. But some remnant of the prudent Methodist maiden her mother had raised her to be kept her feet glued to the floor and her voice silent.

Justin gripped his cane so tightly, he felt the intricate carvings on the handle bite into his palm—and waited for Tess to say something that would explain why but twenty-four hours after they had declared their love for each other he found her in the arms of another man. Or had he only dreamed that moment of magic that had changed his life forever? The disquieting thought occurred to him that he, like Reggie, may have endowed the woman of his choice with virtues and sensitivities that existed only in his own imagination.

"I will bid you good day then, Tess," he said gravely and prepared to take his leave, when he remembered his "talk" with her hadn't been the only reason for his trip to the stews today.

For a long tantalizing moment, he was tempted to forget the telling scene he had witnessed outside White's and let Wentworth reap the rewards of his own stupidity. Why should he care if the pompous ass spent the next few years in Newgate?

But what of Tess? What if she should be swept up in the Watch's net as well? Or what if she truly loved the handsome cit and would grieve for him if he were taken from her? Even now, as deeply as she had hurt him, Justin knew he could never do anything that would cause her pain.

"A word of advice, Wentworth," he said, choosing his manner of phrasing carefully. "I'd think twice about attending that meeting Friday if I were you. Things are tense enough in the city with the Spa Field riots less than a month past, and I have reason to believe that one of your compatriots is a government spy. It appears you and the other leaders of the rally are being set up for arrest— or worse."

"What the devil are you talking about?" Wentworth demanded, his face blank with shock.

"I'm saying one of the men you trust is a ringer—namely that fellow who was with you at the slaughterhouse.

Wentworth laughed. "You're either attics-to-let or the worst liar on the face of the earth. Michael Diehl is the truest friend any man could have. Why, if not for him I might never have thought to enter politics. And as for my being arrested—on what charge, pray tell? There is no law against peaceful public gatherings."

"Are you certain this one will be peaceful?" Justin asked, though he had to wonder why he bothered with the pigheaded fool. "If you had a brain in your head, you'd see you and your friends have been targeted by the men in power on whose toes you're treading."

Wentworth cocked his head as if considering what Justin had said. "What do you suggest I do to protect myself, my lord? Leave London until these 'men in power' forget their grievances against me?"

"It might not be a bad idea."

"Aha! Just as I thought. This so-called warning of yours is nothing more than a devious, underhanded attempt to dispose of a rival for a certain lady's affections!"

He turned to Tess, who stood white-faced and silent beside him. "What think you now of your honorable viscount, sweetheart? As for me, I feel nothing but disgust for a man who would stoop to such trickery to win a woman."

"Why you miserable cur." Justin's hand tightened on his cane. "I would call you out for that slur on my good name if you were a gentleman."

"Feel free to name your seconds, my lord."

"And duel with a common cit and rabble-rouser? Not on your life. I would be laughed out of the House of Lords, and there is too much I wish to accomplish in that august body to risk my good standing."

With a snarl of rage, Wentworth came at Justin with fists raised. "Then prepare to take your beating in the manner we common men employ, you lying, titled libertine."

Instantly, Justin thrust his cane between the cit's long legs, sending him crashing to the floor, to lie stunned and breathless flat on his back.

A flick of the lever at the base of the handle and a razor-sharp knife snapped into place at the end of the stout cane. With the knife at the cit's throat and a boot on his belly, Justin surveyed his would-be opponent through narrowed eyes. "Another word of advice, Wentworth:Never make the mistake of attacking an adversary whose skills are unknown to you. Were I not by nature a peaceful fellow, you would be a dead man now."

A smothered gasp reminded him there was a witness to the brief debacle. He looked up to find Tess backed against the wall, a hand pressed to her trembling lips. "My apology for this display of violence," he said coldly, "but this precious friend of yours needed a lesson."

Another flick of the lever and the knife disappeared from whence it came. At the same time, Justin removed his boot from its resting place on Wentworth's pale gray watered silk waistcoat. He noted with pleasure the muddy footprint now adorning Weston's elegant creation.

The cit still lay on his beck, green about the gills and apparently unable to rise on his own. Justin left him where he lay. "Once again I bid you adieu," he said to the still silent woman, whose horrified expression told him she was not the least bit impressed with his ability as a street fighter.

Heartsick and weary beyond belief, he slowly limped toward the entry hall from which he had exited in triumph but one day earlier. What had gone wrong? Why had she betrayed him with that fool, Wentworth? He would have wagered everything he owned that betrayal was as foreign to her nature as to his own.

Just before he reached the door, he turned back. "There are many questions I would like to ask, Tess. I will not ask them. I accept that you have exercised your God-given right of choice. But one thing I *must* know. Do you believe, like Wentworth, that I would resort to such base trickery to win you?"

Tess's lovely emerald eyes filled with tears, which she quickly brushed away with the back of her hand. "I don't know." She stifled a sob. "With all that has happened in the past twenty-four hours, I no longer know what I believe."

It was not the answer he had hoped to hear.

By the time Tess had managed to coax Drew up off the floor and onto the sofa, her headache had gone beyond excruciating to unbearable. Twin hammers pounded incessantly in her temples and an iron-clad band of pain circled her forehead, rendering her incapable of any thought except retiring to her chamber to die in peace.

"Did you see that?" Drew whined. "Your high-and-mighty viscount actually held a knife to my throat like some common Rookeries' bully boy. What kind of conduct is that for a peer of the realm?" His hands shook noticeably and his face was mottled with rage and humiliation. With a Herculean effort, Tess bestirred herself to pour him a glass of cool water from the pitcher on the sideboard—then changed her mind and drank it herself.

Dipping her handkerchief into a second glass of water, she pressed it to her aching forehead. "What I saw was a man successfully defend himself against an unwarranted assault by an assailant a good two stone heavier than himself," she declared, not bothering to hide her disgust.

"Are you taking that blighter's part against me?"

"I am taking no one's part. Certainly not that of any man. As a matter of fact, I plan to devote the rest of my life to avoiding all contact with members of the male gender. I am heartily sick of the lot of you. Now gather up your things and get out of here before I am tempted to finish the job Justin started."

"Very well, Tess, if that is how you feel, I shall leave. But I must say I am bitterly disappointed in your lack of loyalty to an old friend." Wearing his wounded dignity like a badge of martyrdom, Drew withdrew from the scene of battle, but not before he reminded her that she had committed herself to attending his all-important rally on Friday and he expected her to honor that commitment.

"What was that all about?" Maggie hovered in the doorway with young David in her arms. "His Nibs looked as sour as last week's milk."

Tess proceeded to inform her of all that had transpired between her and her two suitors in the past twenty-four hours. To her surprise, her stoic assistant's sympathies all lay with Justin. "I caught sight of him as he was leaving and I've never seen a soul so weighed down with sorrow. For shame, Tess Thornhill, treating the sweet man so shabbily, and after all he's done for the children, too."

Before Tess could respond to Maggie's accusation, a second voice was added to the disapproving chorus. "Gorblimey, Tess, what did you do to the guvnor?" Danny burst through the door like a small hurricane. "I just passed him on the stairs and mentioned, teasing-like, same as he done to me, that he looked like he'd lost his best friend. Right away he come back with, 'I've lost far more than that, my lad.' Now I asks you, what did he mean by that?"

"Likely he thinks Tess has chosen Wentworth over him, poor love," Maggie clucked, tenderly laying the sleeping baby in his crib.

"Why would he think a dumb thing like that?"

"Because the maw worm poisoned her mind against him and Tess as much as called our viscount a liar to his face, that's why."

Danny scowled. "I don't believe it. What's he supposed to have lied about?"

Too exhausted to do so herself, Tess let Maggie answer his indignant question.

"Something about the rally on Friday and Wentworth's friend, Diehl, being a government spy—but what seems to have set the silly chit off in the first place was he didn't tell her he'd be a duke someday." Maggie shook her head. "It's beyond me what all the fuss is about."

"Well, I can tell you right off, the bit about the government spy ain't no lie. Me own sources come up with it too, only they didn't have no actual name."

Danny's gaze shifted to Tess and his scowl deepened. "And as for the guvnor not telling you he was in line to be the Dook of Arncott, he probably thought you already knew. It ain't no secret. Florabelle twigged me to it the first day he come callin'."

The boy's telling words burned their way into Tess's consciousness like red-hot pokers. Dropping onto the nearest chair, she held her aching head in her hands. Dear God, what had she done? Had she been so blinded by her hatred of the aristocracy, she'd let Drew convince her there was deceit where none existed?

"You drove him away, you crazy woman. You listened to that mealymouthed rabble-rouser and you drove the guvnor away. If I live to be a hunert years old, I'll never forgive you." Danny wiped his brimming eyes with the cuff of his jacket.

It was the first time Tess had ever seen the tough young street urchin cry. If she'd had any doubts about the enormity of her crime, the sight of Danny's tears dispelled them. Hers was not the only heart that would be broken because she'd given Justin a disgust of her.

Between the pain in her head and the pain in her heart, she had had all she could endure. With a strangled cry, she rose from her chair and fled the room but not before Danny's final words dealt her the cruelest blow of all. "Why, it weren't but yesterday the guvnor told me straight out he loved you."

Chapter Thirteen

Rejection was nothing new to Justin. He had suffered it all his life at the hands of members of his family who found it embarrassing to acknowledge one of their own could be less than physically perfect. He'd fared no better at Eton or Oxford; the young blades of the *ton* could be incredibly insensitive when dealing with someone who was "different." Even strangers shied away from him, seeing his affliction as a sign he was devil marked.

Tess, on the other hand, had simply asked if his crippled foot was painful, then dismissed it as unimportant when he admitted it wasn't. Had he been so blinded by his attraction to her he had mistaken careless disinterest for acceptance?

Logic told him he should have become inured to the pain of rejection long ago. But nothing in the past had prepared him for the despair he felt over Tess's betrayal. For the first time in the two and thirty years he'd spent on earth, he had allowed himself to fall in love. It had been a stupid mistake—one he would never make again. Even more foolish had been his illusory hope that the woman of his choice could love him in return. He should have remembered that only in fairy tales did a troll turn into a prince.

But life had a way of going on despite the triumphs and tragedies of a single insignificant individual. And so it was that the pale wintry sun made its appearance on the eastern horizon the morning after his disastrous trip to the stews, just as if his world had not come crashing down around his ears before it set in the western sky the previous evening.

Not one to lie abed and wallow in his misery, Justin rose at first light and dressed himself in the well-worn riding habit that was the despair of his valet. Then, pulling on the gleaming boots Pruefrock had placed beside his bed, he limped down to the breakfast room for a cup of the thick, black coffee to which he had become addicted in Greece.

He felt strangely disoriented, like a man who having lost all he held dear, must learn to live all over again. Unfortunately he could not, like Reggie, find solace in the arms of a willing cyprian. Nor did the thought of burying himself in his ancient books and manuscripts hold the same allure it once had. He had tasted the incredible sweetness life could offer; living it vicariously through the eyes of men long dead no longer satisfied him.

His only thought was to mount the swiftest horse in his stable and ride so fast and so far he would outdistance the loneliness that threatened to overwhelm him. But even at this early hour, he doubted he could safely ride hell-for-leather along the bridle paths of Hyde Park.

All at once, he was consumed with the desire to put the crowded, noisy city behind him. Not for the first time since returning to England, he found himself longing to visit Brandywine, the small estate in Surrey where he'd spent so much of his childhood. There, in the lush countryside, he could ride to his heart's content.

The more he thought about the rolling meadows, gentle streams, and the stands of oak and chestnut and birch that had so delighted him when he was a young boy, the greater his longing became. If there was any place on God's green earth where he could find healing for his wounded spirit, Brandywine was surely that place.

A short time later he was on his way, a hastily packed saddlebag thrown across the rump of the horse he'd chosen from his well-stocked stable. The day was cold but clear and a chill breeze nipped at his cheeks when he gave the sleek little mare her head once they were south of the city. She had obviously not been ridden much lately and was as eager as he to fly along the deserted highway—and fly they did for the next glorious hour.

Justin was a born horseman. He'd been but six years old when the head groom at Brandywine had put him up on his first horse. He'd instantly bonded with the animal beneath him. Even then, he'd sensed that only on horseback could he find freedom from the hated limitations his afflictions imposed on him. Astride a powerful horse, he was as good as any man and better than most.

Gradually, he eased the frisky mare to a slower pace. Much as he enjoyed their all-out gallop, he knew she would soon reach the limit of her endurance at that stride, and they had a long ride ahead of them before they reached their destination.

With but one brief rest stop at a wayside inn, he arrived at the entrance to Brandywine shortly before sunset to find the gates wide open and the gatehouse deserted. An inexplicable uneasiness came over him. The old gatekeeper he had known as a child had probably been pensioned off long ago, but surely he would have been replaced.

He maneuvered the mare up the long tree-lined drive for which Brandywine was famous with the locals. The trees were taller now, their trunks sturdier than he recalled and the grass beneath them was badly in need of cutting. The few flower beds he passed were choked with weeds and the dead stalks of last summer's flowers. His uneasiness grew by leaps and bounds. He could not imagine Luigi, the head gardener, allowing such neglect of the grounds.

Time had obviously wrought its changes on the once lovely estate. Justin found himself wondering what other changes he would find. Would any of the same staff still be here? Would they remember the scrawny lad with the crippled foot who had once been a part of their lives?

He swallowed the lump in his throat, remembering the happy times he had spent here and the affection he'd felt for Mr. Frobisher, the butler, and his plump, good-natured wife. In his young heart, they had taken the place of the parents and grandparents who had done their level best to pretend he had never been born.

Moments later the rambling manor house came into view. The last rays of the pale December sun cast a soft, silvery glow over the mellow stone and ancient timbers, but there was a sad, empty look about the graceful structure, as if no one had lived there in a long, long time. Surely Oliver had not stripped Brandywine of staff and left it abandoned. Even such a careless landowner as he must have recognized the value of such a property.

But no groom leaped forward to take his horse as he would have expected. Another bad sign. He tied the mare's reins to a small bush and warily climbed the stairs, only to find the knocker off the door. Still, he reasoned, there had to be someone acting as caretaker, if nothing else.

With grim determination, he gave the massive carved panels a few sharp raps with his cane. After what seemed an interminable time, the door was opened by a stooped old man with a thatch of white hair framing his gaunt face. Had it not been for the familiar crimson birthmark over his right eyebrow, Justin would never have recognized him.

"Mr. Frobisher?" he asked, when the old fellow looked at him askance. "Don't you remember me?"

Frobisher's eyes widened a notch. "Is that really you, my lord?" A slow smile spread across his face. "The missus and I have been waiting anxiously for you since the news reached us that you had returned from abroad to claim the title. We had almost given up hope that you would find time in your busy new life to visit Brandywine."

Justin felt a stab of guilt that he had been so lax in his duty to these dear people who had been so kind to him. "There were a million and one details I had to attend to concerning the transfer of title," he murmured, hoping the paltry excuse would sound plausible.

Frobisher nodded, readily accepting Justin's word, which made him feel even more guilty.

"What in heaven's name has happened here?" he asked, quickly changing the subject.

"Poor Brandywine has fallen on hard times, my lord, as I am sure you can see. It's a long story, but one I'd best tell now while Sarah is in the village shopping, for there's parts of it no decent woman would care to hear told in her presence." The old man's smile broadened. "But first, come inside, my lord. What am I thinking of, leaving you stand in the doorway like this?"

Leading Justin to a small salon on the ground floor, he whipped the holland covers off two chairs, waited for Justin to seat himself, then perching on the edge of the other chair, proceeded with his tale. "You remember how Lord Oliver was with women—lusting after them all but never caring for any—"

"Indeed I do," Justin interjected. The last thing he was interested in was a litany of his brother's sordid affairs.

"Well, that all changed about three years ago. Fell head over ears for an actress, he did—a rare beauty with the stage name Glorianna. No one, including Lord Oliver, seemed to know her real name. The first few times he brought her here, it was with other gentlemen and their mistresses. A wild, uncouth group they were and Lord Oliver wildest of them all. He flew into a towering rage every time one of the other gentlemen so much as spoke to Miss Glorianna." Frobisher hesitated, as if loath to proceed.

"Go on. Finish what you have to tell," Justin urged, though he failed to see what this had to do with the sorry condition in which he found the estate.

"Then he took to bringing Miss Glorianna alone to Brandywine for weeks at a time. Probably to keep her out of the reach of other men," Frobisher continued. "She was a bit of a flirt, you see. She hated Brandywine. Called it a dead bore. And anyone with eyes in his head could see she was beginning to hate Lord Oliver and his dominating ways as well."

"I should think she would."

"It all came to a head the last time they were here. They had a terrible row one rainy afternoon. Everyone from the upstairs maid to the pot boy could hear them yelling and throwing things around up in Miss Glorianna's bedchamber. Then Lord Oliver rode off in a huff and left her here alone. Of course, being the kind of woman she was, Miss Glorianna immediately took up with one of the grooms—a handsome lad she'd been eyeing for some time.

"Lord Oliver found them together when he came back unexpected-like three nights later. Turned into a raving lunatic, he did. Beat the young groom to within an inch of his life and would have done the same to Miss Glorianna if two of the footmen hadn't held him back. As it was, he turned her off the estate with no more than the clothes on her back—and that nothing but a flimsy nightrail."

"Good Lord. What happened to her?"

"As I understand it, she was picked up by the Earl of Chester, who was driving through Surrey on his way to London. By the time they reached the city, he was so taken with her, he set her up in a fine house and talked the manager of Drury Lane into offering her a part in his latest comedy."

"A fascinating story," Justin said, "but it still doesn't explain what has happened to Brandywine."

Frobisher scowled. "But it does, my lord, as you'll see when I finish my story. Like I said, Lord Oliver turned into a raving lunatic. Miss Glorianna was gone. He couldn't take his rage out on her, so he took it out on Brandywine instead. Said he never wanted to see the miserable place again. Stripped the stables of all the blooded stock and sent them to his estate in Kent. Discharged the entire staff down to the last gardener and kitchen boy, except for Sarah and me, and put the estate up for sale.

"There were buyers aplenty, but as it turned out, some clause in the entailment prohibited the sale, which made him almost as angry as Miss Glorianna had. So, he set sail for France on his yacht to forget the whole sorry affair, though he was warned of a fierce summer storm brewing over the Channel." Frobisher's eyes misted with tears. "You already know the rest of the story, my lord. It's just a shame he had to talk our dear Lady Anne into going with him."

Justin sank back in his chair, too sick at heart to comment on Frobisher's amazing narrative. At long last, he knew the full truth of how he had come to inherit, and a sorry way it was to acquire a title he'd never wanted.

It occurred to him that he should pay a visit to all eight of the Warre estates. If Oliver's treatment of Brandywine was any example of his careless stewardship, there could be problems with the other properties as well. The very idea overwhelmed him. He was ill at ease with strangers; meeting with the managers of all the estates would be a long drawn-out nightmare.

Unbidden, the thought crossed his mind that with Tess at his side, the inspection trip could have been a grand adventure. The stranger had yet to be born who could unnerve her. He quickly dismissed it as too painful to contemplate. How long, he wondered, would it be before everything he saw or heard or thought stopped reminding him of Tess? If this tendency toward self-flagellation was the natural aftermath of an unhappy love affair, God keep him from ever again risking his heart.

He suddenly realized Frobisher was waiting for him to say something. "The first thing we must do is re-staff Brandywine and bring it back to its former beauty and efficiency," he said. "Can such people be found in the nearby villages?"

Frobisher's countenance instantly brightened. Once again he looked like the proud majordomo who had ruled Brandywine with an iron hand during the years Justin had called it home. "Of a certainty, my lord," he declared firmly. "I've but to put the word out that we are hiring and the locals will flock to our door."

"Very well." Justin nodded his approval. "I shall leave that in your able hands then, Mr. Frobisher. Right now I must stable my horse, since my brother saw fit to dismiss all the grooms. Then, if Mrs. Frobisher can find me something to eat and a place to sleep for one night, I promise to get out of your way first thing in the morning and return only when you inform me that Brandywine is once again ready to entertain house guests."

Justin woke at dawn after a restless, dream-filled sleep, in which Tess and her children were somehow tied in with the sorry state in which he'd found Brandywine. It was a riddle that only needed to be solved, his dream counterpart decided, and promptly set about solving it. But just as he'd uncovered the last clue and was about to divulge the solution, he awoke more confused than ever.

It was only a dream, he told himself. Yet the odd feeling persisted that a definite connection existed between the two seemingly disparate parts of his life.

The Frobishers were already hard at work making plans to restore Brandywine to its former glory when, after a substantial breakfast, Justin mounted the trusty little mare. "For the sooner Brandywine is back to normal, the sooner you'll come back to us, my lord," Mrs. Frobisher declared in the no-nonsense voice that had so often made him toe the mark when he was under her care.

With a last wave to the elderly couple, Justin walked the mare from the stable and eased her into a slow canter. There would be no all-out gallop for the lady today; he could tell from the way she moved beneath him, she felt more inclined to take it easy after her strenuous workout yesterday.

A few minutes later, horse and rider topped a gentle rise in the road to gaze upon one of the lush Brandywine meadows in which a dozen or more sheep grazed peacefully. A stand of white birches dominated the far horizon, and it struck Justin that except for the sprinkling of frost on the grass and the absence of the leering god Pan, this could easily be the meadow depicted in Tess's colorful mural.

"The children have never seen a meadow," she'd said, and the sad note in her voice had made his heart weep. And those were the lucky ones whom Tess had rescued from the unthinkable horrors facing the other children in the infamous stews. Justin found himself imagining how this beautiful little meadow would look to children whose normal playground was a garbage-littered street wedged between grimy buildings. He could almost see the wonder in little Daisy's eyes, hear Danny's fervent "Gorblimey."

Was this the connection his dream had foretold? Was he meant to share the meadows and streams and woodlands of Brandywine with the children of the Laura Wentworth Home for Abandoned Children?

A strange sense of peace came over him. Heretofore he had thought only of his own despair and how to find a place where he could escape it. He realized now that no such place existed. He would waste no time trying to outrun sorrow. For the truth was, if he never saw them again, the memory of Daisy and Danny would haunt him always; if he never saw Tess again, he would go to his grave loving the perplexing woman, and no capriciousness on her part could change that love one iota.

With renewed determination, he resumed the long ride back to London. It was Thursday. Tomorrow was the day of the fateful rally. He meant to be there to see that Tess came to no harm, as he'd promised Danny, and he'd take Reggie with him.

If he could never have her as his wife, then so be it. He would somehow learn to live with the grief and loneliness of his loss.

In time, he might even learn to live with the bitter truth that she had rejected him in favor of a pompous fool not worthy of brushing the mud from her slippers.

What he could not live with was the knowledge that her blind loyalty to that fool threatened to place her in grave danger of losing her freedom—even her life.

One way or another, he intended to save the stubborn do-gooder from the consequences of her own folly.

"I don't care wot you say, Tess, I still don't twig it why you think you got to go to this bleedin' meetin' of Wentworth's." Danny shivered, as much, Tess suspected, from apprehension as from the biting cold wind that whipped through the narrow streets and back alleys of London's East End.

She registered his disapproving frown and found herself wishing she'd had the sense to refuse his offer to accompany her on what could well turn out to be a fool's mission. They'd been walking a good twenty minutes toward the designated meeting place in the warehouse district, during which time he'd kept up a constant harangue on this same theme. Her patience was growing thin.

She waited until they'd made their way around two men on crutches, both in the ragged uniforms of the light infantry, before she answered him. "How many times must I tell you, I promised Drew a good month ago that I would support him in this endeavor."

"So what? It ain't as if you was still friends. I seen you shut the door in his face when he come callin' this mornin'."

Tess caught her breath as the unhappy truth of Danny's statement fell like a lead weight on her heart. "You are right," she said sadly. "After a lifetime of friendship, Drew and I are no longer friends. But that's all the more reason why I feel obliged to honor my commitment. It is the last one I shall ever make him."

She glanced around her at the tattered uniforms and gaunt faces of the silent men heading in the same direction as they were. England's finest, gathering by the hundreds to demand tangible recognition for their years of service. "But I have another consideration as well," she continued. "I happen to support this particular cause Drew is espousing. I think the government's treatment of our returning soldiers is absolutely deplorable."

"But what about them rumors of trouble? It could be dangerous, Tess, and I don't know if I can pertect you all by myself."

Tess smiled, touched by the manly concern of her young champion. "To begin with, I am perfectly capable to taking care of myself. I am not some delicate nobleman's daughter who needs an escort every time she steps out her door," Tess declared with considerably more assurance than she actually felt. "You will note I brought my umbrella, though the chances of rain are slim. It has proved a most satisfactory weapon in the past. And as for the rumors, I take little stock in them. As I recall, similar ones have surfaced before every meeting Drew has organized to demand justice for the downtrodden."

"But this is different. I feel it in me bones." Danny searched the sea of faces surrounding them as if looking for someone in particular. "The guvnor promised me he would watch out for you. I just hope he gets here before the trouble starts."

A shaft of pain lanced through Tess at the mention of Justin and his promise. She didn't doubt he'd made it. It would have been the sort of thing he'd have done before she'd destroyed the magical bond between them. "Believe me, Danny, the last thing the viscount is thinking about right now is protecting me." Distress sharpened her voice. "He can feel nothing but disgust for me, and with good reason. In his eyes, I have to look like the worst kind of Jezebel."

"Maybe so. Can't say I'd blame him if he thought you was the dumbest female ever lived—believing all that gibble-gabble of Wentworth's." Danny glared straight ahead, the stubborn set to his jaw reminiscent of a small bulldog with his teeth locked around a bone. "But that don't mean he'll break his promise. It ain't the guvnor's way."

Tess trudged on, too heartsick to argue with the boy. Only now when it was too late to undo the damage she'd wrought with her foolish suspicions, was she beginning to realize the depth of the emotional ties Danny had formed for Justin. And unlike her, the boy's trust in his hero had never wavered.

The monstrous guilt she had lived with for the past two days increased tenfold. She'd been so immersed in her own grief over Justin's loss, she'd failed to realize that like a pebble thrown into a pond, the anguish she'd caused had spread in ever-widening ripples to encompass the people she loved.

They were drawing close to their destination now. The ramshackle tenements so prevalent in the streets surrounding the children's home had given way to the huge, windowless structures that served as warehouses for the multitude of goods and food-stuffs needed to supply a city the size of London.

Tess stared at the sturdy brick and timber buildings, struck by the irony that such things as fabrics and lumber and spices rated these substantial edifices, while but a mile or so away humans were housed in piles of rubble that could collapse with the first strong gust of wind.

Weary of being jostled by the ever-increasing crowd, Danny and she stopped to rest in the entrance to an alleyway adjoining a vast building bearing the name Richfield's Granary. "Never been on this street before. Back alleys is more me style," Danny remarked, obviously awestruck by the massive buildings around him.

"Nor I. But we can't leave it soon enough to my way of think-ing." Tess shivered. "Don't ask me why, but something about this particular spot makes me strangely uneasy." She stared into the dark recesses of the narrow alley and to her horror found two bright, beady eyes staring back at her.

"Dear God," she shrieked and dragging Danny with her, bolted for the street. But not before a rat the size of a large house cat scurried past within inches of the toe of her half boot.

Shaking from head to toe and oblivious of the curious eyes around her, she clung to Danny in breathless terror. It was too much. Her nerves were already raw. How could she be expected to stay calm when she stood eye to eye with this monstrous, grainfed version of her nemesis?

Normally she prided herself on her fortitude; in the past five years, she had managed to cope with problems that few men she knew would have dared tackle. But when it came to snakes and rodents, she turned as missish as the most sheltered darling of the *ton*.

Gulping a breath of air into her parched lungs, she released her death grip on Danny's arm and watched the color return to his ashen face. "Gorblimey, you silly woman, you liked to scare me wits right out of me head." He pressed a hand to his ribs. "And poked me with that bloomin' umbrella of yours as well. It were only a rat fer God's sake; a big un, I admits, like everythin' else around here, but nothin' to get all puddin'-hearted about."

His ginger brows drew together in a frown. "If this is how you takes care of yourself, like you boasted, I got more trouble on me hands than I counted on."

Once again he searched the crowd with troubled eyes. "All I got to say is I hopes the guvnor—"

"Don't even think it, Danny." Tess interrupted him before he could say the words she couldn't bear to hear. For in truth, if by some miracle Justin should suddenly appear in this sea of strangers, she knew full well she would throw herself into his arms and weep all over him—and give him an even greater disgust of her than he already had.

Chapter Fourteen

The leaders of the rally had chosen their location wisely. There were not many places in London's East End that would accommodate the crowd they hoped to draw. This open square in the center of the warehouse district was one of them.

Utilized as an open market of wheeled carts and bins from dawn to dusk, it lay empty all night. The peripatetic hucksters of fruits and vegetables, tinware, and dry goods had apparently closed up shop early this evening. The first shades of night were just descending when Tess and Danny arrived, and already the square was more than half filled with uniformed servicemen.

"Best we stay near the back in case there's trouble," Danny advised. Tess agreed. Trouble or no, she had no desire to be caught in the crush, for she could see more men filing into the square every minute.

"Gorblimey," Danny exclaimed, staring about him in obvious awe, "there looks to be fellows from every regiment of old Hooknose's army here tonight."

Tess nodded, recognizing within just a few feet of her the uniforms of the Hussars, the Light Infantry, the Heavy Dragoons, and the famous Coldstream Guard. Most of the uniforms were filthy, many ragged and bloodstained and with empty sleeves pinned to the shoulders.

As the crowd grew thicker, the stench of unwashed bodies grew proportionately stronger, and Tess found herself wishing she'd had the sense to bring a handkerchief soaked in cologne to press to her nose. It occurred to her that most of these men had been homeless for weeks, even months, with no means of washing so much as their hands and faces. Some even looked to be caked with the grime of battle they'd worn the day they were discharged from the troop ships that transported them from the Continent.

In general, the grim-faced men were eerily silent. Now and then some of those she had fed in the past weeks recognized her and offered a wary greeting. One garrulous fellow in a tattered uniform of the Royal Blues shook her hand enthusiastically, then shouted, "Lookee here, blokes! It's the Angel come to cheer us on!" "The Angel . . . the Angel . . . the Angel" echoed through the crowd.

To Tess's relief, the sound died away before it reached the platform on which the four leaders stood. The last thing she needed was to have Drew spot her and insist she sit with the family group she could see seated off to one side. She would seek him out after the rally so he would know she'd kept her promise. Then as far as she was concerned, any further obligation to him was canceled.

To her surprise, she spied a fair number of women and children scattered throughout the ever-growing crowd. Like the men they supported, the women exuded an air of hopeless despair, and the hollow eyes and hunger-pinched cheeks of the children tore at her heart. She might fault Drew's self-serving reasons for calling this rally, but she could not dispute the need for the message it sent to the Tory government. These men and their families were starving, and something had to be done to alleviate their suffering.

The square was full now—and she could see the satisfied expressions on the faces of the four leaders as they scanned the crowd. With a beatific smile, Drew stepped forward and raised his arms as if in benediction. Tess and Danny exchanged a knowing smile; Drew could always be counted on to do the dramatic. She had long suspected he'd missed his calling. He would have made a superb actor.

"Gallant warriors who followed General Wellington into the depths of hell and back, I salute you," Drew intoned in rich, dramatic tones that Edmund Keene, himself, might well envy. "You gave your all for England in her hour of need. Now, in your hour of need, I demand the men who sit in her seats of power accord you the dignity due you."

Tess groaned. Drew was back on his dignity theme. She doubted these war-weary soldiers would find it of any more consequence than the lady butchers had.

"Dignity won't fill our bellies, nor those of our wives and children," someone in the audience shouted, and murmurs of assent spread through the vast crowd like ripples across a pond. Drew ignored them. Like a child's top that once wound must complete its spin, he droned on and on without saying one word that gave hope to the desperate men he addressed.

Tess could sense the growing restlessness of the men around her, hear their disgruntled muttering. She wondered how long it would be before Drew's audience abandoned him in disgust. Luckily the servicemen lacked the rotting fruits and vegetables with which audiences at Drury Lane pelted performers who displeased them.

She heard a disgruntled soldier near the platform call out, "Stubble it, Wentworth. Get to the point," and for the first time since the rally began, the audience cheered enthusiastically. Drew held up his hands in a gesture that promised he would do as they asked. But no sooner had the cheers died down than a slender fellow some ten feet ahead of Tess, and wearing the uniform of the Rifle Brigade, shouted, "The point is we starve in the streets while the Regent stuffs his belly and grows fatter by the minute."

" 'Tis true," echoed back and forth throughout the crowd, and all at once everyone was talking at the same time. The noise was deafening, but over the babble of voices and the wails of frightened children, the rifleman's voice rose again, "Death to the fat Regent and his Tory Privy Council."

Instantly, a shocked silence fell on the assemblage. Then as Tess watched, a gigantic man in the uniform of the Fifth Northumberland Fusiliers grasped the rifleman by the scruff of the neck and lifted him off his feet. "Here now, none of that sort of talk, little man," the fusilier warned. "This is a peaceful gathering."

Cursing and flailing his arms, the rifleman struggled to free himself from the grip of his powerful captor. To no avail. Not until he'd shaken the smaller man till his teeth rattled did the fusilier set him back on his feet. "Be off with ye now," he said and turning him toward the rear of the square, gave him a swift kick in the pants.

Snarling his anger, the rifleman quickly disappeared into the crowd, but not before Tess got a look at his face. She gasped.

There was no mistaking that gargoyle face, those cold, slate-colored eyes.

The troublemaker was none other than Drew's "good friend," Michael Diehl.

From the spot where he'd stationed himself atop the loading ramp of one of the warehouse buildings bordering the square, Justin could survey the entire gathering without fear of being noticed. Both Reggie and he had felt it prudent to wear unrelieved black in case they needed to fade into the darkness that would surround the square by the time the meeting got underway. Even now, the choice of raiment served him well, for he was just another barely visible shadow against the weathered clapboard of the building.

He had spotted Tess and Danny within moments of his arrival. They stood but a scant thirty feet from him—easily within reach if they should need his protection—and well they might the way things were shaping up.

He recognized two men in the crowd whom Reggie had once introduced as Bow Street Runners, and unless he was mistaken, the twenty or more hard-faced men circling the perimeter of the square were City of London watchmen. Whoever had arranged the police surveillance for this meeting must have stripped every watch house in the East End. But why? Surely one-third this many watchmen would be sufficient to keep the situation under control.

His gaze strayed to the speakers' platform. Wentworth was easy to recognize in his elegant Weston-tailored topcoat and breeches—a singularly inappropriate outfit for a rally of half-starved servicemen, in Justin's opinion. But he had yet to see the cit do anything that would lead him to believe there was an ounce of sense inside the fellow's handsome head.

He didn't recognize the other three men on the platform, which was no surprise. What he did find surprising, however, was the absence of Ferret-Face from the group of leaders. Wentworth had been very specific about the important part his "good friend" had played in organizing this rally. Then why was he missing from the stage? His unexpected absence made Justin more than a little uneasy.

Absentmindedly, he fingered the pistol tucked into his belt and smiled to himself. Between that and his trusty cane, he should be ready for anything that should develop.

As if the mere thought of the odd-looking rabble-rouser conjured him up, he suddenly appeared directly below the ramp on which Justin was standing. Like a snake slithering through a field of tall grass, Ferret-Face wound his circuitous way through the crowd. Justin tensed, aware he was headed toward the very spot where Tess and Danny stood—then relaxed as he passed them by to take up a stand some ten feet ahead of them.

Justin looked again and blinked in astonishment. What was a man like Ferret-Face doing in the uniform of the Rifle Brigade? He would wager his last guinea the slimy fellow had never served side by side with the brave heroes of Badajoz and Waterloo. And why was the acknowledged organizer of the rally sneaking around through the crowd disguised as a common soldier instead of taking his rightful place on the speakers' platform?

Too many puzzling questions; too few logical answers. A familiar sense of foreboding gripped Justin. As Reggie had foretold, something nasty was afoot here, and that fool, Wentworth, was blind to what was going on before his very eyes. In truth, if he carried on his meaningless pontification much longer, there would be no need for Ingraham's minions to cause trouble. Wentworth would drive his audience to violence from sheer boredom.

But something was definitely blowing in the wind. Justin watched Ferret-Face cup his hands around his mouth, preparing to shout something to the speaker, and his sense of foreboding accelerated tenfold. Instinct told him that if Lord Ingraham and his minions did indeed have a sinister plan in mind, it was about to be put into action.

He listened with half an ear, his attention riveted on Tess. She looked so small and helpless surrounded by hundreds of men who towered over her. But there was no ignoring Ferret-Face's voice. It rose shrill as a trumpet over the noise of the restless crowd. "We starve in the streets while the Regent stuffs his belly and grows fatter by the minute."

The provocative words sent reverberations racing through the crowd of desperate men. Everywhere voices were raised in angry agreement. In a matter of minutes the mood of the crowd had shifted from apathetic to belligerent. Was this Ingraham's intention? To stir up enough trouble to provide an excuse to arrest the leaders of the rally?

Justin held his breath as he watched Ferret-Face cup his mouth again. He wondered what more damage the fellow could cause with his catcalls. He already had the disgruntled soldiers on the verge of rioting.

"Death to the fat Regent and his Tory Privy Council." The ugly words burned a flaming path through Justin's shocked brain. As if viewing his own worst nightmare, he watched two of the watchmen draw their pistols and advance toward the speakers' platform. With horrifying clarity, he understood the full extent of Ingraham's heinous plan.

His paid minion had shouted words, the likes of which every English nobleman and member of the Royal Family had lived in dread of hearing since similar words had turned France into a bloody holocaust some twenty years earlier. But no one would remember it was he who had said them. He had already conveniently disappeared into the crowd.

By the time the story reached tomorrow's *Times*, it would be the leaders of the rally—dangerous revolutionaries all—who had called for the overthrow of the government and the assassination of the Regent.

Terror would spread through the *ton* and into the elegant salons of Carlton House like fire through a tinder-dry forest. If Wentworth and his friends had not already been shot on sight, they would be hunted down and hanged for treason. With a minimum of effort on their part, Ingraham and his Tory cronies would rid themselves of the troublemakers who dared criticize their laissez-faire attitude toward the thousands of starving soldiers who roamed the streets of London's slums.

With one hand gripping his pistol, the other his cane, Justin limped down the steep ramp and headed for Tess, only to see her begin frantically pushing her way toward the beleaguered speakers' platform. He was still a good ten feet behind her when the first shot rang out.

If Tess had had any lingering doubts about the truth of Justin's warning, the sight of Diehl's ugly face dispelled them. He was

everything he'd been purported to be—government spy, provoca-
teur, devious schemer. The clever fellow had done his job well.
Unless Drew quickly came up with some brilliant way to bring
the restless crowd under control, he would be faced with yet another disastrous rally—to say nothing of a riot and an extended
stay in Newgate for disrupting the peace.

She stood on tiptoe, hoping to catch a glimpse of him and saw
instead two great hulking brutes advancing toward Drew and the
other leaders with pistols drawn. Suddenly Justin's words rang in
her ears, "You and your friends are being set up for arrest—or
worse."

"No!" she cried. Whatever Drew's faults, he did not deserve to
be shot down like a rabid dog. Using her umbrella as a battering
ram, she shoved her way through the crowd that now appeared
bent on fleeing in the opposite direction. Miraculously they parted
for her.

Behind her she heard Danny cry, "Stop you crazy woman.
You're going to get yourself killed," and another oddly familiar
voice that echoed his words. She stubbornly ignored them both.

She was still a good ways from the platform when she heard
the crack of a gunshot. To her horror, one of the leaders reeled
backward, a startled look on his face and a scarlet stain spreading
across his chest. She recognized him as the Reverend Henry
Huskins, a fiery Methodist minister who for years had involved
himself in every cause aimed toward aiding London's poor and
downtrodden.

With the screams of the poor man's wife ringing in her ears,
she finally reached the edge of the stage, just as the same gunman
raised his pistol again and pointed it at Drew.

"Stop, you murdering dog!" she shouted. Grasping her umbrella in both hands, she raised it above her head and brought it
smashing down across the back of the burly fellow's thick neck.
With a groan, he fell forward, his pistol discharged, and he struck
his head on the edge of the platform.

Even as he crumpled in an ungainly heap at her feet, Tess heard
Drew's cry of pain. "I've been shot," he said, staring straight at
her with shock-glazed eyes. As she watched helplessly, he slowly
slid to his knees and pitched headfirst off the edge of the platform.

Tess lunged forward and grabbed his shoulders, knowing all too well she could never support his weight. "Help me, somebody!" she cried and to her relief, help came in the form of two strong, black-clad arms and a pair of hands that caught Drew's limp body, lowered it to the floor, and propped it against one of the posts holding up the platform.

"Thank you," she said fervently and looked up into Justin's anxious blue eyes.

"That was a very brave and a very foolish thing you just did," he said solemnly. "Are you all right?"

She wanted to say he had done an equally brave and foolish thing, coming to the rescue of a woman for whom he could feel nothing but disgust. She settled for, "I am fine but Drew has been shot."

"So I see. But thanks to you the bullet meant for his heart is now lodged in his shoulder." Justin drew his handkerchief from his pocket and, kneeling beside the unconscious man, pressed it to the wound to stop the bleeding.

To his relief, he saw two Cold Stream Guardsmen subdue the other gunman, but not before he wounded another of the leaders. The fourth leader promptly leaped from the stage and disappeared into the crowd.

"We have to get Wentworth away from here," he said matter-of-factly. "This place is teeming with watchmen, and these two may not be the only ones with orders to shoot to kill."

Tess's eyes widened in disbelief. "These assassins are London watchmen? But why would the law want to kill Drew and his friends? They've done nothing wrong."

"Except point up the fact that the men currently in charge of our government care more for lining their own pockets than relieving the suffering of the poor devils who kept the Corsican monster from setting up housekeeping in Carlton House."

Tess stared about her in wild-eyed confusion. "Dear God, what can we do? We can't just let Drew be murdered because he dared speak out against injustice."

"To begin with, we must somehow get him to my carriage." Justin surveyed the man stretched out between them. "I fear he is too heavy for me to carry alone, and I dare not take the time to send Danny to where Reggie waits. Do you think you are strong enough to hold up your half if we walk him between us?"

"I can certainly try. I am much stronger than I look."

Justin smiled to himself. As usual, Tess was wearing one of her shockingly colorful dresses, and at the moment she looked like a very small, very frightened scarlet bird.

Somehow, between them, they managed to get Wentworth to his feet and drape his arms over their shoulders. Justin could see Tess was struggling bravely to do her part, but they'd not yet taken a step and she already looked ready to collapse.

"Here now, folks, let me help you." The deep voice belonged to the gigantic fusilier who had earlier put an end to Ferret-Face's inciting catcalls. Stepping forward, he lifted Wentworth as if he weighed no more than a child the age of Daisy.

"Lead on, sir, and I'll carry your friend wherever you want me to," he said. "My cronies have created a small skirmish on the opposite side of the square, which should keep the watch busy for a time. But I suggest we move with haste. 'Tis obvious someone in power wants this fellow and his friends dead."

Justin wasted no time in following his suggestion. With Tess and Danny in tow, he led the giant fusilier around the perimeter of the square to the narrow alleyway Reggie and he had earlier marked as a possible escape route in case of trouble. To his surprise, not a single person challenged them. The little skirmish the fusilier's friends had started was now a gigantic free-for-all and every watchman and Bow Street Runner in the square was busy trying to bring it under control.

The carriage was exactly where Reggie had promised it would be, on the backside of the largest warehouse fronting the square. Reggie stood beside it, pistol drawn. "I thought I heard gunshots," he said once Justin came close enough to be recognized.

"You did, and Wentworth carries one of the bullets in his shoulder." Throwing open the carriage door, Justin stepped aside to let the fusilier deposit Wentworth inside, then handed Tess in as well before he turned to hold out his hand to the helpful fellow.

"I cannot thank you enough," he said sincerely.

"Think nothing of it," the giant replied. "I've killed my share

of Frogs in battle, but I've no stomach for senseless murder."
He grinned. "Not even when the victim is a gabble-grinder like
this fellow."

He glanced toward the lozenge on the carriage door. "If
someone like you could speak for us in the House of Lords,
there might be no need for rallies such as this."

Justin nodded solemnly. "I promise you I shall do my best to
bring your plight to the attention of those who can do something
about it."

"That's all a man can ask. Now I'd best go rescue my friends
before one of them ends up in Newgate." With a smart salute,
the fusilier disappeared back into the shadowy alleyway.

"I'll ride up top with his lordship and give him directions,
him being new to this part of town," Danny said, climbing up
beside Reggie to sit on the coachman's hammercloth. "We'll not
be wanting to travel the streets the watch is guarding with a
wanted criminal on our hands, and I knows the back alleys as
well as any cutpurse in the stews."

Justin could find no fault with that plan, except it left him to
ride inside the carriage where he must watch Tess minister tenderly to her dear friend, Wentworth—a scenario he found so
painful, the very thought of it was almost beyond comprehension.

As he'd expected, she sat with the cit's head in her lap, croon-
ing the same tuneless melody he'd heard her croon to baby
David the day he was abandoned by his mother. Maybe that was
the hold Wentworth had on her—he appealed to her overdevel-
oped maternal instincts.

The ride seemed interminable. Justin had closed the window
curtains and lighted the two small, interior lanterns so they
could keep watch on Wentworth's wound to make sure it didn't
start bleeding again. He hadn't counted on how the dim light
would accentuate the dark smudges beneath Tess's lovely eyes,
making her look so fragile and exhausted, he ached to take her
in his arms and comfort her.

Luckily, she was too busy with her patient to notice the
lovesick glances he cast her way. With every bounce of the carriage across the ruts lining the back alleys, Wentworth moaned

piteously. "He won't die, will he?" Tess asked anxiously when he emitted a particularly pitiful cry.

"I doubt it. Shoulder wounds are rarely fatal," Justin said dryly, staring stoically at the window curtain, as if he could see the sights beyond it. Aware she was studying him closely, he finally turned to face her.

"Why are you doing this, Justin?"

"Doing what?"

"Risking your life to save a man you can barely tolerate?"

A sennight ago he might have admitted he did it for her because he loved her beyond all reason. He might even have confessed that he would willingly risk his life to see her happy, even if it meant the end of all his dreams. But the wall between them had grown too high and too thick in the past three days; there was no space left for such maudlin sentimentality.

He shrugged. "Like Reggie, I was ready for a little adventure to relieve the boredom of my everyday existence."

"Oh," she said in a small voice which, if he didn't know better, might make him think his careless answer had wounded her.

The sound of Reggie's "Whoa" and the sudden stopping of the carriage put an end to his senseless ruminations. With the handle of his cane, he tapped on the trap and waited for Reggie to lift it.

"If you're wondering where we are," his friend said, brushing a snowflake off the end of his nose, "we are a few blocks from Miss Thornhill's home. Danny, clever lad that he is, decided he should reconnoiter the area in case the watch had staked it out, knowing she was such great friends with Wentworth. He promised to return within ten minutes."

Only moments later, the door snapped open and Danny poked his head in. "They're there all right, hidin' in every entryway of every building on the bleedin' street. Just like I knowd they'd be, wot with us takin' the long way round, so to speak. So wot do we do now, guvnor? It's Newgate for certain if we're caught hidin' a fellow wots wanted by the law."

Justin was well aware of the danger they were in. He was equally aware that three people for whom he cared deeply were depending on him to make a wise decision.

"As I see it, there's only one solution to our problem. Take him where no one would think to look for him."

As one, three voices asked, "Where is that?"

"Why, to Mayfair, of course. What right thinking watchman would expect to find a rabble-rouser from the stews ensconced in the town house of the Viscount Sanderfield?"

Chapter Fifteen

The trip across town was uneventful, a blessing for which Tess offered humble thanks to God. She would never forgive herself if, because of her, Justin found himself in trouble with the law.

Drew regained consciousness just before they entered Mayfair, stared blankly at Justin, and demanded to know why he was being transported in a carriage with "the knife-wielding viscount."

"Hush, Drew, you should be thanking the viscount, not insulting him," Tess said. "If not for him, you would be lying dead at the site of that regrettable meeting of yours. He and the Earl of Rutledge have put their own lives at risk to save yours."

"What are you saying?" Drew struggled to sit up, moaned in pain, and fell back down again. "What has happened to me? Why do I feel as if I had been trampled by a coach and four?"

"You've been shot by the watch. Thanks to your 'friend' Diehl and his seditious remarks, you are now a hunted criminal. It was just as the viscount warned you—a clever plan devised so you and the other leaders of the rally could be done away with one way or another." Now that she was certain he would live, Tess's concern for Drew quickly turned to anger and frustration with him—and with herself as well.

Drew covered his eyes with a trembling hand. "Good Lord, Tess, never say it was Michael who made those vicious catcalls."

"It was and no mistake. I stood not ten feet from him."

"But why?"

"I believe I can answer that," Justin said. "I observed him

huddled with Lord Ingraham outside White's three nights ago. Money changed hands."

"A spy, bought and paid for by the very men he pretended to despise." Wentworth opened his eyes and met Justin's gaze squarely. "I not only owe you my thanks; I owe you an apology as well. Like a fool, I let my insane jealousy color my judgment of everything you tried to tell me."

"Apology accepted, Wentworth. Jealousy can make fools of the best of us, as I, myself, can attest." Justin smiled that special smile of his that made Tess's heart pound like a triphammer, but this time the smile was directed at Drew. The two men had openly discussed their feelings for her as casually as if she were nowhere around, and she resented it bitterly.

Drew closed his eyes again. "Where are you taking me?"

Tess didn't attempt to answer his question, since it was obviously directed to Justin. Somehow, in the past five minutes, she had become nothing more than a pillow on which Drew could rest his head.

"To my town house in Mayfair. Under the circumstances, it seemed the safest place. Tess's home is already under surveillance by the watch." Justin's voice sounded matter-of-fact, but his taut features clearly showed the strain he was under.

"Add to that the fact that you have lost a great deal of blood and a bullet in your shoulder must be removed before the wound putrefies, and you can see the quandary we were in." Justin glanced out the window. "But as the saying goes, all's well that end's well. It appears we have arrived at our destination."

He consulted his pocket watch. "Perfect timing. The staff should all be in the servants' dining room at their evening meal. If I use my latch key, we should be able to sneak you in with no one the wiser. The fewer people who know of your whereabouts, the better."

"Agreed." Drew grimaced in pain. "If I had the strength, I would walk away from here right now before I exposed all of you to more danger. You can depend on my doing so the minute I am able, my lord."

The statement was so unlike something Drew would ordinarily be expected to say, Tess found herself staring at him in amazement. In the short time since he had regained consciousness and recognized the extent of the trouble he was in, he had matured considerably.

Her eyes blurred with unshed tears of sympathy for her poor friend. In a matter of but two hours, Drew had gone from a man who believed he would one day sit in the House of Commons to a hunted fugitive whose only chance of survival depended on the kindness of a man he had heretofore considered an enemy.

What kind of bumblebroth has the young viscount gotten himself involved in now? Wimple's eye had been pressed so tightly to the keyhole of the library door for the past fifteen minutes, it felt as if it were about to be sucked from its socket.

His vision was restricted, but he could see the Jezebel from the stews, flaunting herself in a gaudy scarlet dress, the likes of which no one but a Haymarket doxie would be seen in. Likewise that dreadful little slum rat who had delivered that note for the viscount yesterday.

He rubbed his eye, then tried again. Now he could see the viscount and the Earl of Rutledge and, God save us, a man naked to the waist lying atop the library table.

His first thought was that the young master and his friend, the earl, had been talked into joining one of those devil's cults he'd heard talk of, and were performing some kind of barbaric ritual. He cracked the door, hoping to hear one of their heathenish chants and heard instead, "Pour a little more brandy down him. It's going to hurt like the very devil, but that bullet has to come out."

A bullet! Wimple couldn't believe his ears. The stranger laid out on the library table had a bullet in him! Had the viscount gone mad, exposing the noble House of Warre to the carrion he collected in the infamous London stews?

Wimple's ancient knees buckled beneath him and he grasped the doorknob for support. He'd heard enough; his duty was clear. A footman must be dispatched immediately with a note to the duke informing him of what was going on behind his back.

As fast as his old legs would carry him, he trotted toward the desk in which he kept his trusty pen and paper.

Reggie set the cut-glass brandy decanter back on the silver tray from which he'd removed it a half hour earlier. A scarce two inches of the amber liquid was all that remained of the original quantity. "Well, that should do it," he declared, "Wentworth is drunk as a wheelbarrow. It's time to get on with the surgery."

Justin nodded his agreement. "Time indeed. Tell me, Reggie, did you learn anything about removing bullets in the years you campaigned with Wellington?"

"Lord no! I left nasty jobs like that to the company surgeon. I just fired the blasted things at the Frogs. I don't suppose you were called upon to practice such surgery anywhere in your travels," he ventured hopefully.

"Not to worry. Tess can do it." Danny grinned from ear to ear. "It wasn't but a month or so ago she pried a bullet out of one of Florabelle's girls after a brawl in the bawdy house."

"The devil you say!" Reggie shook his head in astonishment. "Not the sort of thing one would expect a lady to do, but—"

"Can you manage it, Tess?" Justin interrupted him before he could finish his insulting comment.

"I can try. Since you two stalwart males are so squeamish." She glared at the hapless earl. "I shall need a penknife, clean water, and some clean cloths."

"I have the knife," Reggie offered sheepishly.

"And I have a pitcher of fresh water and an abundance of clean handkerchiefs in my bedchamber which I can fetch immediately, if they will do," Justin added. "Anything else I would have to obtain from the housekeeper, and I would just as soon not involve her."

"Then they will have to do. But I suggest one of you should force the rest of the brandy down Drew. He is a notorious crybaby when it comes to pain." Something close to a smile crossed Tess's face. "The last time I operated on him, I was eight years old and he was ten. He had collected a sliver in a vital part of his anatomy sliding down a banister, and he nearly drove his sister, Laura, and me mad with his everlasting wailing. We finally wrestled him to the floor and sat on him while I extracted it."

Reggie's mouth dropped open from shock, but Justin had long ago grown accustomed to her earthy humor. What startled him most was the band of pain that gripped his heart at this reminder of the years of closeness Tess had shared with the handsome cit. He must have been mad to think he could compete for her affection against such overwhelming odds.

By the time Justin returned with the pitcher of water, the stack of handkerchiefs, and a minuscule amount of his precious hoard of healing powders in a twist of paper, Tess had set up her makeshift operating room with her usual efficiency.

"Danny, I shall need you to hold a candle directly above the wound so I can see what I am doing," she said briskly. "Viscount Sanderfield, I depend on you to hold Drew's shoulders down—my Lord of Rutledge, his legs. It is absolutely essential that he lie perfectly still while I probe for the bullet or I could do him irreparable harm." All three instantly leaped to do her bidding.

Justin watched her take in hand the small penknife Reggie had supplied and bend over the patient. All things considered, he felt a little foolish offering suggestions as to how she should proceed. Still, he felt compelled to mention one thing. He cleared his throat self-consciously.

"I have witnessed surgeries in my travels in the East," he said hesitantly. "It is the custom with many of the surgeons to run the knife blade through a candle flame before cutting into the patient's body."

Tess hesitated, the knife but an inch from the wound. "Whatever for?"

"As it was explained to me, to cleanse it of evil spirits, which I, of course, discount. Nevertheless, there must be something to it, since the incidence of putrescence from such wounds is negligible in that part of the world. Something I understand our English surgeons cannot claim."

"Sounds like balderdash to me," Reggie grumbled.

"Still, anything is worth a try." Tess ran the blade slowly back and forth through the flame of the candle Danny held. "Drew has suffered enough at the hands of evil men this night. He doesn't need evil spirits as well."

She raised her head briefly and her gaze locked with Justin's.

"Furthermore, I have reason to be thankful for the medical knowledge of the men of the East."

"As have I," Justin said, knowing she, too, was remembering the night they'd held vigil together at Daisy's bedside—and celebrated the success of that surgery in each other's arms.

The bullet was lodged against the shoulder bone. Tess had located it almost instantly, but removing it was another matter entirely. Its very position made it nearly impossible to slip the point of the knife underneath it and bring it to the surface.

With each probe of the knife, Drew moaned and fought the restraints put upon him. Tess found herself wondering how much longer Justin could maintain his hold on Drew's shoulders—indeed how much longer she could face the sight of his torn and bleeding flesh and keep her roiling stomach under control.

She could feel rivulets of perspiration running down her back and between her breasts, and the beads forming on her brow dripped into her eyes, blinding her to her task. In desperation, she grabbed one of the handkerchiefs, wiped her eyes and her brow, and tried again.

At last the knife found purchase and slowly, carefully she worked the bullet upward until it popped free. "Thank God," she said, stopping a minute to catch her breath before she cleaned and dressed the wound.

"Bravo, Miss Thornhill. A job well done!" Reggie exclaimed, letting loose his hold on the patient's legs to wipe his own brow. "We could have used you on the Peninsula."

"I'm afraid I wouldn't have had the stomach for it," she said and pressing her fingers to her lips, made a mad dash for the French windows just moments before the library door was flung open and the Duke of Arncott strode through.

"What the devil is going on here?" he demanded. He pointed to Wentworth. "Who is that man? And since when has this town house been converted into a public hospital?"

Justin gritted his teeth, but he calmly finished bathing the wound, sprinkled the healing powder on it, and applied a square of linen six handkerchiefs thick before answering. "It is a long story, Grandfather, and one with which I doubt you would have much sympathy."

"Do not think to put me off, Justin. I want answers and I want them now." He stared about him, as if searching the room for something or someone. "Where is the Thornhill woman? I know she's here. I don't doubt for a minute she's the one who put you up to this havey-cavey business."

The anger that had been simmering inside Justin since the duke burst on the scene erupted into a blazing conflagration. "And how could you be aware of that fact, Grandfather, unless you employed some keyhole peeper in my household as your spy? I have wondered how you have managed to keep abreast of all my activities in recent weeks. Now I know."

"As head of the Warre family, I am entitled to know everything that concerns its members," the duke blustered, the sudden color in his gaunt cheeks a telling confirmation of Justin's accusation.

"Hell and damnation, are all you aristocrats so devious you must employ spies to do your dirty work?" Justin growled. "If so, I take leave to disassociate myself with the lot of you."

He reached for his greatcoat, which he'd tossed across a chair on entering the room, and covered Wentworth with it. "Very well, Your Grace, I shall tell you of this night's work, if that is what you wish. Then I give you leave to do with the information what you will, providing you leave my coachman out of it."

Reggie stepped forward, out of the shadows and into the light cast by the candles surrounding the table on which Wentworth lay. "Here now, Justin, none of that. We stand or fall together. I feel just as strongly as you about this matter. I recognized a good many of those poor devils as men who had served under me. I wonder how I have so long remained blind to their plight."

"Very well. In that case, I suggest we adjourn to the second-floor salon, where we may jointly acquaint my inquisitive grandfather with the facts of life as they pertain to our gallant ex-servicemen."

Justin turned to Danny. "Keep an eye on our patient, lad, and be good enough to ask Tess to join us as soon as she feels up to it."

On the way out the door, he encountered an ashen-faced Wimple hovering in the hallway. The fellow couldn't have looked more guilty if he'd had a sign hung around his neck with the word SPY printed on it.

"Have Cook prepare a substantial tea—a cold collation, in fact—and deliver it to the blue salon," Justin said curtly. "I have missed both tea and dinner and find I am exceedingly hungry."

"Yes, my lord. Right away, my lord."

Justin scowled. "Stop cowering, Wimple. It will do you no good. All the 'yes, my lording' in the world won't put you back in my good graces."

"I am deeply sorry if I have offended you, my lord. I believed I was acting in your best interests."

Justin doubted that very much. Wimple struck him as a man who acted mainly in his own best interests. Still, much as he might wish to, he couldn't bring himself to discharge the ancient retainer. The gullible fellow had merely been a pawn in the power game played by the wily old duke.

But what was he going to do about the duke? There had never been any love lost between him and his grandfather. The old man had frankly stated that, in his opinion, any number of distant cousins would have made more suitable viscounts than Justin. The less-than-perfect relationship between them had been tolerable for the simple reason that Justin had long ago quit hoping for the old man's approval.

But this latest confrontation was a different thing entirely. The duke had walked in on a situation that begged explanation, but Justin had no idea how the consummate aristocrat would receive the information he was forced to reveal to him. Lives other than his own could be seriously affected if his grandfather chose to use that information as a tool to bring his recalcitrant grandson into line.

Justin gritted his teeth, well aware it was just the sort of thing the old tyrant would enjoy doing.

The tense conversation in the blue salon began with Justin and Reggie seated on the small settee and the duke on one of the Sheraton chairs facing it. But once Justin touched on the meeting he had observed between Lord Ingraham and Michael Diehl, the duke rose to his feet and paced restlessly back and forth across the room for the balance of the recital. Why that bit of information should have such a volatile effect, Justin had no way of knowing—unless Lord Ingraham was a particular friend of the duke's.

The arrival of the tea tray, carried by a noticeably shaken Wimple, temporarily interrupted them. Once the butler had retired and shut the door behind him, the duke leveled one of his famous hooded gazes on Justin and demanded he finish his "remarkable story."

"In for a penny, in for a pound," Justin said to himself and grimly soldiered on. "The plain truth is, Grandfather, I am guilty of harboring a criminal hunted by the London watch—a man who has no doubt already been branded a traitor and revolutionary by your fine Tory friends in the Privy Council."

"Charges which, I take it, you believe are untrue."

"I know they are, Grandfather. Wentworth is a pompous self-serving ass, but he is no traitor. With that in mind, I must either do my best to help him escape, or live with the knowledge that I have contributed to his murder."

The duke ceased his pacing to face Justin. "In other words you are setting yourself above the law." He gave a bark of laughter. "And you have dared call *me* arrogant?"

"Hear the rest, Your Grace, before you comment," Justin interjected, "for you will undoubtedly find the sin I plan to commit even more monstrous than any I have already committed."

The duke's nostrils flared. "Good God, what have I done to deserve such tribulation in my declining years?" he moaned, and even Reggie, loyal friend that he was, frowned disapprovingly.

Justin chose to disregard both reactions to his provocative statement. "After much thought, I have decided to take my rightful place in the House of Lords for the sole purpose of speaking out against the hellish conditions our government officials allow to exist in the underbelly of London."

"Have you gone over to the Whigs then, Grandson? For they are the only ones who will listen to you, and their tongues will be firmly lodged in their cheeks."

"Then so be it. I have seen sights in the past few weeks that will haunt me until the day I die unless I make an effort to change them. The plight of our returning soldiers is but one crime for which your Tory friends must answer. Thousands of children living in the London stews daily survive horrors that are beyond the comprehension of those of us born into more fortunate circumstances. I intend to address both problems."

"Bravo, my lord. I hope you raise the roof off the House of Lords with your stirring oratory. It is high time someone with a powerful voice spoke for those who have no voice at all."

Justin looked up to find Tess, pale and somewhat disheveled, standing in the open doorway. He stared into her shining eyes and for one brief instant, the magic flared between them again. Then as if suddenly aware they were not alone, she dropped her gaze and the spell was broken.

Remembering his manners, he rose to his feet and Reggie instantly followed suit. "Your Grace, may I present Miss Tess Thornhill," he said, praying his grandfather would abstain from his usual caustic remarks.

"We have met." Tess and the duke spoke simultaneously, neither looking at the other and both unaccountably flushed.

Justin exchanged a perplexed look with Reggie. When and where had this fateful meeting occurred and how had he missed knowing about it? Before he could pose his question, he was interrupted by the appearance of Wimple at Tess's shoulder.

"You have a visitor, my lord." The elderly butler held out a small silver tray on which reposed a single embossed card. "I informed Lord Ingraham that you were not receiving at this late hour, but he was most insistent."

Chapter Sixteen

Stunned silence greeted Wimple's announcement. Then Justin, Reggie, and Tess all spoke at once.

"Someone must have recognized the carriage and followed us."

"We must have been seen carrying Wentworth from the square."

"Oh, Justin, I shall never forgive myself if you are in trouble because of me."

"Silence, all of you. This is no time to panic." The duke's voice rang with the authority of his rank. Three pairs of startled eyes instantly riveted on the commanding figure dominating the small salon. "I shall deal with Ingraham. I have dealt with his kind before." He resumed his pacing, his brow knit in thought.

"You, Justin, sit there and don't say a word." The duke pointed to the small table on which a new pack of cards lay in readiness for one of the frequent games Justin played with Reggie.

"I will do no such thing, Grandfather," Justin protested. "This is my problem and I will take care of it in my way."

"Damn your eyes, Grandson, whether you like it or not, I am the head of your family. I am also an old man. I demand the respect due me on both counts. Sit, I say!"

Justin sat, his mind in a turmoil. Letting the old man have his way could be dangerous but, all things considered, pursuing the running battle that had been raging between the two of them since his return from Greece could be even more disastrous.

Through narrowed eyes, he watched the duke take another turn around the room, then stop dead before Reggie. "And you, Rutledge, join him and deal out three hands of cards."

Reggie promptly took a seat at the table, reached for the cards, and shuffled them. "What game, Your Grace?"

"What the devil does it matter?"

Next the duke turned his hooded gaze on Tess. "And you, young woman, please be good enough to step behind the window drape."

"The window drape?" Tess echoed, staring at said object as if it were some alien thing totally beyond her ken.

"Move, Miss Thornhill, we've not a minute to waste. And mind you step back far enough so your toes are not protruding."

With an anxious glance at Justin's grim countenance, Tess disappeared behind the drape.

The duke placed another straight-back chair at the table and joined Justin and Reggie. "Very well, Wimple, show Lord Ingraham up—and mind you, if you betray by so much as a flicker of an eyelash that there is anything amiss in this house, I will personally toss you into the street without a change of clothes or a word of reference. Do you understand me?"

"Yes, Your Grace. Yes, indeed."

The duke picked up his cards, studied them, and rearranged two. "I sincerely hope we are playing whist," he said, "because if we are, I have an excellent hand."

A moment later, Wimple appeared in the doorway to announce, "Lord Ingraham."

"So, what brings you out on this chilly December night, Lord Ingraham?" the duke asked, glancing up from his hand of cards.

Ingraham's eyes widened in astonishment. "I didn't expect to find you here, Your Grace."

The duke raised an imperious eyebrow. "Why not? What is so unusual about a man enjoying dinner and a game of cards with his grandson on a Friday evening?"

A brief flicker of anger darkened Ingraham's pale blue eyes. "Are you claiming the viscount and his friend have been with you all evening, Your Grace?"

The duke laid down his hand of cards. "You forget to whom you speak, sir. I cannot imagine why *I* should feel it necessary to claim anything to anyone."

"Then if you will spare me a moment of your time, Your

Grace, I shall be happy to explain it to you." Ingraham hesitated, obviously expecting an invitation to be seated. None was forthcoming, and another look of angry resentment crossed his face at the less than subtle insult.

"For your information, a rally was held in London's East End earlier this evening, ostensibly to air the grievances of certain of our discharged servicemen."

The duke made another minor adjustment to his hand. "I cannot say I find that news too surprising. I have been expecting as much."

"However"—Ingraham continued in a grim voice—"it soon became apparent to those of us who attended as mere observers that this was no ordinary rally. The four leaders were, in fact, dangerous revolutionaries who were using it to call for the assassination of the Regent and members of the Privy Council."

"The devil you say! Did you hear that, Justin?"

"I did, Grandfather."

The duke raised his quizzing glass and studied Lord Ingraham with great interest. "And were these four dangerous revolutionaries apprehended by the authorities, or must we all sleep uneasily in our beds tonight?"

"Two were killed outright; two managed to escape. One of those who escaped was wounded and would have been apprehended had he not been spirited away in a carriage bearing a lozenge, the description of which sounded remarkably like that of the Viscount Sanderfield."

"Indeed!" The duke turned to Justin. "Did you by any chance loan one of your carriages to someone this evening, Justin?"

"No, Grandfather."

"Then we must assume your witnesses were mistaken, my lord."

"There is more, Your Grace." Lord Ingraham made a subtle shift from one foot to the other, as if he were growing tired of standing in one place. "Other reliable witnesses gave detailed descriptions of the two men in black clothing who assisted in the culprit's escape, including such notable facts as the taller of the two was a gangly horse-faced fellow and the smaller one limped and carried a cane." His gaze raked Justin and Reggie, who still wore the same somber clothing with which they had begun the fateful evening. "Can you honestly deny these descriptions are too close to those of the Viscount Sanderfield and the Earl of Rutledge to be considered mere coincidence?"

"Of course not. The coincidence is really quite amazing. But coincidence it is. For we both know it would be a physical impossibility for the lads to be in Mayfair and the East End of London at the same time. Offhand, I would say your so-called reliable witnesses are either in need of spectacles or have had their palms greased by someone with evil intentions toward two innocent young noblemen."

"I wonder if the authorities will agree with you if I am forced to bring charges against the earl and the viscount?"

Ingraham's thinly veiled threat made Justin more angry than fearful. It was all he could do to keep the promise of silence his grandfather had extracted from him.

"And I wonder how much weight the word of paid informants will carry against the word of the Duke of Arncott. You tread dangerous ground, Ingraham. The last I heard, a position on the Privy Council was not a lifetime sinecure."

The smug expression on Ingraham's face quickly deteriorated to one of wary indecision. "Of course, this discussion is merely academic," he declared. "Naturally I have no interest in bringing such charges. The man I want to see brought to justice is the traitor, Wentworth."

"Ah so. Wentworth, I assume, is the wounded man to whom you earlier referred."

"He is indeed, Your Grace, and if I am not mistaken both he and his friend, Miss Thornhill—sometimes known in the East End of London by the unlikely cognomen the Angel of the Stews—are both acquaintances of your grandson, the viscount."

The duke scowled across the table at Justin. "Is this true? Are you acquainted with these people?"

"I am, Grandfather. Miss Thornhill rents one of the tenement buildings I own in the stews, and I met Wentworth when I was overseeing my holdings in that area. While I do not hold the fellow in any great esteem, I cannot believe he is either a revolutionary or a traitor. Someone has made a serious mistake. I suggest an investigation be made to determine who."

"An excellent idea, Grandson. I shall take the matter up with my cronies in the House of Lords on the morrow." The duke glanced at Lord Ingraham still hovering in the doorway. "I vow, sir, you do not look at all well. In truth, you are pale as a ghost."

"It is nothing, Your Grace."

"In that case, my lord, since your business here appears to be at an end, I shall have Wimple show you out." He patted the hand of cards that lay facedown on the table in front of him. "After three hours of losing consistently to these two young scalawags, I do believe I finally have a winning hand and I am anxious to play it."

Once again silence reigned in the small salon until the occupants heard the sound of a door closing in the entryway below. Reggie was the first to speak. "Capital show, Your Grace. My heartfelt thanks. You certainly saved our bacon."

"Humpff!" The duke cast him a baleful look. "A distasteful bit of chicanery which I hope I may never be called upon to repeat."

"Amen to that, Your Grace, but your brilliant efforts on our behalf in this instance are deeply appreciated," Tess said shyly, as she stepped from behind the curtain.

Justin knew he should add his thanks to those of the other two, but his tongue seemed incapable of forming the words. He was frankly baffled by the happenings of the past fifteen minutes. For the first time in his life, his grandfather had stood by him. He had even called him Justin—another first. More important, the old tyrant had accepted his word over that of one of the most powerful Tories in England.

Why the sudden turnaround on his grandfather's part, he could not begin to imagine. He had spent the better part of his youth longing for the duke's acceptance. Now, at the ripe old age of two and thirty, he found it almost too much to believe that the phenomenon had actually occurred.

Still, common courtesy dictated he acknowledge that he was in the duke's debt. "Thank you, Grandfather—" he began, only to have the duke raise an imperious hand commanding him to silence.

"Time enough for that later, Grandson. Right now we need

address ourselves to the problem reposing in your library. Suffice it to say, that while I cannot entirely agree with your methods, I am proud of you for taking a stand against unscrupulous men like Ingraham. You are more a Warre than I had thought. Our family history is filled with men who have rebelled against oppression."

The duke's voice sounded abnormally gruff, and Justin realized his grandfather found the subtle change in their relationship as embarrassing as he did. It was as if the contention between them had been a shield behind which they had both hidden, and stripped of that shield, they were forced to face each other naked and vulnerable.

Luckily Reggie chose that moment to comment, "His Grace has a point there, Justin. What *are* we going to do with the wounded cit?"

Justin hesitated, aware that Tess watched him anxiously. "I'm not sure. I hadn't counted on being followed to Mayfair. The duke may have outwitted Lord Ingraham for the moment, but he is sure to keep the town house under surveillance on the chance we're concealing Wentworth. I suppose we could sneak him out through the back gate in the garden wall. I doubt the watch is aware of the narrow lane between the house and the mews. But what do we do with him then?"

He turned to Tess. "You realize, of course, that Wentworth must leave England. There is no place in the country where he would be safe from a man as powerful as Ingraham."

"I know. But that should not be your problem, Justin. You have done enough. If not for you and the earl, he would already be dead. He should soon be able to travel, thanks to your healing powders. Once he is, his friends in the stews will find a way to get him safely out of England."

Justin desperately wanted to ask if she would go with him. Did she love the handsome cit enough to leave her children to the care of others? He couldn't bring himself to pose the question—not certain he could bear to hear the answer.

Tess tucked a stray lock of hair behind her left ear. "In the meantime, I'd best check on him to see how he fares. Danny is not a very attentive nurse—unless the patient is Daisy."

"I shall accompany you," Justin said. "I, too, am anxious to see how he is coming along."

The duke rose from his chair. "We'll all go. The sooner this touchy business is finished, the better for all concerned." Justin gained the distinct impression that proud or not, his grandfather intended to make certain he didn't take any more risks that might sully the name of Warre.

They arrived at the library to find it deep in shadow. All but one of the candles had guttered out, and it took Tess a moment to realize that the table on which Drew had lain was now bare. Instinctively, she turned to Justin. "He's gone," she cried.

"So I see, but where?" He limped to the armchair where Danny lay curled up, dozing peacefully. "Wake up, lad. What do you know of Wentworth's disappearance?"

Danny sat up, instantly wide awake. "Gorblimey, guvnor, he must've snuck out of here mighty quiet-like while I rested me eyes for a minute or two."

"Or someone else sneaked in through that back gate you mentioned and made off with him," Reggie ventured.

Tess gasped. "Dear God, is it possible? Could Lord Ingraham's minions have done so while he kept us occupied above?"

"Highly unlikely. The back gate is not easy to find." Justin scowled. "But let me light some candles so we can search the room for clues as to what happened." He limped to the massive desk in one corner of the room where Tess had earlier seen him deposit the extra candles after lighting those around the table.

"Aha, this may be our answer." He returned with the candles and two pieces of folded foolscap. "One is addressed to you, Tess, the other to me."

Tess waited until he'd lighted the candles, then read her note. It was very short and in Drew's usual scrawling script.

> Dearest Tess:
> I love you, and shall until the day I die, but I know now
> you were never meant to be mine. I was wrong about the
> viscount. He is a good man and the only one I can think
> of who is worthy of you. Do not let any foolish misun-

derstanding I caused keep you apart. May God bless you
and give you all the happiness you deserve.

Your faithful friend,

D.W.

She looked up from her reading, her eyes swimming in tears
for the handsome, self-centered boy who had been like her
brother—and the man that boy had become. "May God bless
you, too, dear friend, wherever you may go," she whispered
softly.

Justin watched the tears cascade down Tess's cheeks and felt
each one drop like a stone on his aching heart. She had cried
for him once—sweet, sentimental tears which had touched him
deeply. But these tears she cried for Wentworth were heavy
with grief and, there was no mistaking it . . . love.

He picked a handkerchief off the stack that still reposed on
the edge of the desk and handed it to her. "My note simply
thanks me for my help and apologizes for taking my greatcoat,"
he said quickly to hide the pain that engulfed him. "It says
nothing about where he intends to go."

"Nor does mine." Tess folded her note into a small square
and slipped it under the neckline of her dress. He tortured himself with the thought that she would probably read it again and
again in the privacy of her bedchamber.

"Well that is that, my lord," Tess said once she'd dried her
eyes. "Since there is nothing more we can do here, Danny and I
should start for home. If you will be good enough to show us
the secret gate you spoke of, we can walk to where we can hire
a hackney."

"At this time of night? Never. I will see you safely home."

"That would not be at all wise, my lord. Lord Ingraham has
already established that I was a special friend of Drew's. If you
are seen in my company, he will set the watch to spying on you
day and night, which will be certain to cause gossip among
your Mayfair neighbors. Surely neither you nor your grandfather want that."

"Miss Thornhill is right, Grandson, but so are you. She and
the boy cannot be left to their own devices." The duke reached
for his greatcoat, which he had dropped across a chair earlier.

"Therefore, I will see them safely home. My carriage is in the mews. It will be a simple thing to slip them into it with no one but my coachman the wiser, and Joseph is the soul of discretion."

"The dook's got the right of it, Tess." Danny's eyes twinkled with mischief. "I near forgot it was Friday night. He can let us out in that private stable of his back of Florabelle's place, which ain't more'n a block or two from home—and who's to know he's doin' anythin' different from wot he does every Friday night of his life?"

The duke couldn't resist the temptation to do a little boasting to his mistress about how he had outwitted one of the shrewdest and most feared men in all of England. It had been a long time since he'd been called upon to use his wits; the exercise had been unbelievably exhilarating.

Florabelle was all he could ask for in an audience. "Lord luv us, I'd like to have seen that Tory squeeze-crab slinking off with his tail between his legs," she chortled. "He's come in my place once or twice, but last time he came around, I flat out told him to take his business elsewhere. Got so rough with one of my best girls, I had to send the bullyboys in to pull him off her. The poor thing couldn't work for nearly a fortnight. I got no use for a man who takes his pleasure hurting a woman."

She poured them both a brandy and settled her bulk deeper into the cushions of the loveseat she shared with the duke. "Go on, ducks, what happened then?"

"As I told you earlier, I escorted Miss Thornhill and the boy, Danny, here to my mews. The lad claimed he knew a back way into the children's home, which they could navigate without the watch seeing them."

"But what did the viscount do with Wentworth once he was up and about? It's not like he could let a wanted criminal stay at his town house with the beadles swarming round the place."

"Justin didn't do anything with him. The fellow just disappeared on his own while we were dealing with Ingraham. Left a note for Justin and another for Miss Thornhill, but didn't offer a clue as to where he was going. I suspect he's on his way to

Liverpool and a ship for the Americas by now. I know I would
be if I were in his shoes."

"So Wentworth is gone. Well, there'll be none who'll miss
that one."

The duke raised a skeptical eyebrow. "My grandson appears
to think Miss Thornhill will miss the fellow mightily."

"Nonsense. The viscount is the only fellow Tess has ever
been head over ears about. She's just put up with Wentworth
because he was her best friend's brother and because she feels
she's partly to blame for Laura Wentworth's death."

"Oh! How is that?"

Florabelle took a sip of her brandy before answering. "As I
heard it, when Tess was eighteen and living in her father's fine
house in Bloomsbury Square, she struck up a flirtation with
some rackety-titled rake. Being Tess, she could see right off he
was all fluff and no fortitude, and never gave him another
thought when she went off to her fancy finishing school in
Bath.

"Meanwhile, the blighter took up with her friend, Laura, and
by the time Tess came home a year later, Laura had died having
the fellow's by-blow and her parents had disposed of the poor
little mite by dropping it in the Lambs Field night basket. Tess
never forgave them nor her father for encouraging them."

Florabelle tossed her hennaed curls. "If you ask me, her
friend was a silly little gudgeon to be taken in by the pretty fellow, but Tess blames herself for not putting her wise—and
Drew Wentworth has never for a minute let her forget it. No
siree, he won't be missed around here one bit."

The duke's brows drew together in a frown. "In light of what
you told me last time we discussed Miss Thornhill and my
grandson, I made a point of watching the two of them together
this evening. It was really rather comical. When she thought he
wasn't looking, she devoured him with those great green eyes
of hers like he was one of Gunter's prize pastries, and when he
thought she wasn't aware, he stared at her like a puppy who'd
just unearthed a prize bone."

"It's not comical in the least. They've had a falling out—
thanks to that blighter, Wentworth. Unless someone sets them
straight, they could go on forever pining away for each other

and never get together. And that would be a sorry thing indeed. Tess isn't one to fall in love more than once—and Danny claims the viscount's a one-woman man if he ever saw one."

"I don't doubt it. It runs in the family," the duke said sadly, and Florabelle knew he was thinking of his beloved duchess.

She ran her hand down his thigh in a gesture so provocative, she could feel his muscles instantly tense beneath her fingers. He might have loved his duchess, but he had wanted her, Florabelle Favor, with an undiminished passion since the first moment he saw her, and she was not above using that passion to get what she wanted from him.

"Can't you see your way clear to accepting Tess as your grandson's viscountess," she coaxed, "him being the special kind of fellow he is? She may not be a blue blood, but she's a lady, and they love each other."

The duke shrugged. "What choice do I have? It appears I'll never have any great-grandchildren otherwise."

"Oh, Archie, I just knew you'd give in sooner or later." Florabelle clapped her pudgy hands in glee. "Now all we have to do is get them together. Danny and I can work on Tess from this end, but it's up to you to bring the viscount round. You can do it, Archie. You're the most persuasive man on earth once you set your mind to it."

"Am I really, Flora?" The duke looked inordinately pleased at the compliment.

Reaching for her hand, he entwined his fingers in hers, and for a long moment they sat together in companionable silence. "Tell me, Flora," he asked finally, "in all the years we've been together, have you ever loved me?"

His shocking question took her totally unawares. "Well now, Archie, that was never part of the bargain, was it?"

"No, it wasn't. But have you ever loved me?"

She could see he was feeling very old and very lonely tonight and despite herself, her heart went out to him. Besides, with all the brandy she'd consumed while waiting for him and the news about Wentworth, she was feeling unusually mellow.

With a sigh, she laid her head on his shoulder. "Lord knows I've tried not to," she said softly. "What with you being a high-and-mighty duke and me being what I am, falling in love with you seemed the best way I knew to get my heart broken." She sighed again. "But I guess I am just a weak and foolish woman, because the truth is I simply couldn't help myself."

The duke's craggy features softened in a rare smile. Lifting their clasped hands, he pressed his lips to the spot where their fingers entwined. "All things considered, I am a very lucky man, Flora."

Florabelle smiled. "Yes, Archie, I do believe you are."

Chapter Seventeen

A fortnight had passed since the disastrous rally and nothing had been seen or heard of Drew. Tess scanned the *Times* each day for news of his capture, though she felt certain the continuing presence of the watchman huddled in the doorway across the street from her children's home was a fair indication the authorities had not yet laid their hands on him.

She breathed a sigh of relief. Maybe by now he was on the high seas in a ship that would take him to the Americas and freedom.

Meanwhile, life at the Laura Wentworth Home went on, despite the aura of gloom that had settled over its occupants. For Tess had had no word from Justin—not that she'd really expected any. By the end of the second week of silence, she'd quit hoping for a miracle and faced the truth: that brief, magic interval in her life was over, and all she had left to remind her of the fascinating viscount was an aching heart and a few treasured memories which ofttimes were more painful than pleasant.

She could not bring herself to enter the small salon where they had kept an all-night vigil over Daisy—and where Justin had first kissed her.

She had only to pass the spot in the hallway where he'd pressed her against the wall with his strong, lean body and kissed her with a searing, mind-numbing passion—and foolish tears flooded her eyes.

She had even gone so far as to contemplate repapering the wall of the common room because the very sight of the leering god Pan reminded her of how much she missed Justin's quirky sense of humor and quick, shy smile.

It was not easy getting over loving someone, and it didn't help that Maggie wore a perpetual scowl and issued frequent tight-lipped reminders that despite the abominable way Tess had treated him, the dear viscount was still sending generous baskets of foodstuffs for the children.

It certainly didn't help that one gray and gloomy morning Justin's new man-of-affairs delivered the revised rental contract for her to sign and stayed for a cup of tea and a running monologue on what a kind and generous employer he found the viscount to be.

But none of these things bothered her as much as Danny's reaction to Justin's absence. Long-faced and silent, he was a veritable ghost of his former cocky self with no interest in anything, not even his drawing. "I misses the guvnor," he complained one afternoon a week before Christmas as he stood at the window of the common room watching snowflakes drift to the street below.

Tess looked up from her mending. "If it is any comfort to you, I miss him too."

"Do you think he'll ever come back?"

"I don't know," Tess answered honestly. "He's a proud man. I doubt he'll ever forgive me for believing him a liar."

"Florabelle says it ain't that wot's keeping him away. She thinks that he thinks you chose Wentworth over him and he ain't about to court a woman wot's in love with another man."

Tess shook her head. "He can't possibly believe that. I have never thought of Drew as anything but a friend."

"Well how's the guvnor to know that when you took Wentworth's part against him and then insisted on goin' to that bleedin' rally when he told you there was bound to be trouble? Hellsfire, Tess, I seen the look on his face when you bawled your eyes out over that bleedin' note. Don't tell me he don't think you're pining away for the worthless sod! Florabelle was dead right. She always is about things like this."

Tess stared at her accuser in shocked disbelief. Could it be possible that Justin had mistaken her loyalty to an old friend for something deeper and more intimate? Was that what he'd meant when he said he respected her right to make her own choice? The very thought left her shaken to the core.

"I can see from the look on your face that you never once thought how all the dumb things you done would look to a softhearted fellow like the guvnor. You was always so busy motherin' everybody else, includin' that crybaby Wentworth, you never thought about how you was hurtin' 'is feelings."

"The Viscount Sanderfield is the last man on earth who needs mothering," Tess said indignantly. "He's brilliant and resourceful and rich as Croesus—and he's in line to inherit one of the oldest and richest dukedoms in all of England."

"Maybe that's how you see him," Danny said. "Wot I sees is a shy bloke with a gimpy foot wot finally found the one woman he could love and trust. At least that's wot he told me, confidential-like. And he wasn't thinkin' to make you his mistress like any other toff would of done. He was plannin' to ask you to marry him, proper like. But wot did you do the very next time he come around? You called him a liar and throwd his love back in his face, that's wot."

Tess held her head in her hands. "Stop it, Danny. You make it all sound so awful; you make me sound so awful."

"I'm just tellin' the truth as I sees it, like you always told me to," he declared stubbornly.

Tess had spent the past two weeks picturing Justin angry and insulted that she'd questioned his honesty. She'd imagined him thoroughly disgusted with her because of the foolish way she'd acted—so disgusted, in fact, that any tender feelings he'd once had for her were quashed forever. That had been painful enough, but the picture Danny painted was beyond enduring.

She knew now she had lied to herself. She had told herself time and again that a sophisticated man of the world like the Viscount Sanderfield could never be deeply hurt by someone like her. She had convinced herself that hers was the only heart that was broken, because she could not bear the thought that Justin could be suffering the same agonizing loneliness and despair that she lived with every waking hour.

"Dear God, what have I done?" she sobbed. "Justin is the last person in the world I would ever want to hurt."

"Damnation, Tess, don't go all womanish on me. It ain't like all your bridges is burnt yet." Danny crossed the room to stand beside her and awkwardly pat her shoulder. "If you feels about the guvnor like I thinks you do, all you got to do is take a hackney up to Mayfair like you done before and tell him you're sorry for wot you done and you miss him somethin' turrible—and I'll

wager me last ha'penny everythin' will be right and tight again
before you know it."

Tess sighed. "If only it were that easy. Even if all you say is
true and I could make things right between us with a few well-
chosen words, there would still be insurmountable problems."

"If you love him and he loves you, there ain't no problems you
can't solve."

"Love is not all that's involved here, Danny. Think about it.
The viscount and I come from different worlds—worlds too dis-
similar to ever meld together. He could never live in the stews,
and I would be like a fish out of water in Mayfair."

"Then find someplace wot suits you both."

Tess shook her head at Danny's naïveté. "Maybe we could if
we lived in a perfect world—a fairy-tale world of happy-ever-
after. But we live in the real world where no such place exists."

Danny's face crumpled and his eyes grew suspiciously bright.
"You're a coward," he accused, "and you got no faith—not in the
guvnor and not in yourself. If you did, you'd know him and you
together could make things right—and you wouldn't be keepin'
me awake every night listenin' to you cry yourself to sleep."

With the back of his hand, he brushed away a tear that trickled
down his freckled cheek. "You're a sorry excuse for a woman,
Tess Thornhill, and that's a fact. From this day on, I washes me
hands of you."

Late that night, just as Florabelle Favor was preparing to climb
between the silk sheets of her spacious bed, she thought she heard
a knock at her door. Not the door leading into her place of business, which might be expected, but the private door leading to the
alleyway that only the duke ever used. But the duke never rapped;
he used his key. And it was Wednesday; the duke never came to
her on Wednesday.

Cautiously, she opened the door a crack and peered out. "What
the devil are you doing out on a night like this?" she exclaimed
when she spied the snow-covered lad shivering on her doorstep.

Danny doffed his cap and stepped across the threshold.
Florabelle smiled, warmed by his show of respect. Like Tess, this
skinny scrap of a lad always treated her like a lady, and like Tess,
she considered him a close friend and confidant.

"I come to tell you I done wot we talked about," Danny said. "Let out all the stoppers, just like you said I should. I laid it on thick as hog fat when it come to tellin' how she broke the viscount's heart with her foolishness." A frown crossed his thin, freckled face. "I called her a coward, when she's the bravest woman I ever knowd, and I made her cry. I didn't like that—not a bit."

"You did what you had to and it's all for her own good. Did you, as we discussed, suggest she should go to Mayfair to beg the viscount's forgiveness?"

"I did."

"And do you think she'll actually do it?"

"She'll do it. Maybe not tomorrow or the next day. But once the snow stops fallin', she'll go. Tess can't stomach the thought that she hurt the guvnor, and she don't like bein' called a coward."

"Splendid!" Florabelle rubbed her hands together in glee. "You're a clever lad to have thought of that touch. Lord knows how long this unhappy business could go on if we waited for the viscount to get around to coming to her."

Danny nodded. "It were the only way to set it up. The guvnor's the kind to take his time makin' up his mind. Wot with all the hurt he's feelin' over the way Tess treated him, he might stick his nose back in his books and not look up again till spring—and then where would we be? Besides, bein' so shy and slow to move hisself, he admires a woman with gumption. It's wot drawd him to her in the first place."

Florabelle was so elated over this successful launching of their "plan," it was all she could do to keep from hugging the lad—a gesture she knew he'd find excruciatingly embarrassing. She offered him a bonbon instead and happily watched him pop two of Gunter's finest into his mouth.

"You did a fine job, lad, and for a fine cause. If there was ever two people meant for each other, it's our Tess and the Viscount Sanderfield. Even his grandfather, the duke, admits it." She grinned. "And that's my news for you. The old tyrant has agreed to tell the viscount he approves of Tess and won't stand in the way of his marrying her. Now what do you think of that?"

Danny reached for another bonbon, his satisfied grin every bit as wide as Florabelle's. "I thinks that just about clinches it. By the time Tess knocks at his door, the guvnor will be primed and ready to fall into her arms."

The first snowstorm of the winter kept Justin housebound and at loose ends for three days. Without Reggie's daily visits to break the monotony, he felt isolated and lonely and so out of sorts, the servants all avoided him as assiduously as if he'd come down with the plague.

Finally, on the fourth day, the snow stopped falling, a pale sun peeped through the clouds, and a visitor arrived just after he'd finished an early luncheon. He was standing at the window of the second-floor salon when the Duke of Arncott's carriage drew up to the curb outside the town house.

It was the first time he'd seen his grandfather since the night of the rally, and he had to wonder what occasioned this visit. True, they had at last called a truce to their longstanding mutual animosity, but it was an uneasy truce fraught with a painful embarrassment on both parts. He doubted the duke would feel inclined to pay him a purely social call.

Wimple? But no, he'd done nothing in the past fortnight worthy of one of Wimple's missives. The patriarch of his family must have found something to complain about on his own this time. Resigned to his fate, he turned from the window and prepared to greet his unexpected guest.

"So, Justin, how goes it with you?" the duke asked once he'd been seated. His hearty tone of voice sounded so false, Justin felt his skin crawl. The old boy was definitely up to something.

"I am fine, Grandfather."

"Nothing in the *Times* about Wentworth so far. Fellow must have made it to Plymouth all right. Probably on his way to the Americas by now."

"One sincerely hopes so."

The duke fixed his gaze on a small landscape by Humphrey Repton, which hung on the wall opposite him. "And what have you heard from Miss Thornhill? She is not too troubled by the surveillance of the watch, I hope."

"I have not had occasion to communicate with her, Grandfather."

"Not once in more than a fortnight? How odd. It was my under-standing that you had conceived a *tendre* for the lady—and she for you, as well."

Justin felt a twinge of anger at his grandfather's lack of sensitivity. The pain of losing Tess was still too raw to allow him to casually discuss her. "On the contrary," he said stiffly, "Miss Thornhill's affections are engaged elsewhere, as you surely must have noticed on that Friday night two weeks ago."

"You refer to Wentworth, I assume. I saw nothing in her manner to lead me to believe she felt anything but friendship for the fellow."

"She cried for him," Justin muttered between gritted teeth.

"I would expect any woman of tender sensibilities to weep for a friend forced to flee England under such circumstances, and from what I have seen of your Miss Thornhill she has a most sympathetic heart."

"What is your point, Grandfather?" Justin asked, clenching his fists in frustration.

"My point is, a woman supposedly in love with one man does not look at another the way Miss Thornhill looks at you. The woman literally devours you with her eyes. It is really most unseemly. Once you make her your viscountess, you must persuade her to be a little more discreet when it comes to revealing her emotions."

"Once I what?" Justin stared at his grandfather in utter disbelief. "Are you implying that you would approve of Tess Thornhill as the Viscountess Sanderfield?"

"I am. After giving much thought to the subject, I have come to the conclusion that the two of you are eminently suited to each other—a perfect balance, so to speak, of divergent personalities."

Justin raised an eyebrow. "Why do I get the impression that you have rehearsed that particular speech many times, Grandfather?"

"As I told you, I have given much thought to this." A flush spread across the duke's sallow features. "Demme it, Grandson, it is not easy for a man in my position to admit he might have made an erroneous judgment."

The plea in the old man's hooded eyes told Justin that the admission of error encompassed far more than his condemnation of

Tess. For the first time in his life, he felt a true kinship with the haughty aristocrat whose name he bore. The idea was so over-whelming, he felt embarrassingly close to weeping.

"Are you certain you did not misconstrue the way Tess looked at me?" he asked quickly to cover his discomfiture.

"I may be old, but my eyesight is unimpaired. I would wager my few remaining years that the woman adores you."

Too keyed up to remain seated any longer, Justin leaped to his feet and limped to the window to stare at the glistening beauty of snow-covered trees and shrubs and houses that now lay basking in a wintry sunshine. Unbidden, a memory surfaced which had lain hidden beneath the layers of bitterness and pain that had plagued him for so long.

"Until very recently I believed I was incapable of loving any man," Tess had said on that magical day when they'd silently pledged their love—then blushed furiously when she realized what she had admitted to him. How could he have forgotten that telling statement or the fact that she had known Wentworth all her life? Had he been as guilty as she of leaping to conclusions? Was she as lonely and unhappy as he was over their separation? The thought that he could have inadvertently wounded his lovely, free-spirited do-gooder was too painful to bear.

He had never been a man to make impetuous decisions; he made one now and as swiftly acted upon it. Wimple answered his impatient pull on the bell cord so quickly, he felt certain the old snoop had had his eye to the keyhole again. "Have a groom bring my curricle around," he ordered curtly.

The duke's eyes lighted up. "Just like that, on my word alone, you go dashing off to woo your lady. By George, Grandson, you are acting more like a Warre with every passing day."

Justin smiled at what he knew to be the supreme compliment from the old man's lips. "I only hope you were right about that look in Tess's eyes, Grandfather. For if you weren't, I am about to make the world's worst ass of myself."

The duke stood at the window and watched Justin climb into the driver's seat of the garish red-and-gold curricle he had inher-ited from his brother, Oliver. The thought of his deceased grand-son reminded him of the tangible reminder the young rakehell had left behind when he went to his death. Throwing open the window he stuck his head out, and with an uncharacteristic lack of ducal poise, shouted, "Don't forget the child, Justin. Make sure custody of young Daisy is part of the bargain."

Justin's reply was accompanied by a devilish smile. "Don't worry, Your Grace. If I can pull this off, I'll present you with Daisy and a dozen more to keep her company." With a brief wave, he issued a command to his pair of Cleveland Bays and pulled away from the curb.

The duke closed the window, but stood watching Justin until he was out of sight. He felt inordinately proud of himself and of his day's work. He could scarcely wait for night to fall so he could visit Flora. Wouldn't the old girl be surprised to learn that he'd not only given his blessing to the union she so desired—he'd managed to inspire his slow-as-molasses grandson to instantly leap into action as well.

The same pale sun that graced Mayfair's winter wonderland smiled down on the snow-covered refuse littering the streets of the stews. Noon was yet an hour off and already the carts and barrows from which the commerce of the area was conducted had worn countless muddy ruts in the clean white blanket nature had spread outside Tess's window during the night.

Briefly, she watched the frenzied street activity occasioned by the unexpected sunshine, but her thoughts were on anything but the busy tradesmen who had been her neighbors for the past five years.

With agonizing clarity she recounted Danny's impassioned plea that she go to Justin, bonnet in hand, and beg his forgiveness. Could the boy be right? Had she unknowingly broken the heart of the man she loved, even as her own had been broken by their bitter parting?

Where was he now? Could he, as Danny had hinted, have drawn back into his shell of shyness—humiliated by the belief that she had rejected him in favor of Drew? Tears sprang to her eyes at the very thought.

With one of her usual lightning decisions, she knew exactly what she must do. First a brief word of apology to Maggie for leaving her in sole charge of the noon meal, then she donned her pelisse and bonnet, collected her reticule and umbrella, and walked the short distance to where she could hail a hackney.

Fashionable Bond Street was crowded with Christmas shoppers when the hackney Tess had hired entered it on the last leg of her journey to Justin's town house. A day of sunshine so near the holiday was a boon to the merchants, and they made the most of it. The shops were gaily decorated with greens and holly and many of the merchants waited in the doorways to greet favorite customers descending from their carriages to purchase a last-minute gift or two.

The hackney driver was forced to slow his nags to a crawl in the crush of carriages cruising the streets and Tess had ample time to view the tantalizing merchandise so tastefully displayed in the bow windows. Years ago in another lifetime, Laura and she, properly chaperoned by their maids, had frequently patronized such shops as these. The *ton* might close its drawing rooms to the daughters of wealthy merchants; the owners of London's exclusive shops had no such qualms.

With a brief twinge of envy, she ogled the rich fabrics and lush colors of the gowns and pelisses worn by the fashionable women who strolled from shop to shop on the arms of their equally fashionable escorts. As long as she'd remained at home, her father had provided her with the money to dress in the height of fashion, but she had chosen to forgo her life of comfort, luxury, and restriction in favor of one of service, poverty, and freedom. She had no regrets—at least, she admitted honestly, very few.

This was what she must convey to Justin, shortly after she had convinced him she never had and never would love anyone but him. Life in fashionable Mayfair was not for her, just as life in the stews with a dozen abandoned children would never suit a fastidious fellow like Justin. She would propose a compromise. One she had thought never to consider. One so daring, the very thought of it made her blush from head to toe. She would offer to be his mistress. That way he could live in his world, she in hers, and they could have a special world all their own somewhere on the outskirts of London.

"Exactly as Drew foretold," a nasty little voice somewhere deep inside her whispered.

She tossed her head defiantly. "Better a life of sin with the only man I shall ever love than no life at all," she told the pesky voice.

The hackney coach inched forward at a snail's pace in the ever thickening traffic. Impatiently, Tess watched the line of carriages heading in the opposite direction creep by her at the same measured rate. Every kind of carriage imaginable was on the street today. To keep her mind off the shocking decision she had just made, she mentally cataloged them as they crawled past. An elegant black town coach. A small blue tilbury. A dark green barouche and a chaise of the same color close behind it. A gaudy red-and-gold curricle.

Her breath caught in her throat at the familiar sight. Justin was at the reins, his trusty groom behind him. Wherever he was going, he was in a hurry, for his frustration over the crush around him was all too evident in the grim set of his jaw.

Instinctively, she drew back out of sight as he passed, her firm resolve of but a moment ago now as wobbly as a dish of blancmange. What was she thinking of, seeking him out as brazenly as any doxie who walked the Haymarket to offer herself as his mistress, his light-o-love, his whore?

For long, agonizing moments, she huddled in a corner of the stale-smelling cab, cocooned in her own misery, while Justin slowly disappeared into the sea of carriages and elegantly dressed shoppers that surrounded her.

Then slowly the shock of seeing him so unexpectedly subsided and reason returned. She knew she would never find the courage to make this trip twice. Still, she could not accept that she was so fainthearted she would come all the way across London, only to discard her mission at the first setback.

She tapped the roof of the cab with her umbrella, shouted to the jarvey to stop, and climbed from hackney.

"I wants me full fare, madam," the jarvey whined. "This bloomin' fimble-famble ain't none of my doin'." Tess gladly paid him, then looked about her to discover the whereabouts of the red-and-gold curricle.

She spotted it easily, but Justin had made more progress than she'd expected; the curricle was a good half-block away and moving slowly but steadily ahead to where the traffic had thinned noticeably.

She decided there was nothing for it but to run after him, though she was well aware no well-bred lady would ever consider doing such an outlandish thing. "But then, when have you ever let such a consideration stop you before?" asked the same pesky voice that had taunted her before. Without further ado, she picked up her skirt and sprinted forward, dodging carriage wheels and prancing horses as she went.

The cobblestones were wet and slippery from the melting snow. Twice she stumbled, righted herself, and staggered on to the accompaniment of shouts from the angry coachmen whose startled horses took exception to rubbing shoulders with a frantic woman. One particularly excited nag even went so far as to nip at the silk flowers decorating her only good bonnet.

She was within ten feet of the red-and-gold curricle when the bays broke free of the crush and Justin urged them into a trot. "Justin," she screamed, "wait for me!" With her last ounce of energy, she edged forward past an elegant silver-and-blue high-perch phaeton drawn by two handsome grays. To her relief, the groom clinging to the back of Justin's curricle turned his head and stared at her, mouth agape.

Justin heard his groom's grunt of surprise, but attributed it to the fact that the carriage was once again moving. He, too, had begun to wonder if there was an end to the parade of tightly massed carriages. He tightened his hold on the reins and urged the bays ahead, only to have the groom shout in his ear, "There be a woman back there hailing you, my lord. She be on foot and waving her arms like one of me father's windmills."

"The devil you say." Justin reined in the bays and glanced over his shoulder just as Tess stumbled and dropped to her knees some ten feet behind him.

"What the devil!" Handing the reins to the groom, Justin leaped from the carriage and without the aid of his cane, limped back to where Tess still knelt on the wet cobblestones. Her cheeks were flushed, her pelisse mud-spattered, and her hair tumbled from beneath the brim of her bonnet in wild disarray. She had never looked more beautiful.

"Tess, my love, are you hurt?"

"No." She brushed a tear from her cheek and left a streak of mud in its place.

"But what in God's name are you doing here in the middle of Bond Street?" he asked, helping her to her feet. "I was just on my way to see you."

"I was on my way to see you, too. In a hackney. You passed me a few minutes back." She drew in a shaky breath. "I wanted to tell you I love you."

Justin threw back his head and laughed from the sheer joy of the moment. "What a happy coincidence," he exclaimed. "Those were the very words I intended to say to you." Drawing her into his arms, he kissed her soundly. Then kissed her again for good measure.

With a contented sigh, Tess wrapped her arms about his waist and nestled her head on his shoulder, completely oblivious of the shocking spectacle they were making of themselves.

"Perhaps we should adjourn to my curricle, my love," Justin said tenderly, aware that the driver of the blue phaeton had pulled to an abrupt halt, forcing everyone behind him to do the same. As he watched, the carriages that were headed in the opposite direction stopped as well, and from every window in every carriage heads poked, eyes bulged, and mouths gaped.

Tess raised her head. "I'm not sure I can walk. I must have twisted my ankle when I stumbled."

"Not to worry, my love," Justin said, and to a chorus of "Did you see thats?" and "Well, I nevers," swept her up in his arms, limped to the curricle, and deposited her on the passenger's seat.

"There is no doubt about it now, Sweet Tess, you are well and truly compromised," he said with a chuckle as he retrieved the reins from his groom and gave the command that urged the bays into a gentle trot. "You will simply have to marry me."

Tess cast a nervous glance at the groom behind them and slid across the seat until her shoulder brushed his. "That is what I need to discuss with you," she whispered in his ear. "It wouldn't work out, you know. You could never live in the stews, and I could never bear to leave my children to live with you in Mayfair." A furious blush traveled up her throat and across her cheeks. "It would be much better if I became your mistress."

Justin stared at her in mock horror. "You would rather be my mistress than my wife? You shock me, Miss Thornhill. Wouldn't it be better yet if we sanctified our union, then agreed on some-place where we could both live happily?"

She shook her head sadly. "That's what Danny suggested, but no such place exists."

"Ah, but it does, and it is called Brandywine. Do not look so skeptical, my love. It is a delightful little estate of mine situated but a few hours from London, and it has easily enough bedchambers to allow one for each of the children, as well as Danny and your indispensable Maggie."

Noting the stunned expression on her face, he quickly elaborated further before she could utter the protest he could see forming on her lips. "The estate even has a wonderful elderly butler and housekeeper who can help Maggie with the children when we remove to London when the House of Lords is in session. For, of course, I shall need you there to cheer me on when I make my inflammatory speeches."

"You propose to marry me and transport my entire household to this estate of yours to live happily ever after?" Tess raised a skeptical eyebrow. "You must be mad. No man in his right mind would consider marrying a woman with thirteen children."

"Call me a Bedlamite." Justin strove to maintain a somber tone in his voice, but he feared the laughter in his eyes would give him away. "After your scandalous conduct today, I must insist you marry me. For yours is not the only reputation damaged. Mine, too, lies in shreds. By teatime we shall be the chief topic of conversation in every salon in Mayfair. I doubt that even the Prince Regent's latest extravagances or the titillating innuendos about Lord Byron and his half sister will be able to compete with the scandal you caused with your precipitous flight down Bond Street."

He paused for breath. "We will be married tomorrow by special license. I'll drop by Doctors' Commons this afternoon and make the arrangements."

"We will do nothing of the sort. I cannot and will not agree to such an insane proposal, for I feel absolutely certain you would regret it within a fortnight," Tess said firmly. "You will either have to accept me as your mistress or not at all."

Justin merely grinned at her pronouncement and produced the coup de grâce he'd saved for his final argument. "Did I remember to tell you, Sweet Tess, that Brandywine has a meadow?" he asked softly.

"A meadow?" Her entire countenance came alive at the magic word.

"A lush green meadow ringed with stands of white birch trees. There is just a small flock of sheep grazing there now, but in the spring there will be dozens of lambs to gambol about and fluffy white clouds in an azure sky, and I daresay a riot of wildflowers that will take your breath away. If I didn't know better, I would swear the artist who painted your mural had Brandywine in mind."

Tess surveyed him with an expression so solemn, yet so whimsical, it was all Justin could do to keep from dropping the reins and taking her in his arms.

With a grubby hand, she tucked a strand of hair beneath her bedraggled bonnet. "Oh dear, am I never to be allowed to win an argument with you, my lord?" Her voice was heavy with resignation, but the glow in her eyes put the sun above her to shame.

"For what can I say to that? The children have never seen a meadow."